SHEPHARD'S

DRONE

SHEPHARD'S DRONE

Brett Frischmann

Available in e-book and print.
Print ISBN: 978-0-9600519-0-8
Ebook ISBN: 978-0-9600519-1-5
First edition: 2018

Cover art by Jolanta Knap at
www.jolantaknap.pl
Cover layout by Tamian Wood at
www.BeyondDesignInternational.com
Interior design by Kari Holloway at
www.kariholloway.com/khformat

To Kelly, Matthew, Jake and Ben

TABLE OF CONTENTS

Prologue _____ 1

1: Adam's Life _____ 2

2: Questions _____ 16

3: Snakes, Meerkats, and Ants _____ 31

4: Home _____ 38

5: Leads _____ 53

6: Differences _____ 72

7: Crossing _____ 82

8: Trip _____ 88

9: Change _____ 95

10: Coffeehouse Memories _____ 113

11: The Grand St. Louis _____ 125

12: Changes _____ 141

13: Help _____ 146

14: Neighbors _____ 157

15: Conlin _____ 172

16: The Reverse Turing Test _____ 185

17: Jackie _____ 194

18: Progress _____ 200

19: The Grizzly _____ 221

20: Robert Flynn _____ 228

21: Gallows Storm _____ 240

22: Stories _____ 263

23: Friends _____ 271

24: The Vacant Eyes of Ghosts _____ 276

25: Dataswim _____ 290

26: Modification _____ 310

27: A Simple Choice _____ 332

ACKNOWLEDGEMENTS

To write this novel, I depended heavily on the advice, assistance, and mentorship of many incredible people. Fiction writing was new to me when I began, and I doubted I could pull it off. Back in 2010, I told my friend Deven Desai that he should write this story because he had written fiction already and was good at it, but he laughed and insisted that I could and should write my own novel. He gave me plenty of pointers to get me started, and so my adventure began.

While the list of people who helped me is too long to print, I am especially grateful to the following friends and colleagues for reading drafts and helping a novice learn to write fiction: Julie Cohen, Deven Desai, Cathy Dinaburg, Cory Doctorow, Ann Fenton, Lara Freidenfelds, Chad Frischmann, Gwynne Frischmann, Matt Gallaway, Andrea Glorioso, Barbara Kolsun, Orly Lobel, Melissa Rutman, Zahr Said, Evan Selinger, Anjali Singh, Steph Tai, Rebecca Tushnet, and Kathryn Wilham. I thank members of the Fiction Writing Group on Facebook for feedback, writing tips, and support. My deep appreciation also goes to Joshua Cohen, Paul Levinson, and Susan Shapiro for their encouragement and sage advice.

I would also like to acknowledge the incredible work of the following professionals:

Nicole Bokat, Lisa Kaufman, Betsy Maury, and Liz Scheier—editorial services;

Kari Holloway (www.kariholloway.com/khformat)—interior layout and design;

Tamian Wood (www.BeyondDesignInternational.com)—design and layout of the cover;

Jolanta Knap (www.jolantaknap.pl)—cover artwork.

And for their unwavering support throughout the adventure, I dedicate this novel to my family—Kelly, Matthew, Jake and Ben.

PROLOGUE

They now say using technology to design humans is normal. Parents order what they like. If you don't like what you get, you fix it. People make adjustments to themselves and others. Societies use different tech to mold humanity to fit their conception of the ideal. This is called modification.

East Coast bio-mods aim to perfect each individual's body and mind. Even before children are born, doctors carefully manipulate the genetic code, enhancing and adding good traits and getting rid of bad ones. Then throughout life, people make adjustments. Personalized pharmaceuticals provide limitless growth opportunities and experiences.

West Coast comp-mods take an entirely different approach, based on a collective optimization algorithm. They don't mess with genetics, drugs, or anything "bodily" (which they'd say with sincere and obvious disdain). They let nature take its course. Tethered to invisible data networks, comp-mods extend their minds beyond their bodies, leaving physicality to management protocols automated by the comp-sys.

Unmodified humans hide in the Midwest.

Historians believe severing communications is what stabilized the competing mod societies. It took a few decades. Apparently, isolation brought harmony.

ONE:

ADAM'S LIFE

Boston, Massachusetts. May 2154.

She called the maternity ward Santa's Workshop. The nurses were busy little elves, and the doctors, well, she wasn't sure— Santa, maybe, but not quite. The doctors were never jolly or fat. But they did deliver what people wanted, straight off their wish lists. Usually, anyway.

Fredric caught her attention, "Kate, let's go. The woman in Room 542 delivered, and we're scheduled for a prep session. If necessary, just reassure them that we'll only take their baby for a half hour and the shot doesn't hurt a bit."

Kate nodded. "Sure, I'm on my fourth observation. I'm getting the hang of it. I looked over their paperwork last night. Standard mods for their boy, right?"

"Yes."

They left their office, walked down the well-lit hallway, and hit the stairs. Kate had been pleasantly surprised when she learned that Fredric also preferred to take the stairs. They both liked the exercise and hated elevators. Kate felt she had to make up for her pretty mediocre physical condition.

Compared with most bio-mods who had heavy physical enhancements from Day One on the genetics side, as well as continued enhancements throughout their lives on the pharmacological side, Kate felt like a wimp. She couldn't lift twice her bodyweight, run a ninety-minute marathon, or swim like a goddamn dolphin. Her parents were scientists, very successful ones, and they'd put a heavy emphasis on her intellectual capabilities, especially her cognitive capacity and fluid intelligence. She was grateful, of course, because it had helped her become a rising star in the genetics field. Her physical condition was fine. Generations of significant biomedical improvements were part of her basic composition. But she still felt the need to squeeze in exercise whenever she could, to make up for whatever deficits she might have. Maybe Fredric felt the same way. He also was quite intelligent, even if a bit of a goofball.

Nicola Gwynne and family were inside room 542. Fredric knocked gently, and they waited. A young nurse opened the door. She was cute and bubbly. Kate recalled a rather dumb girl back in college barely dressed in a retro fantasy costume. Similar face, same fake smile. In a surprisingly not-so-high pitch, the nurse said, "Ah, here they are, just on time. Mr. and Mrs. Gwynne, let me introduce Doctor Stroud and Doctor Genet."

Fredric reached out his hand to Mr. Gwynne, a thin, light-skinned, middle-aged man wearing what Kate was beginning to recognize as the tired, blissful look of a brand-new parent. They shook hands. "It's a pleasure." Kate caught something in

Fredric's eye, but she couldn't figure out what. It passed too quickly, like a lightly struck nerve.

"I'm Doctor Fredric Stroud, the pharmacological mod specialist. I administer the cocktail. Let me introduce my associate, Doctor Kate Genet. She's a geneticist who also works for Biomen. She conducts research on pharmacogenetic modifications in adults, but she's doing a three-month rotation in the maternity ward. She's here to observe."

Kate stepped forward and extended her hand to Mr. Gwynne. He shook her hand weakly. "This is my wife, Nicola, and our son, Adam." He stepped to the side, and Kate saw Nicola holding the newborn. For a moment, she lost her breath, started to sweat, and felt a pull within her stomach. She smiled as she stared at the two of them on the bed. And then the feeling faded, her breathing resumed, and all was normal. Did anyone notice? Not likely.

"Hello. Thank you for allowing me to share this moment with you. Congratulations on your beautiful boy." Her eyes returned to Adam. They got what they wished for all right.

"Thank you," each replied.

Her eyes lingered. He really was beautiful. Adam had those dull bluish eyes and wrinkled, raisin skin that all newborns have. He looked healthy. He was very quiet and almost odorless. She lifted her gaze, surprised by a sudden desire to hold him. She almost said so, but luckily Fredric started his routine.

Fredric took out his notepad and called up Nicola's chart. "Let's go over the basics first. I need to dot the I's and cross the

T's as they used to say, and I still do." He smiled at his joke. Everyone else grinned politely.

"Let's see. Nicola, your bio-mod profile. Your parents have A-type genetic profiles, which mostly passed to you, and you've passed to Adam. They modded you pre-birth with an emphasis on increasing cognitive function. They didn't do much more."

"More?" Joseph interrupted. His face was blank, eyes wide, like a schoolkid's. Nicola looked at him with eyebrows raised, her lips closed. Kate couldn't tell if she was annoyed or worried. He had a good deadpan look. He was messing around with Fredric.

Fredric played along. "Well, no extra physical, behavioral or emotional mods, nothing beyond the standard genetic changes everyone did at that time to keep on track." He coughed and then proceeded in a school teacher voice. "Lots of their generation did the same. Today, there is so much more variation in the pre-birth mods people choose. It used to be mostly cog mods, and then for a while, behavioral and emotional normalization was very popular, but now it's all over the map. Parents want to design their children to give them a leg up. Only so much you can choose to do, of course."

"Why is that, Doctor?" Joseph asked, his face still deadpan but his voice carrying genuine notes of curiosity. "I mean, why can't we choose to have it all?" Kate leaned forward. It was a decent question given progress made in the past few decades.

"Sorry, I didn't quite put that correctly." Fredric responded. He took a breath and lost the school teacher voice. "We do get it all at the most basic level. For generations, we've made a wide range of genetic improvements. You know, you're superhuman in most respects. We all are." He clenched his notepad, flexed his arms and shoulders, puffed his chest, and held the pose for a few seconds. Kate almost laughed aloud. Fredric continued. "It's the targeted enhancements, where parents place a greater emphasis on specific capabilities, which are only potentials, really, possibilities that can be developed and exploited in life. These push mods, as we call them, are the ones I was referring to, really. Studies show that push modifications dilute each other; so parents must choose. The science is quite interesting, and ..."

"OK, Doctor, thanks. I get it," Joseph intervened. "We didn't choose push mods."

"No," Kate almost said, "don't kill it there. Let him go on." She bit her lip instead. It'd be interesting to see how well Fredric would explain the scientific studies, which were inconclusive as to the cause and thus a mystery for researchers like her to solve. She'd ask him another time.

"Alright, then, we'll go over your choices in a minute. So your parents relied mostly on post-birth pharmacological interventions, probably so they could make adjustments over the course of your childhood and adolescence, which I see they did. OK, so I want you to take a quick look at the form I have, verify the mods you've had, and sign the bottom."

She browsed and signed with her finger.

"Excellent. Now, Joseph. Let's see. Your parents have the same profile as Nicola's ..."

"Had."

"Huh?"

"Had. My parents are dead. But yes, they had the same profiles as Nicola's parents. Anyway, go on." Kate shuddered at Fredric's mistake. It was in the documentation, for goodness' sake.

"OK, sorry. Where was I? Your parents didn't mod you much pre-birth—just behavioral controls, nice—and uh, they also focused on pharmacological mods. You've had a steady series of cog-mods. Looks like Adam is going to be a little Brainiac. Here take a look, verify, and sign this."

Joseph looked it over, much more carefully than his wife had, and signed. Kate shifted her position, stepping closer to Joseph. In contrast with the others she'd observed, he actually read the details. She stole a glance at Adam, who lay peacefully, oblivious. Kate couldn't help but smile at him.

"Let's see what you've done with Adam, and what we're going to do. Ah, so you followed your parents' paths. Only the standard pre-birth mods. You're going the pharmacological route. Excellent. We can work with you on setting up the protocols for monitoring and adjustments over the next decade. All we have to do today is give Adam the basic pharmacological cocktail, essentially to plant the seed. It's important that we do this today."

"Why?" Nicola asked. Kate concealed a smile. Mothers always asked why at this point in Fredric's routine, even though they knew the answer.

Fredric answered. "It needs to be done within 48 hours of birth for safety and efficacy. Standard practice. So let's see what mods you've chosen to include in the cocktail."

Fredric looked down at his notepad, nodded, and held it out so the Gwynnes could confirm the mods they'd chosen. Joseph took the notepad and read it carefully. He looked over at his wife, nodded, and then signed. He handed the notepad to her. She browsed and signed. They suddenly looked very tired, almost frightened. Their heads hung a little, like dolls. Or maybe more like dogs. They looked sort of like Zito, the droopy-eyed puppy Kate's father had brought home when she was six. Kate instantly wanted to comfort the couple, but she retained her distance. She left it to Fredric.

"Don't worry about the procedure. It isn't a big deal. I do it every day, dozens of times each day. Never had a problem. It's a simple, old fashioned series of injections with a hypodermic needle. Three little pinpricks. I won't lie to you. It hurts a little, but just a little. He'll barely feel it. And then we'll need to hold him under observation. We'll watch his vitals, make sure he's received all the juice he needs. We'll have him back in your arms half an hour later."

They picked their heads up, smiled and seemed a little better, but not happy, not the happiest people in the world. They should be. He's perfect.

"Any questions?" Fredric asked.

"No. We understand the procedure. It's just hard to let him go, you know," Nicola said.

"I understand. But don't worry. He'll only be away for a short time. We'll be back in about an hour. In the meantime, if you have any questions, you can buzz me." Fredric turned to leave.

Kate followed Fredric down a long hallway and then down two flights. On the stairs, he stopped and turned. "What did you think of them?" He didn't hesitate long enough for her to answer. "She was alright, but he bugged me."

"Well, what do you expect? You didn't know his parents had passed. I mean, …"

"Huh? That wasn't a big deal." He shrugged his shoulders. "It happens. Didn't even faze him. No, I mean before that. From the beginning." He paused, scratched his neck. "I couldn't figure him out." He began to turn but stopped and gave her a chance to respond. She shook her head and said, "He seemed a little anxious, I guess."

They continued down the stairs and went to the special room in the hospital where the drugs and biologics were kept. Strict biometric security measures were in place for this room, not that Kate could see any of them. Only Biomen employees were admitted. Hospital employees couldn't enter the room— too many trade secrets, too many valuable and potentially dangerous materials, and some very expensive, high tech equipment. Security measures like these only curtailed the black market for pharma mods. There was just too much demand, especially among the middle class without employer sponsorship. Kate pictured the bubbly nurse for a moment and shook her head; she'd be covered. Of course, the recipes were easy to come by. You could reverse-engineer them from a legit dose, but printers needed raw materials, and those were tightly regulated and expensive.

Fredric told Kate that she was free to watch him put the cocktail together but suggested that there was nothing interesting to see. Kate agreed. She'd seen it before. She got most of it the first time, and all of it the second time. If there was nothing challenging, then there was nothing worth sticking around to watch and learn. She felt very differently when meeting with the families. That was challenging. It wasn't intellectual, not the sort of theoretical puzzle or cutting-edge lab research that really grabbed her attention. It was more emotional and uncomfortable. No, she wouldn't watch Fredric do his calculations and tests on the formulations.

Instead, she'd go back to Room 542. She didn't say anything to Fredric as she left the room, not that he would have noticed. Her heart pumped more now as she walked the hallway than when she'd run up the stairs. Could be me, she thought. A husband, a child, maybe two. She blew the hair out of her face. It was too much though. It was not like she even had a boyfriend. No, she was too busy, and didn't really try anymore. Besides, she would have to endure too much, and she'd already decided against that. But these past few weeks in the maternity ward had stirred something inside her. It wasn't surprising, but she hadn't expected the feelings to be this strong. She avoided dwelling on it though, not much to diagnose and no harm in letting the feelings linger. Natural emotions for a 33-year-old woman, that's all.

It raised some interesting questions that she'd never thought about before, questions she understood and could reflect on. She considered what mods she would choose for her own child. Most likely, she'd have followed the same path as her parents—nothing very exciting or out of the ordinary. But then she wondered what that would even mean; what would be an exciting set of modifications? Sure, there were some people who gambled with their children, or perhaps for their children. But did parents really have a clue about what mods actually would give their kids an advantage when everyone was modified in one form or another? Better to stick with a conventional, balanced mod program with an emphasis on whatever particular competencies were already genetically advanced in the parents and naturally passed down the familial line. So, for her, heavy cog mods. She'd have raised a little scientist and shared with him everything she knew and loved, her life passions. These thoughts made her feel good and a little selfish.

Then, an odd idea crossed her mind: what would it be like to start fresh, to be unmodified, just plain human. It seemed like such an antiquated idea. There were some non-mods in the Midwest obviously, and for a moment, she thought she might get a kick out of seeing what they were like.

She arrived at Room 542. She stood just outside and peered in the room through a small glass window. They were talking quietly but not saying much. They seemed so anxious. Fredric arrived a few minutes later. She walked into the room with him. "We're all set. Any last minute questions?"

"No," whispered Nicola. She wore a thin smile, and then looked into Adam's eyes, touched his nose with hers gently. Time slowed for what seemed the most intimate of kisses.

Kate stepped toward Nicola. As the nurse approached to do her job, Kate tensed. She stepped aside and let the nurse scoop up the baby from Nicola's arms. Without Adam in her arms, Nicola seemed to shrink, and her eyes darted between Adam and the nurse as she put Adam in a little padded cart and wheeled him away.

"Alright, then. We'll be back soon." Fredric said.

Kate walked with Fredric down the hallway in silence. They entered the room where the nurse had taken Adam. Three shots and a wailing infant later, Kate wondered whether they really needed to observe the babies in this room, away from the parents, for medical reasons. Maybe it was just to save the parents the distress of her hearing their babies scream like banshees.

As promised, they wheeled Adam back within a half hour. Fredric said, "Everything went smoothly." The parents relaxed. Nicola took Adam from the nurse and held him tightly. "Thank you, everyone. We're so happy." Kate longed to stay and bask in their joy, but snapped out of it as Fredric tugged her toward the door. "We'll leave you three now. We'll be in touch in three months to set up a follow-up meeting, just to check how things are going. In the meantime, you are in good hands here. Get some rest. And congratulations!" Kate smiled, "Yes, congratulations."

Back in their office they fell into their routines, Fredric recording the details of Adam's cocktail while Kate checked the paperwork for the next meeting.

A loud beeping noise startled Kate. She had been daydreaming at her desk, but she couldn't remember the dream. The beeping prevented any recall. Fredric popped up from his chair. "Let's go. C'mon, Kate. Room 542." Only then did she notice the little red light flashing on his desk; the beeping was coming from somewhere on his desk too. They ran, the beeping noise ringing in Kate's head. No one else in the hallways seemed to hear it. They didn't get out of her way.

When she entered room 542, Kate felt an intense wave of biochemical feedback, jumbled emotions heavily laden with confusion and dread. The loud rhythmic beeping was suffocating. She spotted a flashing red light in a corner of the room. She stepped to the side as another nurse rushed in. Nicola was crying. Fredric was beside her. Joseph was shuffling, two steps to the left and then back to the right, staying as close to Nicola and Adam as he could without getting in the way of the medical professionals who surged into the room.

Adam was oddly quiet. He was breathing slowly, but otherwise seemed fine.

To one of the nurses, Fredric asked, "What happened? What triggered the alarm?" She stared back at him, shook her head, but said nothing. Another nurse turned her head toward

Fredric as if she were about to answer him, but she turned away and stared at a screen. A third nurse, who had one hand on the bed while she leaned in and stared at Adam, popped up and responded, "We're not sure. Vitals are fine. We're checking."

The second nurse, who stared at the screen, shifted her stance and tilted her head. "Doctor Stroud, do you see anything?" Fredric rushed over, looked at the screen, and shook his head. He murmured, "Where the hell is he?" and then told the nurse, "Get Doctor Schmidt."

Suddenly, the baby turned a dark, purplish grey color. His blue eyes were open, and they stayed open, staring blankly. It progressed so rapidly, so abruptly. Everyone in the room froze. All of the air in the room was sucked out; the beeping was gone. All eyes were pulled into Adam's frozen blue eyes, like light into a black hole. No one moved. No one could have, even if they tried, but no one tried. The stillness seemed to last an eternity, an eternity of painful disbelief and wonder in a split-second.

It broke.

The parents were screaming. The nurses had never seen anything like this before, and it showed. The masks they had carefully constructed for moments like this were cracked, broken, useless. Death, they'd seen, been prepared for, but only death of the elderly or by accident. Not an infant, not like this.

Tears flowed down Kate's cheeks. This can't be happening. He can't be dead. She looked to Fredric for an answer, but he was lost in his own mind, muttering to himself—Where was Schmidt? Was there an incompatibility that he hadn't seen? An older doctor came running into the room, saw the dead infant, and stumbled backwards as if struck hard in the chest.

Kate looked to Adam, his perfectly round head, tufts of black hair. The eyelashes she'd been envying earlier. He stared back with dead blue eyes.

Two:

Questions

Kate slept uneasily, cycling among intense dreams. She relived her last sexual encounter in horrid, slow motion and extreme detail. Over a decade old, the memory remained, no matter how hard she wished to forget it. It had been worse than her previous sexual experiences. The dream accentuated the chaotic aspects of the sex-driven hallucinations she'd had, the parts she hated most. Most bio-mods thought the intense ecstasy was divine. But it was too strong for her, made her dizzy and nauseous. The dream she was having slowed and amplified everything, putting the end out of reach, even further outside her control than it had been. She felt like she was drowning, suffocating, sinking, but too damn slowly. She could see poor Johan above her, absorbed in delirious pleasure, but oblivious to her distress. His demon eyes plastered pink; his breath crimson hazed; his smile crystalline. She shuddered, her muscles twitching involuntarily, which he must've misunderstood as indicia of success. With every thrust, her revulsion toward this lover who had unwittingly become her tormenter grew. Let it be over. Please. Not again.

That's when she knew she was dreaming, and it only made it worse, much worse, because she knew it could go on forever. Maybe she'd die in the waking world but never reach the end of the dream; infinite torture through a finite dream. She woke suddenly in a panic, sweating. She sat up.

Disoriented, she looked at the clock. It was only 2 am. She remembered little of the dream, like an old breeze. It lingered in the back of her mind, hiding, waiting for another shot. She lay back down in her damp bed and drifted asleep.

She was back in Room 542. *No, not again*, a sliver of her consciousness moaned. "Congratulations," she slurred, and then she was walking with Fredric back to their office. "Only two more today." *No, that was a lie. There would be no more this day, not for her.* Loud beeping startled her, but she did not wake. It penetrated in ear-splitting bursts, pressing her body to move, and then blended into a dull, continuous ringing, as she ran down the hallway in a daze. The door was open. She entered the room. The nurses inside faded into the background in between shadows. She barely noticed. There were others, but she was drawn to him, to his blue eyes. Adam was looking for her. He was alive. He was aware and searching. Their eyes met. He drew her in with his eyes, an intense gravity, somehow familiar. He called to her silently. What did he want? He couldn't speak, but he wanted to, it seemed. She wanted him to speak, to say something. "What?" She shouted. The rest of the room was chaos. The nurses' faces were cracking under an intense pressure. Fredric muttered like a madman. No one heard her, except Adam. She shouted

"What?" again and again at the infant who stared at her. She saw something move on his face, and she stopped yelling and listened, straining to hear. His lips clenched, his mouth opened and then closed, lips clenched again, forever. He died instantly. She mimicked him, a simple mime, and recognized his only word. "Mom." He spoke it to her. It was her word too. Tears spurted from her eyes, and her heart broke. She echoed Nicola's screams and felt her unbearable pain. Oh, how she felt it! Motherhood lost seared her. Instinctively, Kate tried to process what was happening and how she felt, but her intellect was useless, completely absent, as if destroyed. She'd experienced motherhood for a tantalizing second; it had expanded within her as the universe had in its first moment. Seemingly limitless hope and love, purpose and meaning. But then it was suddenly lost in an immediate reversal, as her universe crashed in on itself.

It was like nothing she'd ever felt before, a deep pull from her entire torso: her heart beat intensely—not fast but hard with a fury, her lungs collapsed as air seemed impossible to get and then she had to breathe deeply just to get some but not enough, her stomach dropped and churned, and even her kidneys ached as if squeezed dry. She turned to Nicola, who clenched Adam to her chest and sobbed. Joseph was holding his head in both hands, weeping, muttering to himself. She tried to make out what he was saying, but couldn't.

The dream started over again. The steady beeping again carried her into room 542. Adam only stared. He had no weight. Instead, it was Joseph who drew her attention. He shone brightly and seemed the happiest man alive. She felt the joy and smiled. Then he broke. Such a sudden, ruthless wrenching of emotion caused her to weep. She wasn't weeping for Adam, but for Joseph. His head dropped into his hands, and he sobbed as he shook his head. "No," he sputtered in a low, guttural moan. It ached. She felt it pass through her, a physical echo inside the hollow places of her body. Then he began muttering. She couldn't understand all that he said. Something about a storm. "How could this happen? Why? I knew it couldn't be true. I couldn't be this fortunate. To have Nicola and Adam. Oh, God, it's too much. It's my fault. I know we shouldn't have done this."

The dream started over again. Room 542. Elves in white danced about the room with bells on their shoes. Fredric was jolly, old Santa in a red suit, with a big white beard, and a fat belly. He held out a white porcelain doll and handed it to Nicola. She shied away. He pushed it toward her, and when Joseph stepped between them, Fredric dropped the doll. It shattered and broke. Only its small head remained intact. The blue eyes fixed on Kate. She woke in a panic and sat up.

5:30 am. She got up and went to the shower. The hot water pelting the back of her neck felt incredibly good. It woke her mind. She began to recall what happened the day and night before. It was a blur. Did Adam speak to her? Of course he couldn't have. Did Fredric say something about an incompatibility that he didn't see coming? He seemed guilty, fearful. Was that from her dreams last night or the hospital room the day before? She couldn't say for sure.

Even if she only noticed it in a dream, it could have happened. Sometimes, Kate recalled things through lucid, vivid dreams. Many biomods did. It had something to do with their expanded capacity to access memories.

But now, she was confused. Her dreams from last night didn't help her. They were too chaotic and unreliable. Something went wrong, obviously. Infants didn't die. Her stomach twisted, a false hunger. She needed to figure out what happened. She owed it to Adam, who had called her mom, whether in a dream or reality didn't matter, didn't register.

***

Kate returned to the hospital. She had three observations on her schedule. She met Fredric in their office. She often thought of it as their retreat. Besides some of the top executives' offices at the hospital, theirs was much nicer than the other offices in the hospital. Biomen took care of them. It was actually two offices adjoined by a sitting room with comfortable couches, a glass coffee table, and a stocked kitchen off to the side. They kept their office doors wide open most of the time. Fredric was sitting at his desk when she arrived, and he called to her as soon as he saw her.

"Why do you look so ragged?"

"Thanks, Fredric. I couldn't sleep. I had terrible dreams."

He started to laugh, probably a joke forming in his head, but he stopped himself. "Sorry. I understand. But look, don't worry. It isn't a big deal. Unfortunate, sure, but not something to stress over, much less lose any sleep over. It's incredibly rare, but it happens. An allergic reaction that causes an extreme anaphylactic shock and sudden cardiac arrest. ..."

Goddamn animal. He wasn't even bothered by Adam's death. He continued talking. She barely listened. Maybe *they're* right. We are animals. We say comp-mods have lost their humanity and become machines. But what's worse? Machine or animal?

Kate had never doubted the path the bio-mods were on or doubted their superiority. They were human, absolutely, but more advanced than the unmodified humans hiding in the Midwest. Bio-mods had evolved rapidly and vastly improved the human species in countless ways, maintaining a rich diversity and continuing to play Darwin's game. She knew the comp-mods regarded bio-mods as degenerate drug addicts who had regressed into subhuman animals, but she had never given those views the slightest weight, not even as much as a playground taunt. They were calculated propaganda generated by whatever AI machination was in charge of the comp-mod machines. There was no hint of truth in such propaganda. Or so she had always thought, until now.

Fredric was still talking. "Kate, you should also know that the doctors already ruled out any fault on our part. There's no need to worry about liability. It's just a very rare allergic reaction."

"But why wouldn't we be responsible?" Kate interjected. She'd taken the oath, and so had Fredric. "We gave Adam the drug cocktail, and he had an allergic reaction to it. Shouldn't we have known about the risk?"

"Of course not, Kate. It's impossible to know ahead of time. Well, I mean, we know that one out of every 25,000 is going to have an allergic reaction, but we have no way of knowing which one. There is nothing we can do to avoid the random death."

"It is not random," she said fiercely. We are in control. Her scientific instincts, training, and intellect rebelled against his claim. Biomodification was a strictly controlled process, honed carefully for over a century. Random deadly mistakes couldn't happen.

He stood up, and his chair hit the wall behind him. "Yes it is, Kate." They stared at each other like predators. The standoff lasted less than a minute. He relaxed and sat down. "Look. I understand how you feel. This is awful. I have never seen it happen before. I'd read about it a long time ago, and last night, I spoke with the doctors and did some research. I can forward you what I found and the report, and possibly even the autopsy, if I can get the parents' permission. But I'm not sure that would be a good idea right now. You seem very upset. Why don't you take a day or two off?"

Kate shook her head, her eyes shut, and took a deep breath. "No. I'm fine." She took another less obvious one and made eye contact with Fredric. "Maybe I'll have a look at what you found later this afternoon. We have two this morning and one this afternoon, right?"

"Yes. You sure?"

Kate assured him and then went into her office and shut the door. She put her head down on her desk. Her head throbbed as she tried to process Fredric's explanation and casual attitude, and her own reaction. Why do I care so much about this?

Fredric's explanation didn't make sense from a scientific perspective. An allergic reaction seemed implausible. Her cheek pressed on the flat cool surface of her desk while her feet tapped an irregular beat on the floor. A strong urge to develop hypotheses, investigate, and conduct research pulled on her attention. She recognized the rational part of her brain doing its ordinary work. Yet, to her surprise, she felt an equally strong pull towards something else; she couldn't quite name it. Compassion? Sorrow?

Adam. Why do I care so much about this particular baby? She'd felt connected to him when she'd seen him in the room with his parents; she'd even felt connected to them. But it hadn't been different than other families she'd observed. Or had it? There had been something, something that drew her to him. She'd assumed it was just biochemical feedback within the room, tripping her hormones and emotions, accentuating the maternal feeling that had been emerging since she began the ward observations. But now, after his death, it seemed different, more intense and stable, not the transitory wave from biochemical feedback.

She sat up, pressed her hands on the lip of the desk, arched her back, and held the pose to stretch her lower back muscles. If not an allergic reaction, then what? Hypotheses danced just outside cognition. Not worth pursuing, though. They'd surface when she had more time to think and less emotional noise. Better to focus on more immediate tasks. Three procedures to get through, that's all.

The first two procedures went smoothly. Kate was in a daze throughout. During the second, her mind wandered, and she imagined herself lying in the bed, holding Adam. The dream lasted only a moment, however. After the third procedure, when they returned the little girl, Abigail, to her parents, Doctor Schmidt arrived in the room. He greeted the parents and explained that he was just checking in on them. He gave the baby a very quick look-over. "Looks great. I'll see you three tomorrow morning before you check-out." He turned to leave. When his eyes met Kate's, he smiled. She smiled back. As he left the room, he glanced back at her. She decided to follow him and quickly excused herself. When she caught up to him in the hallway, he was surprised.

"Can I talk to you about the death yesterday?" She let her smile dissipate slowly.

"Of course, Kate. Not now because I'm booked all afternoon. But we can grab coffee or something next week? When are you available?"

"I'm not sure. I just want to chat briefly. I mean, I …"

"Look, Kate. It was an awful accident, that's all. I know you're not a medical professional and so you're not used to death. But you've got to understand that it happens, even sometimes, although only very rarely, to infants. Death happens. But so does life, and that is what we need to focus on, life. Right? I've got patients." He turned away from her, ready to rush off.

But she put her hand on his shoulder and said, "Thanks, Doctor Schmidt. Has the coroner performed an autopsy yet?"

He turned back, and her hand fell. His warm eyes replaced. The sudden biochemical feedback was intense. Kate felt his strong sense of superiority and frustration, as well as anxiety. "Yes, of course. Last night. Nothing more to report, Kate. Allergic reaction to your company's drug cocktail." He edged closer to her. "The parents signed the appropriate forms, acknowledging and accepting the risk, just like everyone does."

***

Kate wandered the hospital. She couldn't get her thoughts straight. She felt compelled to accept Doctor Schmidt's explanation. After all, weren't doctors the ones with the relevant expertise, years of training and experience? Who was she to second-guess them? She'd expect the same respect in her own field of research. Besides, doctors were trustworthy. They took the oath, of course. She'd always trusted them without reservation. Everyone did. Given the number of medical interventions in their lives, they really had no choice.

Yet as she began to settle on this equilibrium, her stomach rebelled, the pores on her neck, armpits and lower back moistened, and her vision shifted focus. She blinked rapidly and breathed slowly to regain composure.

She stood outside the room with all of the newborns. They were sleeping, and they looked healthy. She watched them for a few minutes. They were so peaceful, so beautiful. Suddenly, she heard a ringing and the hairs on the back of her neck stiffened. Then the sleeping infants all turned a dark, purplish grey color. She tried to scream but nothing came out. She looked for help, saw nurses in the room, but they weren't doing anything; they were just standing and talking. She looked back at the babies, and they were all fine. She shook her head violently and left.

Kate thought about trying to get her hands on the autopsy, but she decided not to bother. She knew what it would say. Instead, she took the steps down to the basement. The file room was a subterranean labyrinth, but it was secure. She passed through security and headed straight to the file clerk's desk.

As she approached the desk, something about the clerk piqued her curiosity. He looked ordinary, like he fit the position. How did this guy end up as a clerk in the basement of this hospital? Why him? Why this job? Did his parents gamble and lose when they modded him? He didn't have the exaggerated muscles or looks that usually accompanied such a gamble. No, he looked quite normal, as handsome and fit as anyone else, except for his somewhat large ears, which were almost cute. Nothing more stood out. He couldn't have incredible mental capabilities, or he wouldn't be a clerk in the basement. His parents probably didn't have the resources, couldn't afford more sophisticated mods or recurring payments for pharmas. He got the basics that everyone got. Fortunately, since he worked for the hospital, he'd probably get better access for his children. They'd have a chance to advance. Maybe that's why he ended up here, to give his kids a chance.

"Hi. My name is Kate Genet. I'm working in the maternity ward and doing some research on allergic reactions to the Biomen drug cocktail. Can I take a look at the infant mortality data for this hospital, and if you have it, any aggregate data you have for the region?" She stopped for a second, and he looked at her with eyebrows raised, as if more explanation was required. So she went on. "I know that infant mortality rates are usually calculated in terms of the number of deaths of infants under one year old per 1,000 live births, but I'm really very interested in the number of deaths of infants under one week old. I'd like to know the cause of death, if possible. And I would like to know how close in time the death was to the administration of the Biomen cocktail." He coughed to interrupt her. Or had he yawned and covered it up with a cough?

"Ms. Genet, I need to see your authorization. Do you have a signed T-120?"

"No, I don't," she answered, and then, "How could I?" more to herself than him. "Listen, an infant died last night. I was there. I need to complete this assignment for my employer as soon as possible. I don't have time to get a T-120 authorization. That will take weeks. Look ...." She took out her Biomen identification card and pushed it toward the clerk. It gave her a very high level of clearance at the hospital.

He took the card and examined it carefully. "Oh, very well, I see. I can get you aggregate data for this hospital as well as the region, and heck, if you'd like, the entire East Coast. But I can't get you any individual patient files. Not without a T-120."

"That will be fine. Thank you very much. Should I come back later or …?"

"No, don't bother. It will be just fifteen minutes or so, maybe less. You can wait over there." He pointed to an empty waiting area.

She sat at one of the worktables and took out her notepad. She finalized her notes for the three procedures she'd observed.

Fifteen minutes later, the clerk approached her. "Here you are, Ms. Genet." He handed a sheet of paper, folded in half. She took it from him and thanked him. "You can keep that, by the way. It's a disposable copy."

She laid the sheet flat on the table, activated the visualization features with a wave of her hand, and began scrolling through the three-dimensional images projected above the table. He had given her a comprehensive report on infant mortality. The first section covered infant mortality at this hospital over the past fifty years. All patient identifying information had been scrubbed and replaced with generic codes. But it did provide the age of the deceased infant as well as the cause of death. She was surprised to see this information. She dug through, flipping to internal pages of the report, and saw that he had also included twenty-six additional sections, including similar data for twenty-five other hospitals on the East Coast. The final section provided aggregate statistics and analysis. She browsed that section and then returned to the first.

The data suggested that infant mortality rates were incredibly low and actually steadily declining within the bio-mod community. The rates were more or less the same across bio-mod hospitals. Very few infants died within their first week of life, about one in 25,000. The Biomen drug cocktail had to be administered within forty-eight hours, and so it was to be expected that the rate would be about the same as the rate Fredric had suggested for allergic reactions. She was partially relieved. She folded the paper, tucked it in her bag, and returned to her office.

Fredric was waiting. He held out a white rose. "You're back. I'm sorry about how I was acting this morning. I guess it bothered me too, but I was trying to blow it off. Are you feeling better?"

"Actually, no, Fredric. I think you were right, that I need some time. I don't know." She glanced at the dull grey flooring tiles. They had an odd white swirl that gave a brief illusion of depth. "Doctor Schmidt was right. I'm not a medical professional, and I'm not used to death." She hesitated and looked to Fredric. Then her voice squeaked a little, like a country bird, "You know what? I don't want to be. I think I might head to Rochester for a while. Get myself settled."

"You sure?" His eyes puzzled, his voice wavering with a trace of sadness buried beneath his surprise. Kate shrugged and nodded. "Well, I guess you are. Good luck. Come back when you're ready."

"Thanks, Fredric. I will." He handed her the flower, and she took it with a smile. He recovered ground in her mind, and that relieved her.

THREE:

SNAKES, MEERKATS, & ANTS

Mr. Shephard stood in a sunlit boardroom. His mind extended.

Omniscience was divine. Or was it the other way around. It didn't matter. Either way, he felt like God. As one of God's children, a son of God, shouldn't that be what he aspired to? A deep, exhilarating desperation crept up, from his loins to his heart and head. He filled his lungs. He wanted more. Mr. Shephard knew or could know almost everything about his community, his family. He was the CEO of CompSys, after all. He could share his godlike awareness and understanding with them, give them access to parts of the comp-sys data flows, and he did, at least to a degree. He gave them what they wanted, what he thought they could manage. He exhaled in a sigh as his hunger subsided, not disappearing but slipping into the background. He shifted his attention to the people sitting around the white table, waiting for him.

"So here is what I want. I'm willing to grant $750 million to each group to support this R&D competition, but I want it done my way, carefully and accurately. No shortcuts. There is plenty more to follow this initial seed funding to whichever group is most successful. I alone determine the winner, and I alone own everything both teams generate. If you want to play, you work for me. It begins once we adjourn and ends in exactly nine months. Questions?" He glared around the table. He knew they were on board. They'd already signed the contracts.

The Stanford team had more women than men. He immediately placed his mental bet on Stanford. He knew that both teams were incredibly talented and would do well, but they approached the competition differently. Berkeley was mostly comp-sys tech experts with a single non-tech, probably a historian or anthropologist. Stanford had a few non-techs, obvious from their appearance—they had a little more color and weight to them.

"Will there be a more complete spec sheet?" It was one of the chippies. "The specs are rather abstract and don't specify the data agglomeration protocol, which we obviously need if we're supposed to construct the environment, and we don't even know how far back we should go or how much to pre-specify. Moreover, I wonder ...."

The rest of the Berkeley team glared at him, and the Stanford team watched Mr. Shephard with a calm confidence. Yes, Stanford would win.

"No. I will not provide a more detailed spec sheet. Look, kid." The chippy was 28. "It isn't hard to imagine what I want, that is, if you have an imagination and don't need me to supply it to you. It's simple, really. I want you to develop an all-inclusive, immersive, interactive world history. Livable history, get it? We already have a near limitless range of perfect experience tailored to our each and every want. Right?"

The kid nodded.

"No, wrong." Mr. Shephard sighed. "C'mon, you know there are vistas we can't quite get. I want one in particular. I want human history. Our past. Understand? We should be able to wander through and experience it—a self-directed, fully immersive museum tour."

The kid nodded, but still looked confused.

Mr. Shephard continued. "We've got bits and pieces, of course. We've got the simulations and various reconstructions of past events. Shit, every kid relives bits and pieces, and they get a decent education. We do a pretty good job, if I do say so myself. But I want something much more grand." He immediately made direct eye contact with each person in the room and spoke directly to them through the system, leaving the simulation of audible speech behind. "Look everyone. I currently have working prototypes, which I cannot share with you. I don't want to bias your approach or distort your projects. Fresh starts are best. But let me be clear, I have wandered down memory lane and relived my past experiences, my father's and his father's past experiences, all the way back to my great-great-great grandfather's experiences. I've lived parts of their lives, and I've witnessed them, like a ghost and like God above. I've even lived some of your experiences." He grinned for all of them, but he gave that one chippy an especially devilish smile. "Look, what I've got works with stored memories, and as you probably know, we've been storing that data for decades. It's big, and it's a good beginning, but it's not the end."

He could tell that the wheels were turning, gears triggering, heck, even a little smoke from the ears. He'd lit a spark. He conjured a memory from Jonathan Shephard, his great-great-great grandfather, their Founder, and decided to share it with the teams, a glimpse to inspire them. "This was our beginning ...." With a command thought, he sent it.

**

Jonathan stood in a coffee shop on Vallejo Street in San Francisco. A 2030s-era roborista delivered his double espresso on a fingerless hand-tray. It was mid-summer. He watched hundreds of people walking down the sidewalk in neat lines like ants.

So much had changed in such a short time. He pictured the same street a decade ago. Hundreds of people walking, but the sidewalk was mobbed, and one out of every three walkers was a stumbling, bumbling idiot—either meandering like a snake or stopping suddenly like a meerkat, chatting away on a cell phone or worse, swiping and thumbing a screen on their mobile devices, oblivious to everyone else around them, not giving a shit about anyone beside themselves and whoever it was that they were interacting with, if it really was an actual person and not the latest cat video. Meandering snakes and sudden stop meerkats, he thought, were fucking annoying.

Jonathan smiled. So much had changed. From snakes and meerkats to ants in just a decade.

He shook his head. There was something lurking beyond his comprehension—an itch, a story, a puzzle, an answer. The orderly procession outside seemed slow as his mind raced. He began to put the pieces together. There were only a few. It began with cars, not people.

He recalled I-80 rush hour, back in 2015. Thousands of people congesting the highway like maggots on roadkill. Murderous rage and frustration, and for some, desperation—those poor souls who had to pee! He laughed. Bumper to bumper traffic swelled and surged and then suddenly stopped in a flash mob of red taillights. Another snake-meerkat metaphor popped in Jonathan's head, but he rejected it and searched for something better, a boa choking down a deer, no, that wasn't right though it stuck in his head for a few seconds, and then he returned to the meerkats and thought of a huge swarm of them running full speed and then freezing at the first sign of danger. Close, but not quite; according to some video he'd seen, that was an efficient and orderly response to a perceived threat. Highway congestion was a shitfest.

A few years later, though, maybe 2020, I-80 during rush hour looked and felt quite different. Rage and desperation were replaced with calm satisfaction. As he thought about this shift, Jonathan felt a tingling sensation along his arms and midsection; he filled his lungs and held tight, his ribs pressing hard, and then slowly exhaled. He could see it now, an orderly network of humans and machines. Traffic was moving, managed, in synch. Ants. The cars were equipped with auto-drive systems and received data from the highway sensor network. Ants. Elegant sensing, communicating, cooperative management systems. Content ants.

The next pieces came together in 2022. Google announced a new version of Google Glass. It was a game changer. Revolutionary. So long cell phones, smart phones, hand held mobile whatevers. There had been healthy competition. Since its resurrection in 2019, Google Glass slowly gained modest market share in the mobile communications and computation sector. But this new version changed everything. Remarkably, Google had kept it quiet. No patents. Maybe they weren't necessary because the company had patents on the underlying technologies, and no one expected the synergistic combination. Or maybe they were in the works.

The glue technology, the one that made it possible, was the motor function management software and the interface through Google Glass with the human brain and body. Initially, researchers developed the tech as a small independent project to help accident victims who were paralyzed or lost control of certain parts of their bodies. No one paid it much attention, except the victims, of course.

Jonathan stared out the window at the beautifully synched bodies, better than any ballet. He marveled at the ingenuity; who'd have thought to combine the three technologies—Google Glass, self-driving cars, and the motor function management system? Brilliant. *Snakes and meerkats to fricken' ants.* Just like the cars. Utterly brilliant.

Still staring out the coffee shop window, awe flooded Jonathan's brain, as powerfully as when he first met Anna. Startled and excited, he let it settle and expand. He'd put together the puzzle, reached the present, finished the story, or so he thought, but then he began to extrapolate. It hit him, and he whispered, "Hallefuckinlujah." The new Google Glass had been revolutionary, but it was only the beginning, a birth. Jonathan saw a glimpse of the future he'd build.

***

Mr. Shephard stopped the stroll down memory lane. There was more, much more, but he wouldn't show it to anyone, not yet. It was his. He knew that the segment served its purpose. He felt the energy. The data was unambiguous.

He spoke to them. "An early comp-mod. Maybe the first. You see how it emerged. You feel how he felt." He paused. "These memories, how we experienced them, the reality, the history, the significance, I want that to inspire you. It's just the beginning, a glimpse of what you can construct. Do you see?"

He took one last glance around the room, nodded, and then he dismissed them.

FOUR:

HOME

Kate had been excited to return home. She'd missed the rolling green hills of upstate New York. She grew up in Rochester, went to the University of Rochester for her undergraduate studies, and returned after completing her doctoral work at M.I.T. She loved Boston and Rochester, but she had only ever called Rochester home.

The upstate New York Biomen campus was huge, much larger than the Massachusetts campus. It had more or less taken over the University of Rochester. The science, mathematics, and engineering departments as well as the medical school were filled with Biomen employees, or in some cases, University employees who so heavily relied on Biomen funding for their research that they were Biomen's employees in everything but name. Kate had two offices on the campus, a big corporate office near the "lab" and a small academic office, which she used mainly for meeting with her doctoral students. She preferred the small office, which was mixed in with a dozen graduate student offices in the pharmacogenetics building. She supervised some doctoral students who studied genetic resistance to pharmacologically induced change in adults. This was her area of expertise and supervising students kept her fresh. Besides, she loved her team of young geniuses. The best of them also worked on her lab team. This office was also her retreat, a place she could dig into something without being disturbed.

Instead of her office, she went to their suite.

"Kate, what are you doing here?" her mother said. "Roger, come quickly. I have a surprise for you."

"Hi Mom. It's good to see you. I'm back for a while." They hugged, and Kate kissed her mother's cheek. The embrace brought a surge of comforting warmth, like a shot of whiskey.

"Is everything alright? You seem, I don't know, down." She stepped back from Kate, and Kate tried to smile. "No, I can feel something's bothering you. What happened? Wait, a second. Roger. … Roger, take your head out …"

"Mom, it's OK. Not a big deal." Her voice was flat, like she was reading a script from her teenage years.

"What? What do you want? Jackie, did you call me?"

"Yes, Roger, I did. Come out here. I've a surprise for you."

A tall man with dark grey hair and brilliant green eyes skipped into the waiting room. "Oh my God! Kate!" His face lit up, and it reminded her of Joseph. Kate shuddered. Her face dimmed, as if his joy sucked the light from her.

"Kate? Are you alright?" Her mother's face tightened, revealing her age. "What's wrong?"

Her father took three quick steps to her and took her in his arms, and hugged her tight. "Kate, are you OK? You don't look so good." He shuffled her back a step and to the side so she could sit on the couch. The cold corkine fabric felt good against the back of her neck and legs. She breathed out heavily and recovered. Her father sat with her, and her mother rushed over and sat on the other side of her.

"I'm fine." That script voice again. After a moment, she added, "Just tired."

"Kate, you never admit to being tired, even when you're on the verge of collapse." He put his hand to her temple and looked into her eyes. "Kate, we're so happy to see you. Tell us why you're here. What's going on?" Then he got up, grabbed a chair and swept it under him so he could sit in front of her. His eyes never broke from hers.

Why had she come straight here, to them? She had even brought her bags. What had she been thinking? Was she thinking at all? Of course, they would be worried and want to know everything. She sat still and silent, not defiant but unsure about what to say next, where to start and how far to go. Her parents loved her deeply, she knew that, and they would support her in whatever she chose to do. But that was the problem; she wasn't sure what she was doing. She didn't have a plan, possibly for the first time in her life.

"Kate, darling." It was her mother. "Did you meet someone?" She looked half-worried and half-hopeful. The mixed emotions showed on her face in a weird contortion of eyebrows twitching from raised in hopeful expectation to furrowed with worry, and a thin smile that showed just a hint of teeth between pink lips.

"No, Mom. You know that I'm not ... I'm not looking for that anymore." A hint of anger, frustration slipped into her voice. She hadn't meant to let it.

"I know Kate, but sometimes it happens precisely because you're not looking. That's when God might step in and enter your life, bringing love. You know, your father and I ..."

"Seriously, Mom?" She shrugged her shoulders and twisted her head to relieve the stiffness in her neck. Why did she insist on going down this path, again?

"Jackie, please, not now. That's not it, can't you tell? There's no need to go down that path again." He looked to his wife. It had always been backwards, her father understanding her need for control while her mother struggled. Kate smiled. Fortunately, he understood her mother's needs as well.

After a moment, her mother turned back to face Kate. "I'm sorry, Kate. Really, I'm very sorry. That's not it, is it?"

"Don't worry Mom. Not a big ..." She stopped and reached out to hold her mother's hand. It was warm. "I mean, I know what you're thinking, what you want, what you want for me. I really do understand. Now more than ever before ..."

Her mother's face shifted from worried toward hopeful, though not completely. "What do you mean, dear?"

"Kate, we're here for you. Just tell us what's on your mind." He knew when to just listen. Could've been a successful psychologist. How many times had she confided in him as a child? She'd end up in his study, looking up at him, eyes pleading for his support; he'd pull two chairs next to each other, sit, and listen. It was like confession, but without all of the Catholic ritual. He never broke her trust by discussing what she'd said or done, unless she brought it up first, and even then, he'd feign surprise. When she finished her confession, he'd offer to help but always insist that she should work out a plan first. He'd help her to think it through, to think methodically, and to face whatever consequences must be faced with her head high. That's what she always seemed to need from him. All she really wanted was for him to listen and offer to help, and that was what he gave.

She hesitated, stretched her legs and pressed her neck against the cool corkine, and thought about making up something. Of course, nothing came to mind. So she told them everything that had happened in room 542. She wasn't sure what she'd done wrong. She was just an observer, but it felt like her confession. Adam died.

Her parents didn't interrupt. They just sat and listened.

Kate felt oddly relieved. She had cried a little while telling the story, but not much; she spoke mostly as if giving a report, in a formal, newscaster voice. But they must have felt her distress. They didn't say anything, though. When she finished the story and returned to the present, she looked to her father. He stared back at her with compassionate eyes, but he said nothing. He just waited for her to continue. She wasn't sure what to say next. "That's what happened. That's it."

"I don't understand." Her mother said. "Why did the baby die? He was born healthy, with no sign of any problems?"

"Right. It was an allergic reaction to the drug cocktail. Incredibly rare, but apparently unpredictable and unavoidable."

"Well, that's terrible." Her mother said. "Hard to believe, in this day and age. I would've thought allergies were modded out decades ago. I don't think I've heard of anyone having an allergic …"

"It really is awful, Kate. But why has it got you so unsettled? Tell us what you're …"

"I don't know, Dad." Kate took a deep breath. "I feel responsible somehow. I know it's crazy, but I do." With another breath, she relaxed a little, but there was still something, a knot that wouldn't come loose.

"Go on."

"Adam was so damn perfect. I don't know. He wasn't supposed to die. It doesn't make sense. Like Mom said, we modded out allergies a long time ago, right? I understand that we can't get it perfect, that there are still things that we can't predict or control. And maybe that's a good thing. I mean, Darwin's game and everything. But allergies? To the basic cocktail? I don't know. It just doesn't feel right."

"You think that maybe …"

"Jackie. Don't. Kate, go on."

"What do you want me to say? Dad." Her voice cracked and fell. "I don't know what happened. Maybe something went wrong with cocktail, or with Fredric's process, or … I don't know."

"Kate." He just looked at her.

She understood. She wanted to tell him how she felt, she wanted to tell him everything, to just let loose, to pour it all out, like she did the last time she confided in him, years ago. Back then, she had needed him so badly, to help her, but she'd been afraid to talk about sex with him. It was weird, uncomfortable. She had no one else and was on the verge of losing it. Her pain trumped the discomfort, and she went to him as she had all her life.

***

Kate was almost seventeen. She knocked softly on his door. Perhaps he wouldn't hear. He was probably busy. Maybe she should come back, or try to deal with this on her own. She started to turn, and the door opened slowly.

"Hey there. I thought I heard something," he said. It only took a moment for him to recognize something was terribly wrong. The feedback was intense. "C'mon in, Kate. Tell me what's bothering you."

She knew just where to go. She sank into the couch and tried to relax, breathing slowly. He pulled up his chair, and just looked at her, eyebrows raised, lips together, sadness in his eyes despite his effort to maintain control, to keep his own emotions in check. He felt her distress.

"I'm not sure what to say, Dad. It's hard …"

"I understand." He waited.

"It has to do with Johan, with …." How could she explain or talk to him about how she was feeling? She didn't know how to begin. It was embarrassing in a juvenile way, as if she was five years younger when the topic of boys, much less sex with boys, was her taboo.

Kate could tell that he wanted to say something, to ask her a specific question, probably whether Johan had hurt her or something like that, but instead, he just waited. His lips held together tighter; his eyes saddened a little more, perhaps. But he waited.

After a long minute, she took a deep breath and took the plunge.

"Sex, Dad. We had sex. And, I just, I just hated it. It was terrible. I can't stop it from coming back, pushing me, haunting me. I think I'm losing my mind." She held her head, fingers pressing her temples, eyes open wide.

He waited, and then asked, "Did he force you …"

"No! Not at all." Kate dropped her hands from her head and stared at him. "He didn't do anything like that. He didn't do anything wrong, Dad. We loved each other, and we, we decided to have sex." Kate looked down at the floor.

Again, he waited and then asked, "Did you take anything, before or during?"

"No. We talked about it, but it was our first time together, and we thought it'd be better without enhancements."

"Alright. That was probably best, although some enhancements can depress the hormonal and emotional reactions that we have, you know, make the experience less intense and chaotic."

"I know. I thought about that. They wouldn't help me. This was different. We weren't coupling and tuning into each other like we're supposed to. The neurological and biochemical exchanges were completely distorted. There must be something wrong with me, Dad. I mean, the experience became hellish, a slow torture, and the whole time, Johan enjoyed it. I don't think he even knew what was happening to me. That's not how it's supposed to happen. It should have been wonderful."

He shook his head, confused, his face leaching pain no matter how hard he tried to maintain his composure. "There's nothing wrong with you, Kate." He muttered. "It's not you, not your fault."

She went on. "Well, it's not his fault. It was me. I wasn't …" She hesitated. "It doesn't matter. We're done. He has no idea why, but I broke it off. I couldn't even look at him without feeling intense fear and a strong need for retribution. I hate him now." She sobbed, and tears flowed freely. "I don't want to, but I do."

He put his hand on her shoulder. "I'm so sorry, dear."

Kate caught her breath and then looked straight into her father's eyes. "The experience, those feelings, they linger, Dad. It doesn't make sense, I know, but the hell lingers in my head, in my dreams, nagging me when I'm awake."

"Now? How long?"

"No, not now. It subsides, especially when I'm working or focused on other things. It creeps in my head when I'm idle or when I think about him."

Kate flinched. It had been different than the other times she'd gone to him for help; it was the one time that when he insisted she work out a plan, she shook her head, "Dad I can't. I just can't. It's too much. I, I …" He'd immediately taken her in his arms, hugged her, and helped her work out her plan. If her mother only knew that he had helped Kate decide on celibacy, a life of science as he had called it, she'd flip. Fortunately, the plan worked, the feelings receded, and her mother didn't know.

***

Kate straightened her back, pressed her shoulder blades against the couch, and took another deep breath. "I feel responsible. Adam shouldn't have died. I don't know what I could've done. Something, anything. He shouldn't have died. God, shit, what happened? Adam was healthy. I don't understand it, but … I love him. Really, I did, I do, from the moment I saw him, I guess. But when he died, it hit me, like my soul was sucked clean out of me. He looked at me. He called me Mom. I mean, he called me Mom. Mom. Me." She fell forward and wept uncontrollably, sobbing. Her father caught her and rested her head on his shoulder. He said nothing. Her mother leaned over and clung to her as well. She was weeping too. "Oh, Kate," she softly cried.

It was such an odd moment, unbelievable. The three of them wept in a bundle on the couch for five minutes. It didn't make sense, to any of them.

Her father broke it. "I want you to listen to me carefully."

She sat up and slowly straightened her back. "OK."

"I have a question. But I want to be clear with you first. I don't doubt your connection to Adam. I don't fully understand it. You haven't explained it. But I don't think I need to, and I'm not sure that even you do, at least not now. But that doesn't matter. I don't question it at all. I felt it, through you. But what is your plan?"

"I'm going back to work. I can't stay at the hospital; that I know. It would be too stressful and too depressing. But my research, there's tons to do. And I have a half-dozen doc students to check on. That's my plan, Dad."

"No, it's not. We both know that."

Her mother had recovered, but she only watched.

"What do you mean? It seems like a good plan to me. Keep busy. Avoid the source of conflict or depression or whatever. I mean, what else would you expect?" Her weak voice betrayed her.

"Kate. I'm here to help you whenever, however, and forever. Your mother too, of course. You know that. "

"Yes, I know."

They sat for a few minutes.

"Dad, do you know anyone who knows anything about allergies?"

***

Kate resumed her genetic research with ease. The team in the lab was thrilled to see her. Everything was rolling full speed ahead, as expected. Sometimes she worried that she wasn't really needed, that the project could go on without her, no worse off. It was probably true. It had legs. Biomen had put together an incredible team of scientists, dedicated a small building on the U of R campus, and built a state-of-the-art lab. It had legs alright. Over the past few years, they'd published a steady stream of scientific papers in BioScience and other leading peer review journals, and they'd churned out an even larger number of internal studies circulated among Biomen researchers worldwide.

Kate had been the first person to recognize and then systematically study genetic resistance to pharmacological modification. In her doctoral thesis, she had proven that some adults between the ages of forty-five and fifty-five who shared a particular genetic profile actively resisted certain pharmacological modifications. For decades, it had been well understood that some pharmacological modifications were difficult to achieve because of physiological constraints, essentially upper limits on how far one could modify certain characteristics and capacities. Kate's discovery of active genetic resistance to pharmacologically induced change was heralded as one of the most important scientific discoveries in pharmacogenetics. Her paper, *Genetically Coded Resistance to Pharmacological Modifications*, was published in Science and read by virtually everyone in the field.

What fortuity! What goddamn luck! She happened upon the discovery, while looking for something else. She'd been trying to understand the physiological constraints for men in their early fifties (then her father's age) when she spotted something in the data, or maybe it was more of an intuition; she knew that something wasn't quite right, didn't fit. She thought of her rival Trevor, pictured him examining the same data, and her vision blurred and refocused in a slow blink. Then the idea of an active genetic resistance just popped in her head. She was excited and immediately knew she had something, but she wasn't sure what exactly. She spoke with her father the next day, he listened, and he simply asked her, what he always asked her, "Kate, what's your plan?"

"Scientific method, Dad, plain and simple." She worked for one year setting up the study, developing her theories and hypotheses, figuring out how to gather reliable data, set up reliable experiments, and secure funding. Then she spent two and a half years buried, busy, and happy. It was thrilling, and the hard work paid off.

She discovered a significant resistance in about ten percent of the adults in the studies, and specifically, different cohorts of adults who shared a particular genetic profile exhibited resistance to different types of pharmacological modifications. The resistance manifested as an absolute block to particular modifications, but otherwise had no negative health consequences, which is probably why no one had noticed.

Trevor Blair had come close. Most people didn't know it, but she barely beat him. They'd met early on at a Harvard-M.I.T. grad student mixer. Trevor cornered her near the bar, and she disliked him immediately. He gazed upon her, like she was being served with the food, and introduced himself with a smug smile. He was fishing, but she wasn't sure what for. Possibly he was just flirting; there was some lustful interest that she picked up on, although it didn't have the usual biochemical signature. After a few minutes of casual convo, his mood shifted. It wasn't even subtle. His smile faded as his voice became hard and calculating, inquisitorial. He asked about her thesis topic and research methods as if he was her advisor and not another graduate student from a rival school. Apparently, they'd both been granted access to the same classified Biomen data. Neither revealed much more. His smile returned when she admitted that she hadn't formulated hypotheses yet; she resisted an urge to smack him. That was the beginning of their bitter rivalry. It ended when she successfully defended her thesis and Biomen offered her a dream job as Research Scientist at the upstate NY campus. She could return home, be close to her parents. Trevor switched fields.

***

She'd been in daily contact with the research lab team while she was in Boston on the maternity ward rotation. Mostly, they had reported to her, told her of any progress made as well as the latest gossip. Some were upset that she'd left because it meant more work for them. But most were supportive. She'd explained that to understand the roots of genetic resistance, they had to move beyond adults; they had to study children and infants, probably conduct prenatal studies. But to move in that direction, they needed to tread carefully. They needed to build alliances with other Biomen groups, including the folks at the MA campus. Plus, she wanted to begin the exploration of this new territory fresh, in a setting where she was not a superstar. The U of R's Strong Memorial was a world-class hospital, and she would be welcome there. But Kate wanted to be a fly on the wall.

For the first week back at the lab, she caught up, followed the work-flow, and intervened only occasionally, despite the temptation. She was busy, but not stressed. No one had expectations for her. She had meetings with various members of the team—the project manager, the scientists and the lab techs. They were conducting a comprehensive series of studies across a wide range of adults. Everything was on track. She felt proud because she had planned most of this, and it was going according to plan. She almost wished for a hiccup. For the first time in the past eight years, she was bored in her lab

FIVE:

LEADS

She walked over to the hospital. It was a large complex, and her lab was part of it. She thought of her lab as separate from the hospital, even though they relied heavily on doctors, nurses, and other hospital staff when conducting their studies. She crossed a boundary, and she knew it, she felt it. Her senses became more alert, and she breathed more slowly, taking in more air and then letting it work itself out.

She had scheduled a meeting with Villa Spencer, a maternity ward nurse. They both attended Brighton High School and were friendly acquaintances back then. A few years ago, one weekend, they ran into each other at a coffee shop on campus. Villa was a dark beauty with pale hazel eyes, impossible to forget. Kate had seen her at the coffee shop, instantly recognized her, and thought for a long moment how enticingly attractive Villa was. Then Kate had walked over to her and initiated a conversation that turned into lunch and dessert. They were surprised to learn that they worked within five minutes of each other and hadn't run into each other before. When they parted, they vowed to keep in touch, to get together soon. They hadn't. But upon returning to Rochester,

Kate remembered Villa and arranged to meet her for lunch. She felt guilty, a little fake—why now— but she reminded herself that she really did want to see Villa. Villa only had a half hour break, so they met in the cafeteria.

"Villa, it's so nice to see you. It's been too long, and I'm sorry about that." She meant every word.

"No worries. I'm just glad you called, glad to see you." She smiled, a warm invitation, and tilted her head toward the food line. "Let's grab something."

They bought sandwiches and filled their water cants. Villa spotted a seat near the window. The window was floor-to-ceiling and offered a nice view of the Genesee River. They sat, and Villa immediately unwrapped her sandwich and brought it up to her mouth. "I don't mean to be rude. I only have twenty minutes." She took a bite, crunching cucumbers and crisp romaine, and continued, "I'm so glad to see you. We should go for a walk on the canal or something. It would give us more time. But tell me, what have you been up to?"

"Villa, eat, please. Don't worry about it. I, uh, I'm just glad to see you." Kate unwrapped her tomato and egg salad sandwich, pausing to swipe a chunk of egg with her finger and pop it in her mouth. "I've been in Boston for a few weeks, and when I got back, I thought of you. I spent a few weeks in the maternity ward at Mass General." Had it only been a few weeks? It seemed more like a few months.

Villa perked up, put her food down. "Really? What for? I thought you were into adult mod tech. The pharmacological versus genetic tradeoff or something like that, right?"

"Well, yes, sort of. Not the tradeoff exactly, although I have been learning more about that from the perspective of, uh, the choices parents make. But no, my normal focus is genetic resistance or blocking of pharmacological modification. And, well, I'm just starting ... I'm at the beginning of an entirely new research program that might look into children and even infants. So I just went to the maternity ward as an observer, to watch and learn, to get my bearings, you know."

"Uh, I guess, but why not here? You should have come to me. We could've set something up here no problem."

"Yes, that's true, and I would've loved to do that. But I wanted to be completely in the background, somewhere that no one really knows me. Just a fly on the wall."

"Like a small camera, or a sensor?"

"Not exactly, ... well, maybe. I hadn't thought of it like that, but yeah, like a sensor, anonymous." Kate felt like she was lying, just a little bit. She hadn't really been anonymous. No, she needed to rely on her credentials. She thought of the record clerk.

Villa's soft hand settled on her arm. "Kate? You alright?"

"Sorry," Kate fumbled, "Thought crossed my mind. You know me, remember back in high school, how I'd get distracted?"

"Yeah, that's right." Villa laughed, coughed, and then took a sip of water. "If you'd ever like to hang in our maternity ward, let me know. You could tag along with me." She smiled. "I got to go in a sec."

"I might take you up on that, Villa. But let's definitely run the canal, maybe down to Pittsford."

"Sure. Sounds good."

"Look, can I ask you a quick question?"

"Sure."

"What's Andre DeGrassi like? He's the pharmacological mod specialist who administers the cocktail."

"Right. Andre's a good guy. Why?"

"I need to talk with him, that's all. Anything I should know about him?"

"He does his job well, been here for years, married with two kids, all the normal stuff. He's a talker, really likes to engage with the patients, sometimes too much if you ask me. But it's his routine. Anyway, I can introduce you, if you want."

"That's alright. I'll be fine. Thanks Villa. You probably need to get back. Run, Saturday morning at 8am? I'll meet you where the Lehigh Valley trail hits the Canal Trail. What do you say?"

"Perfect. See you them."

Kate watched her leave and smiled. She looked forward to the canal run.

***

He stood up and quickly stepped around his small desk to greet her. "Ah, you must be the young woman that Villa mentioned." Kate smiled. He extended his hand, which she shook. "She said you were an old friend and that makes you my friend too, you know. What can I do for you?"

Andre may have been forty, not that much older than her. Kate glanced at pictures on his desk as he returned to his seat. The kids were cute, both under ten. They looked more like his wife, shared her more delicate features. The arrangement of the pictures on the desk, angled for both him and others to see, reflected a sense of pride and contentment, which made Andre seem less ordinary.

He sat down, and they both looked up. His eyes were sharp, and his mouth seemed ready to launch, like a paused vid. The feedback she caught was simple happiness spiced with slight anxiety, probably because he was excited to talk. He reminded her of Fredric, but she didn't expect the goofball humor. She hadn't realized how much she missed him until now.

Kate pressed on with her plan, which was rather straightforward. Get him talking and guide him toward the question of bio-mods having allergic reactions and specifically, reactions to the cocktail.

Andre was talkative and prone to go on and on and on. She gently steered him, letting him veer off here and there to keep the momentum, but she maintained control. She did not tell him details about Adam's death, but she described the event in broad strokes. She expressed no hint of suspicion or doubt in the explanation Fredric and Doctor Schmidt offered. Instead, she framed her inquiry as a purely scientific one, motivated by her own drive to develop a solution, a method for prediction and managing the allergic reaction. Andre wasn't suspicious either. He reiterated what Fredric had said, that infant deaths occurred incredibly rarely because of an odd allergic reaction. Kate's shoulders sank. She was surprised and disappointed at the consistency in the explanations. It ruled out one hypothesis.

Andre finished, "… despite our best efforts, we have no way to predict when it will occur."

"Best efforts? Has someone done research and tried to develop a diagnostic tool to be applied during prenatal testing or genetic modification?" Andre stiffened a little, chest up, head lifted, shoulders pulled back. Kate continued, "Or something that could be used prior to administering the cocktail? Or even right after since there was about a half hour lag between the shots and the sudden death. Or perhaps there is something to be learned from the parent histories? These are just some of my ideas, things I'm interested in developing for Biomen, so we can avoid these deaths. But I haven't seen any research."

Andre shook his head and grimaced, his left hand open palm up. "We don't have any of that, any means for predicting allergic reactions to the cocktail. At least, so far as I know." He scratched his neck, just below his left ear, put a finger on his chin, and stood still for a moment. "Look, I've only read about the allergic reaction. I haven't seen it. I dread the day. I hope I never see it. It's really quite rare. From what I remember, we're supposed to know it could happen, mainly so we can deal with the aftermath: the parents, nurses, doctors, and so on. Us too. Knowing it could happen, at least we're on notice. But I don't think there is anything that can be done, at least not yet. Maybe you'll ..."

"What about incompatibilities? Fredric mentioned ..."

"They're different." He stated in a calm voice. "When I look for incompatibilities, when I'm testing the drug formulations against the parents' genetic profiles and what they're requesting, I'm using all of the tools at my disposal. It's well documented and captured in the programs. But even if someone makes a mistake and missed an incompatibility, it doesn't cause death. I've never had a baby in my care die, but I have made mistakes and missed an incompatibility. It just causes some of the mods to stall. The baby might not get all of the modifications that the parents requested, that's all. If I hadn't made the mistake, I could've given them more from their list, that's all. No adverse health consequences. Not death."

"Yes, I understand. Thanks, Andre. This is super helpful, and oddly encouraging. I think there's room for the research I have in mind. Are there some other people you think I should talk to? Any doctors or research scientists who might have studied these issues?"

He gave her a few names, all of which were already on her list.

***

Kate had been surprised to find out that no one at the hospital focused on allergies. She'd assigned one of her doctoral students the task of locating any allergy specialist at Strong, and when she came back without a single name, Kate asked her to figure out why. Two days later, she had a short report. Apparently, allergic reactions were a thing of the past. Bio-mod immune systems did not become hypersensitive; they'd been optimized about seventy years ago through the modification of genetic coding in lymphocytes. It was one of the first genetic modifications that became standard. Allergies were modded out.

Kate stared at report on her desk. It had the grim bearing of an autopsy, as if allergies had been killed off and she was sad about their demise. But that wasn't it. Should she be looking at the genetic coding in lymphocytes? Had anyone taken samples from the infants?

Kate scheduled meetings with each person on her list. She met with everyone who specialized on the drug cocktail and potential side effects, as well as all of the nurses who worked the maternity ward. There weren't many. A dozen or so altogether, but they all told more or less the same story about the allergic reaction. Same as Fredric, Doctor Schmidt, and Andre.

One nurse, John, had worked in Philadelphia before moving to Strong Memorial, and he had actually witnessed an infant die. He described how he was in the room with the parents, the infant, Jessica was her name, and the pharmacological mod specialist whose name John couldn't remember. Everything had gone smoothly. "Jessica whined, but in a cute way," John said. "Suddenly, she died, the ugliest color, a grey-purple." John stopped to catch his breath, his eyes watering.

"It's alright, John." She wanted to say more, to ask more, but she couldn't. Her chest tightened. She just stood there with her hand on his shoulder. Is this what her father would do? No, he would've been deliberate about it, not paralyzed like her. He'd probably tell himself, "Let him work it out, but be there for him in case he needs you."

John waited for a minute or so, shook his head. "Sorry, it was just so sudden, and there was nothing I could do. But I felt like I should've been able to help her, to help them. But I couldn't. It's the worst feeling for us, when there is nothing you can do. You learn to deal with it, to block it out, to keep focused on what you can do, and to help everyone else, especially the other family members. We've got to keep it together, that's what we do—build a mask and put it on. But, you know, that day, I couldn't. I didn't do my job. I struggled to get a grip."

"I know, John. I know. I felt the same. Everyone in the hospital room felt like that." Almost everyone, at least. Had Fredric?

They didn't say much after that. John probably didn't have any more to add, and Kate didn't feel like pressing him. "Thanks so much for your time, John. And I'm very sorry to have brought you back to that day."

"No, don't be sorry. I relive that day often. It helps to talk with someone about it, to be honest."

"Well, if I can ever be of any help to you, John, just let me know." She left him and the hospital.

***

She sat in her little office with the door shut. Frustrated because she hadn't expected to hit a dead end without any leads, she reworked her plan. It had taken three weeks to squeeze the meetings in, on breaks and at the end of shifts. Her drive remained strong. Adam remained with her. When she closed her eyes, she could see him, his blue eyes, his little mouth. Fortunately, for the past two weeks, she had not returned to room 542 in her dreams.

Who might know more about allergic reactions to the drug cocktails? No one focused on the issue because it was so rare and apparently, there was nothing to be done about it. Her father suggested that her best bet was the hospital, but he also mentioned the Biomen scientists who worked on formulations in the pharmaceutical labs. Maybe one of them would have some information.

So she scheduled meetings. More of the same. Nothing new until she met with Matthew Gondrum, a biomedical statistician. Matthew worked across research groups at Biomen. He was one of those general-purpose guys who was needed everywhere. She'd been referred to him by one of the pharmacological biochemists she'd spoken to. "If you want to talk to someone who knows about the various studies we've done, rare events, and whether there are statistical anomalies, well, you should talk with Doctor Gondrum. He's seen it all, I bet."

Kate met him in his office. He was manipulating data flows floating in front of him, projected from his desk screen below. She stood in the open doorway for a moment and just watched. It was fascinating to see data, always entrancing.

"Doctor Genet?" he called in a deep voice. He was about forty. He was heavily modded on the cog spectrum, not much on the physical. He was thinner than most men and even showed slight signs of age, lines on his face, a stoop. Interesting. "Doctor Genet?"

"Oh, hi. Kate, call me Kate, please. I was admiring the visualization." It disappeared instantly.

"Right, I could see that. Look, I'm incredibly busy. What can I do for you?"

Kate told him the basic story. She had fine-tuned her presentation over the past month and found the one-minute version sufficient to get the ball rolling.

"Yes, Doctor Genet. I understand your concern, and I do know about the reaction. It falls into what I like to call the 'weird, don't fight God anomaly' category. No, not a technical term, I know." He smiled. So did Kate.

He continued. "Or you might call it the 'reality's complicated anomaly.' It exists, it happens, but we don't understand it and can't seem to catch it in any clinical studies. This isn't the only one, mind you."

"There are other such anomalies? With infants?"

"Well, with infants, let me see. ... Maybe. I mean, yes, there are other incredibly rare sudden death events, such as cardiac arrest but not many. The point I'm making is that the allergic reaction you witnessed occurs very rarely, one in 25,000 or so, if my memory serves me, and it only occurs in the field. We've never seen it in a controlled study, and we've done many studies as you know. Never seen an infant die after being given the shots in a clinical study. As you know, clinical settings don't capture all of reality. The field is just more complex."

"Has Biomen, or anyone else, tried to do a field study, or to gather data from the deceased infants?"

"No. I don't think so. It's incredibly rare. Of course, it could be done if we banked the genetic samples."

"Why don't we?" Her voice cracked. "Seems an obvious thing to do. I mean, babies don't die, not here."

"I'm not sure, Kate." He shook his head, looked away from her, distracted, and mumbled something about "backlash."

"What?"

He turned back to her and continued. "Nothing, I was just thinking about how people might overreact, if the incredibly small risk were blown out of proportion. Just imagine people refusing to use the cocktail, like the anti-vaccination movement back in the twentieth century."

"Yes, that could be a problem. But that can't mean we wouldn't want to know, to do the research?"

"No, that's right." He still seemed distracted. "In any event, it could be done. We could take genetic samples, but it's probably not worth it, at least from Biomen's perspective." He hesitated, his jaw moving side to side. "According to all of the doctors' reports from the field, the babies appeared to be doing fine and then die within an hour of being given the drug cocktail. It happens so rarely, and only in the field, mind you. We don't know the cause of the reaction, but the symptoms point toward an allergy."

"Right. But how do they know, how can we know that the infant deaths are actually allergic reactions? What if it was something else, some other cause?" Agitation crept into her voice as her mind began to race. "And if there are concerns about people overreacting, can we trust the reported numbers? Are they accurate?"

He raised his hands, fingers splayed. "Kate, I'm not sure what you're getting at. Allergic reactions shouldn't occur—we modded 'em out. But they do occur, very rarely. You saw that." Kate began walking toward the door, as he continued. "Maybe it's a reminder. Don't fight it, I say. Don't fight God. She works in mysterious ways."

"Forget that," Kate muttered to herself as she walked out. She headed straight across campus to her little office and slammed the door.

So much for talking to people.

Kate connected to Biomen's electronic research system and spent the night learning everything she could about allergic reactions. She'd done some background research earlier, but this was more comprehensive. It was fun, like graduate school. She enjoyed being a student again, learning something different. First, she reviewed what she had previously learned—the basic medical knowledge about allergies, the role of the immune system, lymphocytes, and so on. Then she surveyed the scientific literature. Multiple sources confirmed what she had already learned, that in the bio-mod community, allergies had been modded out generations ago. Immunoglobulin E, the antibody that drives hypersensitive allergic reactions, is much more tightly regulated in bio-mods. Apparently, the basic set of universal genetic modifications had done what Darwin's slow process could not.

She also learned some new information. She found an internal Biomen report that suggested the comp-mods still had allergic reactions, which made sense biologically. What was surprising was that comp-mods had allergic reactions much less often than a century ago. She wondered why. Probably, the decline in allergies corresponded with the decline in their human quotient. Machines don't have allergies. She laughed. So perhaps comp-mods still have a little humanity left in them.

As so often happened in the past when she'd set her mind on an intellectual puzzle, she had a flash of insight. Unmodified humans still had allergies. They must. There was no discussion of unmodified humans in the report, and she found no other source of reliable data. Why was that? Why wouldn't Biomen study unmodified humans, and even comp-mods, and their medical conditions? She winced at the thought of comp-mods. But the answer was obvious enough upon reflection.

The communities didn't interact with each other much anymore, hadn't for a long time. They'd severed the connections between their communication networks out of fear. The bio-mods worried about comp-mod surveillance and control over the networks, and the comp-mods claimed they wanted to avoid contamination. Did the unmodified humans have anything to say in the matter? They probably were happy to disconnect and remain isolated and free. The communities had agreed to self-governance, and as far as Kate knew, there wasn't much commerce between them. No one she knew had met an ordinary human or comp-mod or been further west than Cleveland.

She knew she was on to something. She felt like the addict of comp-mod propaganda, compelled by the reptilian part of her brain. Instinct, curiosity and raw emotion drove her forward. She continued her research and found an old medical text discussing human allergies. It was like reading history, though. She needed to do some fieldwork.

***

"Kate, when you first came back from Boston, you said something that caught my attention. I mean, besides Adam's tragic story. You said you understood what I wanted for you, that you understood better now, or something like that. What did you mean? I've been thinking about that."

"Mom, I want to be a mother. Like you. It's that simple. Adam made me realize that. And I understand why you want that for me. I get it. I want it too." Kate's shoulders relaxed, and she let out a breath that seemed to have been caught in her lungs for years. "But I'm afraid. I wouldn't want to do it alone." Kate looked away from her mom, toward the wall at nothing in particular. "No, not on my own. I know it can be done. Some people do. But that's not what I want. I guess, it isn't just Adam, not only about having a baby. No, there was something more about the whole experience. I want what they had, what Nicola and Joseph had, what they had with each other and with Adam. The whole thing felt right." Kate's eyes returned to her mother's. "Like what I thought it should be like, I guess. It's confusing. I don't know exactly." Again, she looked at the wall and then returned. "But I want to be happy, with a family."

Something had happened, had passed between them. Kate smiled, and so did her mother. They embraced. Kate had wanted this, perhaps more than anything.

She decided to hold off a few days before telling her parents of her plan.

***

Kate decided to take a trip to St Louis. She could drive there in a day or two, depending on whether she stopped for the night. She wasn't sure about what to do. Maybe a stop in one of the border towns like Cleveland would be worthwhile. She could arrange a hospital visit or even better, visit Biomen's food research and operations center. But that would take time, and she was anxious to begin her fieldwork. It was exciting, like her first visit to the maternity ward, but even more foreign and somehow liberating. Before she could make any concrete plans, however, she had to deal with work.

Kate anticipated an obstacle: her supervisor at Biomen. Aruun could be difficult. Like her, he preferred to be in control, and he expected a lot from her and her team. When she returned from Boston, he had understood, or at least he seemed to. He didn't say much. But she knew he wanted her to get back to work, to get moving with the series of genetic resistance studies on adolescents, children, and infants. She'd persuaded him, after all, about the critical importance of this new research path. He strongly believed in her, and he was anxious to see her complete the maternity ward rotation and move on to the next steps of her original plan. He'd probably lecture her about her ongoing genetics projects and how important it was for her to get back in the saddle. He wouldn't want her to leave.

She met him first thing on a Monday morning. Not the best time for such a meeting, but she wasn't given an option. He greeted her with a brief nod.

"Kate. I read your memo." Like a breeze, his calm welcome relaxed her.

"Thanks for meeting on such short notice. I'm glad you read it." She sat down. "As a follow-up, I'd like to propose a research trip. I'd like to go to St. Louis."

"Not a problem." His demeanor shifted, and Kate picked up his concern, possibly sympathy. "I understand you're still shaken up by the accident at the hospital, and if you can find out anything about the allergic reactions from doctors in St.

Louis, then Biomen and the entire bio-mod society would benefit."

Kate leaned forward, as if she hadn't heard him, and put her left hand on the edge of his desk. Why wasn't he worried about lost time? Persuading him about the maternity ward had taken time and effort. This was too easy. Her heart beat faster. Maybe she was missing something. Despite her efforts, nothing came to mind. She'd expected resistance and instead got nothing but support. Aruun seemed genuine. Was it her? Was she looking for an argument or for someone to stop her?

As these thoughts raced through her mind, Aruun continued, "Look, Kate. This won't be a vacation." His voice deepened as he became more serious. "I expect a comprehensive report on everything you learn. Allergic reactions is an area we've ignored for decades. Our genetic code eliminates errors that cause hypersensitivity in the immune system. But obviously, we're not perfect, as you know firsthand. There is much that we could learn, and possibly we'll even be able to offer the unmodifieds some help, maybe even bring some of them on board."

"Sure."

"That's not all. We want you to report on everything you learn about them, not just medical information about allergies. Keep detailed observational notes. You understand?"

"Yes, I get it. Not a problem. I'll leave this weekend, and sort things out at the lab before I go."

"Perfect."

***

Her parents were surprisingly unsurprised. They were prepared. They spoke mostly about the heat, how unbearably hot the Midwest had gotten, and how careful she would need to be. Her father emphasized that humans had a lot to teach her, but she would have to gain their trust, and that might not be as easy as she might think. "They're baking in the Midwest for a reason, Kate, to avoid modification, to avoid bio-mods and comp-mods. To avoid us, Kate." He hesitated and then looked her in the eyes. "Just remember to listen to them, Kate." Her father hugged her tightly. "I know you've got a plan."

She didn't tell him the truth: she was winging it.

SIX:

DIFFERENCES

Despite the hype in the twenty-first century, sex robots never really caught on. The industry seemed ready to take off when Sexplicant introduced its line of sensuous androids. Venture capitalists showered funding on start-ups, and the market got excited, too excited. That bubble burst, and many investors lost everything. They got the timing wrong.

Mod tech outstripped the sexbots, relegating bots to more routine tasks. This couldn't have been a surprise to anyone, at least anyone without a robofetish.

For if there was one aspect of human life a society would try to optimize with modification technology, it had to be sex. What may have been surprising was how different perfect sex turned out to be. You see, optimization depends on some conception of the ideal, and on that, opinions and technological paths diverged.

San Francisco, California. August 2154.

Orgy isn't quite the right word. But it was close. He scanned for the right word, but the instinct to describe what he was experiencing was quickly suppressed by the experience itself.

It was sex, and there was a group, a large group of people having sex. They were together, networked and sharing and triggering sensations in ways that could only be described in sexual terms—ecstasy, orgasm, intimate physical and emotional and for some spiritual relations. It had a rhythm, a give and take. But not an orgy. Henry was only in bed with her.

Earlier that evening, he'd met Sophia for the first time, at the grocery store. He smelled her before he saw her. This was natural to him. His nose was a powerful sensor on its own, of course, but the olfactory chip coupled with local processing enhancements and additional data contributed from the network and its sensors put him on par with a hound. Useful for his police work, but also for so much more, he thought.

She smelled of baked copper skin and salt from the ocean, probably blown through her hair in the breeze. He licked his lips. She had ridden her bike to the store and taken the path by the beach. He was excited to see her. He waited an extra second in aisle two, and she turned the corner. He saw her and smiled. She smiled back and walked toward him with the same determined look that he had. Her eyes were soft, sky blue and her hair strawberry blond; her nose was cute, and her smile intoxicating. She was athletic, a biker for sure. Her legs were lean and copper. She was an excellent match. They left the grocery store together and went to a nearby Japanese place for an early dinner. They exchanged information and had an excellent meal of sushi, cold soba with shrimp, and Hamachi. Throughout dinner, they were completely tuned into each other. They muted everything else and spoke softly aloud but passionately in each other's heads. The attraction was palpable. Beneath the smell of the foods, which he filtered with a thought, he smelled her desire for him. It fed his desire. A virtuous feedback loop, if ever there was one. After dinner, they went back to his place to intercourse.

The two engaged each other in physical foreplay. Sight, smell, taste, and touch went into overdrive while hearing faded into the background. They consumed each other. He remembered the taste that had lingered on his lips in the grocery story—salty, hot sun-baked skin; it had teased him, whet his appetite. He looked into her eyes and saw her hunger and satisfaction. Gradually, their sex reached a plateau and then it shifted. Their comp-mods now integrated. The enhanced senses remained active and salient, but became more a part of the background, the environment for their continued intimacy. The physical, sensory, and emotional combined and intensified. Different brain activities took center stage, and the result was a complex mix of emotions. A torrent of intimate feelings that bound them together in what could only be love at the most basic, emotional core. They thought they were making love. It didn't matter that it was constructed because in the moment it was perfect.

But even this plateaued. The individual comp-mods and localized, two-person network they had formed maximized its output, akin to a perfect shared dream. Once more, it shifted.

Their network expanded. Their lovemaking combined with others at similar stages, others on the comp-sys network.

They joined the community, not an orgy exactly. It was different than that. It was stable, safe, familiar, and controlled, though exhilarating and pleasurable beyond measure. Their senses reached others. They easily found others to whom they were attracted, and they were joined, forming smaller networks within yet still connected to the whole. The compsys network provided a stable, optimized environment and shaped the experience and opportunities to interconnect based on the wants and needs of those participating. They touched and tasted many at once. They shared cumulative orgasms. The couple stayed together throughout, physically and emotionally linked, as they climaxed.

They slept soundly for the rest of the night.

Cape May, New Jersey. August 2154.

It was hot, and the sand almost burned the bottom of her feet. Villa walked slowly toward the water. She knew she was being watched. It didn't bother her. She was looking too. Her eyes soaked in the sights. It was an adult beach, and there were many men and women to gaze upon. Such physical beauty, exquisite bodies and tantalizing faces. So many different shades of perfection, different combinations of features. Most were dark-skinned, like her, and all were physically fit. There was not an inch of fat on the beach. But there was variety in height and weight; people certainly were different sizes, she laughed, especially in certain places. She had small breasts, but the beach displayed many of the larger variety. Most of the men were of the larger variety. But it was in the faces that she saw so many different, beautifully cut gems. She thought the reason had to be related somehow to the bio-mod technologies, perhaps it was just too difficult to control facial features; again, she laughed, therein lies the beauty and irony!

It was a gorgeous afternoon, hot as usual, but bearable. Her skin never burned, of course. She sweated profusely, however, and had to keep drinking water to keep from getting dehydrated. The sweat made her shine, glisten, moisten. She waded into the water and walked along the beach for a while. Her eye caught a glimpse of a man watching her. She pretended not to notice and walked on, but after a minute, she turned around as if she were simply heading back to wherever she had started, and she took a good look at him. He was looking out at a sailboat on the water. He was her type, for a man: not too tall but tall enough, ripped with muscles but not bulky, dark hair left free to fly about in the wind, and dark, thoughtful eyes. She felt herself slow down and heat up. She was barely walking and her breathing had also slowed and deepened when he turned toward her and smiled. Had he known I would come? Somehow, she felt he knew. He walked toward her. She stopped, letting her feet sink in the sand. She felt the sand slowly creep up between her toes, and that felt really good, erotic. She felt her body sweating more, making her glisten everywhere. He was about 10 yards away, and his smile grew as he approached. It wasn't just his smile. He wanted her too. She smiled back but in a mischievous way, and then she bolted for the water. She ran until it reached just above her knees, and she dove under. The cold water awakened her. It felt incredibly good. It also slowed her down as she had hoped it would.

After a decent underwater push, graceful like a dolphin, she surfaced, stood up, and turned back toward the shore. He had left. She was incredibly disappointed, almost heartbroken. She wanted more from him. She sighed and thought that at least the water felt refreshing. Besides, the beach was full. Perhaps she'd meet a woman instead. Suddenly she felt something brush against her left leg, on the inside of her upper thigh. She shuddered and a rush of feeling returned, even stronger than it had been before she hit the water. Jesus, she uttered. He stood behind her, and pressed up against her. She felt all of him. He whispered in her left ear. "I am not Jesus, although you may call me that if you wish."

Jesus, she uttered again, as he brought his hand further up her thigh. It must be his hand, she thought. She slowly let her feet sink a little in the sand as her legs slowly spread, keeping her balance. His hand found what it was looking for, and she spasmed slightly. Again.

Her eyes were wide open, as was her mouth. She breathed deeply. The air expanded within her, and her bloodstream became active, swelling, working. Their hormones kicked in. They drove each other. Biochemical exchanges escalating and intensifying their intoxication. Sex was the bio-mods' most potent drug.

She faced the beach. People swarmed over the sand, but no one noticed them in the water. They were oddly alone in this public place. She saw them no longer as people but as odd flowers, beautiful, dark stemmed flowers with purple petals bursting from the tops. The hallucination warped her environment.

She felt the Atlantic, its waves rushing to meet and wash over her. Each wave brought an incredible sensation of pleasure, originating deep inside her and washing over every inch of her body, through each and every pore on her skin. The salt water cleansed her, and she felt new. She felt her skin opening to receive the salt water, and she felt it swishing within her pores, filling and cleansing each one. It felt so good. She was one with the ocean itself, so powerful and alive.

Though the sky she saw remained clear with only small wispy clouds, she felt a storm coming, as the ocean stirred and became agitated, more chaotic. The waves began to increase in size and strength, and the undertow, the pull back as waves receded, also grew more powerful. She welcomed it at first. After all, she was one with the ocean. They were one.

But as the intensity grew, she became worried. Why weren't people leaving the beach? She wanted to scream out to them that they should pack up and leave because a storm was coming, maybe a hurricane. But when she screamed, no one heard. What could she do? Lightning struck a dozen different spots on the beach, sizzling. She saw people carried off in huge gusts of wind; they were screaming. No, she yelled.

She directed her attention to the ocean. Its waves were the size of houses. She had lost control, and this made her nervous. She wanted to slow it down, but it was beyond her. She remembered her partner. She called out to him. "Yes," he replied, "I am with you. This is intense, but we'll be fine. Ride it out together."

She reached with her hands to find him, and when she did, she gripped him tightly. "Yes, together. What a wondrous storm. The ocean is alive." The rhythm of the waves continued to increase, although the height of the waves did not. The waves peaked, plateaued, and eventually settled. What a ride, she muttered.

Though the couple had sex for less than an hour, it felt like a month long voyage. For most of the experience, each lover felt an intense euphoria.

Boston, Massachusetts. August 2154.

Nicola and Joseph were still mourning. They were in their home. It was a rainy Saturday afternoon. They were trying to read, but neither one had made it past a few pages. They sat together in their bed, sipping tea and barely speaking. They had not said much to each other in the past week. It had been especially difficult because Joseph had to return to work and Nicola struggled when alone.

Nicola had begun crying. Joseph tried to comfort her. He moved closer to her, reached out and gently took hold of her and pulled her to him, laying her head down on his lap, and then he stroked her hair, slowly caressing the scalp just over her ears.

"Nicola. I love you. Everything will be OK, in time. At least we have each other, my Nicola. My dear." He continued to stroke her hair and she stopped crying.

"I know, Joseph."

"Nicola."

"Yes."

"Nicola, I'm so sorry. It's my fault, I know it is …"

"No, Joseph …"

He started to weep. At first, his eyes just moistened, a thin wet lens on each, but in a moment, tears streamed down his cheeks. He sobbed. "I'm sorry, Nicola."

She pulled herself up, using his shoulders for support. She wiped the tears from his cheeks with her index fingers, tracing a gentle path. She pulled his head forward, resting his forehead on her lips, and she softly kissed him, a dozen slow, soft brushstrokes. He raised his head. Their eyes locked in an intense embrace, expressing their deep love for each other.

She kissed him on the lips fully. "Make love to me, Joseph." She leaned back and pulled him toward her. "Are you sure, Nicola? It hasn't been two months since…"

"Yes, Joseph. I'm sure."

They had sex for the first time in months. Joseph was worried that she would hurt, that she hadn't recovered fully, but she told him it was alright. It did hurt at first, and she whimpered. He stopped and said he couldn't do it. She insisted, made it happen. She took control. They did need to stop and start, and it was not particularly erotic or stimulating. Joseph finished early, and apologized.

"I'm sorry, Nicola. It has been a while and …"

"Stop, Joseph. I'm happy. First time in a long time, and there is nothing to apologize for. It is exactly what I wanted. It felt good."

"I'm ready to try again if …"

"I know you are, but let's wait a bit. It was perfectly fine."

He smirked. "Perfectly fine." She laughed, and he laughed.

They lied naked, holding each other tightly, looking out the window at the rain, happy. An hour or so later, they made love again, and they almost climaxed together.

SEVEN:

CROSSING

"So you're leaving again? Where to? Back to Boston."

"No. Not Boston. I'm heading to St. Louis."

Villa stumbled a little and then caught her balance and within a half second, was back at Kate's side. The canal trail was quiet. It was a beautiful morning for a run, a little overcast and a nice breeze kept it cool. Kate preferred this weather for running. Still, they passed only a dozen or so runners this morning, and no bicyclists.

"Are you running?"

Kate stumbled and then caught herself as Villa had done. "What? No. Why would I? I mean, running from what?"

"I don't know. Nothing, I guess. I just thought …" She hesitated but didn't break her stride.

"What?"

"I just thought that's where I'd go, if I ever decided to run."

"What? Why would you ever run?

"I wouldn't, no, that's not what I mean. I'm good, you know. Everything is fine. And it has been nice these past weeks reconnecting with you. I just mean that if I was going to run, if I ever had to, you know, then maybe St. Louis. It's a place I had thought about, or dreamt about, I guess, as the place I'd go. Sort of, back in time or something."

"Oh, I see."

"I think other people have the same idea, you know. I don't know of anyone that has actually been there. But I have heard people talk about it. I mean, I've talked about it with friends. Like a vacation we wish we could take or something." She looked ahead at the canal trail and the shreds of blue in the distance. Kate kept glancing at the canal. It was absolutely amazing that this part of the Erie Canal was still around and functioning. It wasn't used anymore for moving cargo or people, as it had been centuries ago, but people still used it for recreation. Kate loved to run and bike on the paved trail that ran alongside the canal. She had done it as a teenager, and as an adult, it was her only vacation.

"Well, I'm not going for vacation, and I'm not running from anything. It's just work, a research project, basically. I'm going to visit some of their hospitals, I hope."

"Maternity wards?" She perked up.

"Maybe. We'll see." Kate thought about confiding in Villa. But why bother, she thought, why make Villa worry or sad.

"I wish I could come with you. We'd have an adventure."

"That'd be nice, really. But I need to go alone." The shreds of blue slipped behind the clouds.

Villa slowed and looked away from Kate, toward the tall green trees that lined the other side of the canal. "Sure, I understand. I couldn't get off anyway. So when are you leaving?"

"Tomorrow."

Villa stopped and put her arms above her head, folded them and then put her hands behind her head on the back of her neck. "Seriously? Tomorrow. Well, that's sudden." Her face tensed, her eyes intense and beautiful, but in a moment, her face was soft again. "Are you ready?"

"Mostly. I just need to finish packing and load up my Personal Transport Vehicle. I'll sleep the whole way, I hope."

"You kidding? No way. Don't you want to see what it looks like when you cross over?"

"Yeah, I do, but then again, I can catch it all on the way back. Plus, I'll have plenty of time to explore when I'm there. But I need some sleep. I'm a little behind this week. It was crazy at work."

"I bet. They can't be happy about …"

Kate went on, "I'm a little nervous about what it'll be like. What they'll think of me."

"Don't worry. They'll accept you, and they'll like you. Heck, how couldn't they?" She had such a genuine, cheerful look on her face that Kate almost relaxed.

"It's not that. I don't know. I'm worried that it will be too much of an adventure, if you know what I mean. I want things to go smoothly, according to plan." Why was she lying? What plan? Was she worried about St. Louis or the fact that she didn't actually have a plan?

"My guess is that you'll be surprised no matter what. Plans are made to be broken." They embraced for a long minute. Neither, it seemed, wanted to let go.

***

Kate thought she would sleep for most of the drive. Her PTV would do all of the work. Her little box on wheels was fully charged, programmed, and ready to go when she woke at 5am on Sunday morning. She slept very little the night before she left.

She'd had a technician over Saturday afternoon to check everything, from the mechanical to the computer systems. She had him go over the VAC (ventilation and air conditioning) system with her and explain how the PTV could be operated manually, so she would know what to do in an emergency. He gave her the "sure, crazy lady" look when she asked, and only when she asked him whether the navigation system covered the Midwest, did his eyebrows drop and that look disappear. "Of course, Ms. Genet. The system will sync with their regional GPS network."

She suspected that this was not exactly correct, and her mind wandered: Whoever ran the system for bio-mods must extract the data and replicate the other regional GPS networks before syncing with the PVT system. Just as they'd done with all of their other computing networks, the bio-mods had built their own systems and avoided interconnecting with the comp-mod systems, or the comp-sys as they called it. Both communities must have preferred it this way. Many decades ago, they'd collaborated in a major joint venture to develop deliberately incompatible networks. The bio-mods wanted to be secure from comp-mod surveillance or interference, and the comp-mods did not want bio-mods congesting their networks, or worse, infecting them with impure technologies. The comp-mods had too much invested, as they became part of the network itself.

"Ms. Genet? Hello, hello there." She shook her head as if waking from a dream.

"Oh, yes, sorry." She smiled. He probably thought she was on some pre-trip trip. She never used hallucinogens. Many people she knew had. Her parents used them occasionally, recreationally. She wasn't tempted enough to give them a try. She worried it would be too chaotic. Some of the high-end cocktails, the kind you couldn't just pick up at the local store or print yourself, they were supposed to be a good way to develop perspective or creative insight. Among a certain crowd, they competed with a niche set of pharmacological enhancements.

She caught herself just in time, as he began to fidget. "Just thinking ahead, about the trip. You know, running over my to-do list."

"Sure, no problem. Well. I'm all set here. You're all set, that is. Your PVT is ready to go. Just be sure that if you're gone for more than three weeks, especially if you're using the VAC system daily, you need to charge the system. You can use the solar top, but that requires the PVT to be stationary for 48 hours in order to charge fully. Otherwise, you've got to find a station. I don't know if they have them in the Midwest. They must, right?"

"Yes, of course." She had no idea.

EIGHT:

TRIP

Kate looked out the windows as the PTV left Rochester. The roads west to Buffalo, and then south and west to Cleveland, would be lightly traveled, and the scenery beautiful. Tall trees lined both sides of the highway. Kate loved the woods, and there was something special about the wooded tracts along the highways. For almost one hundred years, they'd been untouched. The great reforestation project had set aside substantial corridors of woodland along most highways, and the result was magnificent—a mysterious place of natural beauty that induced reverence and curiosity, especially when seen from the steady remove of her PTV. It reminded Kate of a vid, except flipped, like she was in the motion picture, looking out at a still audience basked in darkness.

Kate peered through the trees, seeking something hidden in the depths, some movement, a hint of the life she knew to be there. Her attention was drawn away by the sight of birds flying above the trees, but when she lowered her gaze and peered within, she saw only a sanctuary of shadows. She knew they were there, deer flitting among the trees with squirrels, rabbits, and chipmunks; she remembered these well from her hiking trips in the Catskills as a kid. She did not search for these animals though. Had she seen one, it wouldn't have excited her much, or so she thought. She looked for something else, but she wasn't sure what exactly. It also lurked just beyond recognition within her mind. She could smell the dirt and death that hung on it, a shiver ran the length of her spine, and she suddenly knew it must be a large beast for her head thrust forward and pressed against the window upon sight of what turned out to be a large boulder veiled in shadows. For a moment, she believed she'd seen it, and only when she realized she hadn't, she remembered the black bear she'd encountered when hiking with her parents.

***

"Kate, stop, shh." Her father whispered in a commanding tone.

Kate slid on gravel and stopped dead, turning to face him with a grin on her face as she played statue. He didn't acknowledge her though, just looked past her. So she quit and turned back to continue the hike. He grabbed her shoulder with one hand, the other on her mother's.

"Look, both of you, down there, across the creek. See it. You've got to be still."

Kate saw a huge black beast sniffing and pawing at something on the ground. She couldn't see what it was, but she could smell it. Death, meat, blood, urine, something oddly sweet, a flavor that smoothed out the repulsive smells. A pit opened up within Kate's midsection, working her stomach, heart, and lungs. It pulled inward physically, stomach churning, heart pumping, and lungs drawing breath, all more intensely to feed the sudden vacuum, while simultaneously pushing out her biomod senses. She saw the bear crisply against what now seemed a dull yellowish-brown background; the smells intensified, but these details seemed less worthy of her attention as she began to feel something different, coming from the dark mass. It was calm. The purity surprised Kate. She'd not expected it, but as soon as she felt it, the pit left her. Her father let go of her shoulder.

After a few hours or minutes—it was hard to tell, the bear ceased its investigation and moved on. For a moment, it seemed as though it would head in their direction, and at that moment, Kate felt the pit returning. But it turned away from them and slowly disappeared into the woods.

***

When the PTV turned south and passed Buffalo, she grew tired of peering. The inviting gaps between trees solidified, like fence turned to wall, and with that, the depths of the woods were lost to her.

She obscured the windows and played an old vid that she might have seen long ago, perhaps in school. Her assistant had found it in the archive and sent it to her before she left Rochester. It was an educational vid that supposedly explained the different societies. That is what her assistant had promised. Kate thought it might help to see how the unmodified humans lived, how their society functioned.

The vid opened with a narrator standing in the front of a classroom. Her voice was calming yet commanded attention, like an opera singer or a good politician. It was like she was sitting in the front row of the classroom and the narrator was talking directly to her. "The end of the twenty-first century was tumultuous. The United States split into territories and the Northeastern bio-mod society rose to its current prominence. We'll discuss this history and reflect on lessons we've learned. We'll also discuss the hubris of comp-mod society." Kate fidgeted in her seat, stretching her hamstrings. "To get a sense of ordinary life in modern bio-mod society, we begin with scenes from Philadelphia, a relatively large bio-mod city." Most of the scenes seemed familiar and boring. Bio-mod scientists engaged in cutting edge biotech research; extreme athletes running super-ultra-marathons over days; an emotionally charged audience listening to and participating in a jazz concert with biochemical feedback flowing in the arena somehow tinted different shades of yellow and green in the vid.

One scene caught Kate's attention. It showed school children smiling and singing, while playing outdoors at a playground. The sun shined brightly, but the heat didn't bother them at all. The kids were in constant motion, running around, leaping from equipment and over various obstacles, swinging and flipping over bars, all while still smiling and singing. They were incredibly fit and though it probably wasn't the intent of the vid producer, they seemed like super-powered animals, like monkeys, panthers, even birds, but in a good way. Not like the image the comp-mods put on us of degenerate reptilian animals, monsters from old mythologies. There were no reptiles among the children. We are the beautiful ones, Kate whispered.

Her mind again returned to the magnificent bear she'd once met in the woods. It had triggered her biochemically enhanced senses, first from fear but then calm understanding. She stared at the obscured PTV window imagining the woods beyond, home to the bear, and she again walked the woods in the dark gaps between the trees, searching without a purpose and mindful of some uncertain weight in the air that laid on her like a heavy blanket but felt feather light.

"Singularity is the term some used to describe the melding," the narrator said, grabbing Kate's attention. "The point at which machine and man become one." Kate vaguely remembered the name, Turing, and felt confused. She focused on the vid again. There was a scene with human bodies lying on barely visible cots with wires connecting their heads. The wires fed from behind each ear and drooped between the cots. Kate couldn't tell where they went though. The vid camera panned out and the single row of ten cots became three rows— the thirty cots faded further and disappeared—and then it panned out to show ten rows. Kate gagged at the sight of one hundred heads with dangling bodies and drooping wires. The camera panned out again and again and again. Ten thousand wired heads. Kate put her hand over her mouth; the tip of her thumb caught her tear.

The narrator started to explain how the wires were only necessary in the first decade. But Kate wasn't interested. She'd heard it before and only revisited it involuntarily in nightmares. She skipped past the comp-mod history, telling the vid player to find unmodifieds.

To her surprise, there wasn't much. Apparently, her assistant hadn't watched the vid. "The unmodified humans do not communicate with bio-mod society. Accordingly, in making this educational vid, we respected their wish to be left alone. Unfortunately, we do not have much data on their recent history." Almost apologetic.

"The unmodified humans fear technology, especially modification technologies. To remain free of technological modification, they congregated in the Midwest and isolated themselves. They concentrated in the old Midwest cities, such as Chicago, St. Louis and Omaha, and rebuilt the cities as best they could to deal with the intense heat. Some speculate that networks of tunnels were built so people could move about during the daytime without being scorched by the sun. Technophobic idealists, we suspect they maintained many of the old cultural and societal traditions that predated the rift between bio- and comp-mod societies." The narrator's tone had shifted. She spoke about unmodifieds with affection, like they were the younger siblings of the school children she addressed.

"Throughout history, human conflict has involved Us and Them. In our modern context, bio-mods and comp-mods may seem to fit these roles, although it is important to note that direct conflict has been eliminated. Unmodified humans, however, have remained on the sidelines." The narrator went on without saying anything Kate didn't already know, and then she referenced other sources to consult, including other vids. Unfortunately, Kate didn't have any of them.

Kate shut down the vid system, darkened the interior, and slept.

NINE:

CHANGE

Kate woke to a beeping noise. Her heart stopped. Adam. Bile crept up her throat. A hot, burning sensation trailed. She forced it down and shook her head. Had she been dreaming? She didn't think so, but couldn't be sure.

"Final destination, 20 minutes." A soft voice informed her. Her heart settled, and her vision cleared. She looked out the windows anxious and amazed. She turned off the alarm.

She had imagined something apocalyptic, straight out of a late 20th century science fiction novel, where most of society was destroyed by a superflu or nuclear war and small patchworks of communities lived in barren cities and towns. After all, that is more or less what had happened in the Midwest. No maelstrom of death or destruction, but an unbelievably intense heat wave that never really let up and made life unbearable, coupled with the technological mod revolutions that took place on the coasts. Most people just moved East or West, and some north to Canada, and only a few stayed. The unmodified humans chose to avoid bio-mod or comp-mod societies and broil. She half expected ghost towns with dilapidated, well, everything. No traffic on the roads, streetlights down and not functioning, houses abandoned, and so on—all of the hallmarks of a decaying civilization.

Yet rationally she knew this wouldn't be what she'd find. That's why she chose St. Louis. She knew it was one of the large Midwestern cities still functioning. Yet the sci-fi apocalyptic fantasy lingered.

As she approached St Louis, she was reminded of Rochester. It looked very much like home, at least from what she could see from the PTV. There wasn't much traffic on the roads. But then again, that was often the case in Rochester on a late Sunday afternoon. And there were some PTVs. They didn't look the same as hers. Older versions probably. But they were moving alright.

She was still on the highway, an old interstate, but not for much longer. Perhaps when she got a closer look, it would still meet her original expectations. But she doubted that, based on the look of the highways and the traffic alone. You could always judge a civilization by its infrastructure, she remembered someone saying. Would St. Louis be just like Rochester?

She reset Mercy hospital as her final destination. She'd planned to go to a hotel, the hotel actually. The Grand St. Louis was the only hotel that her assistant had been able to identify as open to bio-mods and approved by Biomen. She'd rested enough in the PTV and could afford a slight detour to the hospital, just to look around, and then she'd settle in at the hotel. Kate leaned her forehead against the slightly cool window and closed her eyes.

She opened her eyes as her PTV exited the highway and settled into the local system. She began to notice differences. There was no traffic. A few PTVs, no bikes, and no pedestrians. The streets were empty. Where was everyone? Only then did Kate notice the temperature reading for outside the PTV---118 degrees Fahrenheit. Everyone must have been inside, keeping cool, or at least, avoiding the heat. Then she noticed how remarkably clean everything was. Again, it reminded her of Rochester.

"Arriving, final destination." The PTV pulled up to the designated lane just off the road and prior to entering the hospital campus. From the outside, it looked a little like Strong Memorial, but not much. Different style of construction, and different layout for the hospital complex. This was much more closely packed, and didn't seem to be integrated into an old university campus. She noticed that there were indoor corridors connecting all of the buildings, making a giant spider web.

Kate took manual control of the PTV and found a parking garage. It was tricky to get inside. There was a series of three, one-way segments connected by sharp 180-degree turns, pivoting around a wall. She heard a dull vibration and deep whah-whah-whah noise, and felt a strong breeze blowing against her PTV, first from the front and then from the back. Some sort of VAC system, she guessed. When she turned the final corner, she saw the lot with hundreds of PTVs parked. Her heart beat a little harder. She slid into a slot.

She sat for a few minutes and thought about a plan. What should she do? Who should she try to see? Who should she say she was? Kate, you're an idiot for not thinking this through ahead of time. She decided: Go to the front desk, and tell the truth.

She exited her PTV and immediately felt the weight, like a cloak. The air was warm and thick, though not humid exactly. It was musty but without an identifiable odor. She felt a light breeze, but thicker, more like a slow, steady current in a stream. Again, she heard/felt the dull vibration, in the background. She was impressed; it was a sophisticated VAC system, definitely not old school.

She wasn't sure where to go. The only light came from a strip of luminescent material on the ceiling that ran down the center of the drive and walkways. They seemed to reflect light rather than generate it, and Kate stood staring at the strips, puzzling over where the light actually came from.

Finally, she decided to take the nearest walkway and head inside the hospital. Again, she had to weave through a winding series of one-way walkways with alternating air currents. She wondered whether there was a separate entrance for emergencies. She imagined people covered in blood, stumbling over each other, rushing down each of the corridors, racing to get ahead of each other. It was a gruesome free-for-all. She shook her head. There must be a separate entrance. As she exited the final corridor, she readied herself, excited to return.

It looked very much like Strong Memorial, except for the colors. Plenty of white, of course, but mixed with light orange and light green to create a dreamlike atmosphere. Sherbet heaven. It wasn't very crowded. She followed the entrance hallway to the lobby and went straight to the front desk, where two clerks were sitting. One was speaking to a couple and had a short line of people waiting.

The other did not have a line. The clerk was busy talking to an elderly man with wild white hair that did not hide his bright red scalp. Mesmerized by the man, she approached from behind. When she was about five feet away, she noticed little red droplets on his neck and his head. Beads of beet-colored sweat formed and did not run. She stared. She wanted to reach out and touch one. Would it pop and run? Her stomach churned at the revolting thought. He glanced back over his shoulder and saw her disgust. He smiled lazily, turned, and stepped toward her. She froze.

"Mr. Salonich." The clerk called. "The doctor will be right out to see you. Grab a seat." The man grunted and took another step toward Kate. "Whatchyouwan, smomma." He said, inching closer. His rancid breath was overpowering; she felt like it burned sheets of skin from her face. "Youwan, youwansommathin ahhme." She gagged. He smiled. "Youbetcha, smomma, desint, thas me, thas right. Ahgotchayou asommathin, agif. Alill un." He swerved past her, walked to a row of seats, and plopped.

"Miss. What can I do for you?" The clerk said. "Miss? Hello. Are you alright?"

"Oh, yes, I'm fine. Can I ask you -what was his problem? That guy." She motioned with her eyes without moving her head.

"Can't say. Might be drunk. Might've stayed out too long. That's my guess, between you and me, but what do I know." He studied her. "Where are you from, mam?"

"Rochester. New York."

"Ah, of course, that makes sense. A little too much, a little too dark. You're going to need to change it up a bit." She must have looked puzzled. "Your clothes, mam." Only then did she notice that everyone was wearing white, off-white, beige, those awful light green and yellow (lime and lemon sherbet), and other light-reflecting colors. Their clothes were all loose fitting, except for some type of elastic or pull string thing at the neck, wrist and ankles. Of course, everything had to be designed to cope with the extreme heat. She had chosen what to wear with the heat in mind and had packed intelligently, or so she'd thought. She hadn't thought how she would stick out, and now she'd have to buy all new clothes.

"So you're fine. You're here on business? Do you have an appointment?"

"No, no appointment, but I am here on business. I'm studying medicine and doing research on allergies. I came to the hospital becau ..."

"Wait, hold on." He looked to his monitor. "Can you excuse me? Just grab a seat over there." He motioned to the waiting area and continued. "I've got to take this. I'll be right with you."

Kate nodded, "Sure, no problem," and she turned toward the waiting area. Mr. Salonich sat there, leaning back in his chair, watching her, waiting for her. He smiled and gave a slight nod. She almost went to him. That smile seemed genuine, made her curious. But then she saw him wobble left to right and lurch. No, thank you, hanging with a drunk bleeding out his pores and breathing death spores was probably not the best move.

Instead, she found a spot to stand, not too far from the clerk's desk. The man she'd just spoken with was looking down at the monitor on his desk and talking with someone. She looked around, trying to be discreet, a fly on the wall, but doubting it was possible. She realized that she stood out like one of Fredric's raunchy jokes—"you know," he might say, "like a slowly squeezed silent fart; it's noticed alright regardless of how quiet you might be, har har." Her clothing must have screamed, "I'm a fricken mod!" And what about her skin color? The clerk had said she was a little too dark. She hadn't seen any dark-skinned humans. Of course, she hadn't seen many people and didn't have much to go on. But so far, she had seen skin tones ranging from copper tan to reddish white. Due to base genetic mods as well as pharmacological triggers, most bio-mods had a rich array of highly active melanocytes in the bottom layer of their skin, and this led to a much darker hued skin—usually, a rich dark chocolate—and increased protection from UV radiation. Most midwesterners would evolve in the same manner, as had occurred with many cultures in the past, but just much more slowly.

The waiting room seemed familiar, like all of the other hospital waiting rooms she'd ever been in. Anxious patients and families sitting, some chatting to pass the time and others lost in their own thoughts or just wound too tightly to engage with others. Amid the throng, Kate spied a pregnant woman and her heart skipped a beat. The woman looked strong, confident. Then Kate caught Mr. Salonich's eye on her. He smiled and nodded approval. Kate turned away from him and back to the pregnant woman. Her husband stood next to her, holding her hand. They were talking. Nicola and Joseph had looked into each other's eyes like that. Kate thought of Adam. She started to walk toward the couple in the waiting room.

Two men, obviously security guards, emerged from a small corridor to her right. They stopped her. "Miss? Will you come with us? We have a few questions." They were calm and looked trustworthy, with those bright eyes. She glanced at the clerk, who shrugged—as if to say "sorry, protocol." The guards escorted her down the small corridor and stopped at the third door on the right. It had no label, no number. She felt her heart quicken. A holding pen? Inside was a plush waiting room that reminded her of the common area of her suite with Fredric. She sat where they pointed, on the couch. One of the guards sat down in a chair nearby, and the other asked: "You want a drink? Water? Something else?"

"Water would be fine." Kate replied. He left the room, which was odd. There was a small kitchen in the room.

The sitter didn't say much. He sat rigid, looking at her but not saying anything. She looked back and after a minute or two started to get worried. Why wasn't he saying anything? What was he thinking? Did he think she was a threat? She shifted her position and tried to sit back and relax, but this couch was not like her parent's. It was stiff. Had the clerk contacted them? Or had security been watching and listening? The hospital probably had sensors and security monitors, just like Strong. Was she assessed to be a threat because of her appearance? If so, why hadn't they come sooner?

She broke the silence. "So why am I here? Did I do something wrong?"

With the slightest shrug and eyebrow twitch, he said. "You tell me."

"Well, no. I didn't do anything wrong. So can I go?"

"Sure, go ahead. See ya."

She considered it. Should she test him? No, probably not the best move. It would either lead to a confrontation, and possibly serve as confirmation of their fears, or she'd walk out and have nowhere to go. Surely, she wouldn't get past the clerk's desk without first dealing with security. So she waited.

Again, she broke the silence. "What's your name?"

He looked down at his left shoulder. Regis, a tag on his shirt read.

"Regis, I'm not from around here, obviously. How long have you lived here?"

"All my life. Born and raised, desint louis. Where are you from, mam?"

"Rochester, NY. Born and raised." She smiled. He didn't. "How long have you worked at this hospital?"

"About five years. Security detail the whole time." Anticipating her next question, he said. "I like it. This is a good place. Good people. My family."

She believed him. A calm happiness settled on his face, a sheen. Along with those bright eyes, it made him quite attractive, actually. Cute in a certain fashion, and not a fashion Kate had paid much attention to before. She was puzzled yet curious, mostly about herself, her own feelings. She'd not felt much attraction toward men in years, and here of all places with this human security guard, she felt something—only very slight, a soap bubble—but still something.

"You alright, mam. Tell me if you got a fever. That I need to know." His tone matched the sudden intensity in his eyes.

"No, I'm fine." Embarrassed, she pulled her head and limbs back inside the shell.

He relaxed.

In a few minutes, there was a knock on the door. The second guard returned with a cant of water. Behind him was an older man in white. His thin face was all angles, almost chiseled, his eyes squeezed between cheekbones and brow.

"Here you go, mam, your water." The guard handed her the cant and then retreated to a corner of the room where he stood very straight, watching.

"Good evening, Miss, uh, Miss?

"It's Genet, Doctor Kate Genet."

He smiled and his eyes disappeared, crushed. "I'm here to welcome you, Miss Genet. We don't see many B-mods at this hospital, and so I hope you understand why security brought you here." He smiled again, and instinctively, she shuddered at the thought of his eyes being crushed like grapes. She recovered quickly: "Sure, I understand. Look, can I …"

"Excuse me, Miss Genet. But we need to run some tests. Then we can talk about why you're here. A nurse will be here shortly. I kindly request that you consent and cooperate with her. OK?" His tone was soft, almost warm at the end.

"What tests?"

"OK?" He repeated, sharply. She saw his eyes now without obstruction. Dark, strong eyes, almost handsome in strict command. She shook her head but said, "OK, but I would like to know what tests before I consent. You understand, right, doctor?"

"Look, Miss Genet. We've a protocol to apply, and we are going to apply it, whether you like it or not." He hardened and snarled, "You know what happened to the Native Americans, don't you, when the Europeans came, don't you? Jesus, I don't know why I bother." He shook his head violently. "Look, Miss Genet, you're here, in our hospital, and you're compromising all of us. Sit tight, mam. I will return to complete the examination." His disgust was palpable. The guards didn't move a muscle or say a thing. Silent observers, nothing more.

The doctor turned abruptly and left. A minute later, the nurse arrived. She was no elf or angel; she was more like a little piggy. Her nose turned upward at the end, and her hair was bright red. Her pink uniform completed the picture. She smiled to Kate and said, "Good evening, Miss Genet. I'm sorry about your exchange with Rolf. He can be testy. It's best to just say yes when dealing with him. Don't upset him. I'm going to take samples and run them down to the lab for testing. We should be done in about a half hour or so. Assuming everything checks, we'll have you to your interview before waking hour."

Kate nodded, "Alright. Thank you. What tests are we running? I'm a doctor, and I have a right to know. He mentioned a protocol."

"Yes, the B-mod protocol. You're a B-mod, right?" Kate nodded.

The nurse went on. "Well, it's pretty simple. B-mods can be carriers for all sorts of nasty stuff for us humans who haven't tampered with our bodies. Frankly, God forbid, but you could wipe us out, bring the next plague, you know. I'm not really supposed to tell you this, but this room is a full quarantine station. The guards and I, we're part of the special unit. So is Rolf. He's in charge. We're all risking our lives, you know. Anyway, I don't mean to make a mountain." She opened a cabinet and pulled out a shelf. "But bear with us, alright? We do this because we have to, and you're the cause. You came here, right?" The shelf extended out to form a table, an examination table, with legs that folded down from underneath. Without missing a beat, she asked: "Can you take off your clothes please? You can put them in this box. We'll need to send them to be analyzed and sterilized." She pulled a box out from the cabinet.

Kate stammered. "Wait. What tests? I mean I get it, why you need to check. But I want to know exactly what you're going to do. And I'm not going to ..."

"Miss Genet. Please cooperate. We don't have time." A military mask, stern and strong, commanding, but Kate sensed worry, a little crack. What was she scared of? Me? No. Rolf.

"Miss Genet. He'll send others. They won't be like us, not volunteers. And they'll do their job, alright, you'll be tested and thoroughly examined, but they'll be drafted to our unit, and they won't be happy ... or gentle." The crack widened and her concern seeped out. Kate could almost taste fear, pity, and pain.

"I'll cooperate." She started to remove her clothes. She glanced to the guard.

He noticed and said, "I would turn away, but I can't. I have to keep my eyes on you. But I'll focus on your green eyes. I promise."

A chill ran over her exposed limbs. Goosebumps remained, freckling her skin. He just likes my eyes, she assured herself, and continued to undress, hoping he would keep his word. She knew the room was being monitored and there could be a roomful of people watching, or her disrobing could be broadcast to all of St. Louis. It didn't matter to her, so long as he focused on her eyes only.

"Thank you, Miss Genet. Please hop up on the table." The nurse said relieved. Kate moved to the table and contemplated the most awkward climb of her life. Hopping on the table seemed wrong. Her naked flesh was not meant for such a move. Sliding seemed better until her skin caught and stuck to the plastic surface. In the old days they used paper sheets to make it more comfortable and easier to clean, but paper was too expensive nowadays. If only they had a stepstool, she looked but saw nothing of the sort. What the hell? She sprung with some agility and some swaying flesh. The landing was not very graceful. She didn't care. She laughed.

"Very nice, Miss Genet. I haven't seen it done that way before," the nurse said.

Kate looked to the guard whose eyes were fixed on her.

He hadn't even noticed, or if he had, he didn't let on. The nurse continued. "Please lie down."

The nurse completed a rather conventional examination, using standard equipment and recording everything on a notepad. She also took a number of samples, including blood, tissue from various places, saliva, and hair. All of these were tagged and placed in small vials or tubes and then placed carefully in a box with various compartments. "I need to take all of this down to the lab." Kate thought of her own lab, wondering if she should have stayed. "I'll be back when it's completed, probably 15 minutes or so." The nurse left with bits and pieces of her in two boxes, clothes and body.

Kate felt oddly relaxed. It was almost over. She propped up on her elbows and looked to the guard. The corners of his mouth rose a little. How odd that she felt so peaceful naked on a table with this stranger watching her! This morning she was in Rochester. Calm, unusual serenity washed over her.

It broke.

Rolf entered the room. He wore a smile. He pulled out a notepad. While reading, he said, "You can go, if you like." Not to her. To the guard. "We're almost done here."

"No, that's alright, sir. I should stay. This is my post."

Rolf turned to Kate and stared at her. A different smile, just for her. He turned back to the guard. "No, you're not needed here. I've got it. Just the final part of the examination to wrap things up. She's not a security threat, of that I'm quite sure. You are needed, however, outside of room 245. Now!"

"Yes, sir." The guard nodded to Rolf and walked to the door. He looked in Kate's direction, their eyes met, and he winced.

Kate tensed. She was sitting, ready to jump down. No fucking way I'm going to let this bastard ...

He said calmly: "Lie down, Doctor Genet. This will only take a moment. The nurse is running tests on all of your samples. I just need to complete the mental examination." Huh? What is he talking about? Mental examination? Was this some sort of test?

"Doctor Genet. Lie down, please, and tell me why you are here in St. Louis. No appointment, no business. Allergy research, you say? Really? You could do better. Allergies don't exist in B-mods. Even I know that. Really, why are you here?" He had moved beside her, softly placed his hands on her shoulders, and guided her to a flat position on the table. Confused, she did not resist.

"I don't understand," she replied. "Why are you asking me these questions now? Like this?"

His eyes disappeared as he smiled. "Simple, Kate. The truth, that's all I want. And around here, I get what I want. After all, you're in my quarantine station, bio-bitch." Suddenly, his left hand shot from her shoulder to her neck and gripped her throat tightly, and in the same moment, his right hand pressed firmly against the wall, his elbow jabbed into her midsection. She screamed but little noise escaped her mouth. He grinned wickedly. "You'll learn obedience."

Both of her fists shot out with incredible force. Left hook shattered his nose and a short straight right hit his solar plexus. He doubled over, blood pouring out his nose. Kate leapt off the table, snarling. She backed away from him and looked for a weapon.

He had crumpled, but he recovered and stood tall. Hatred oozed from his face. "You're dead, bio-bitch." He walked to the cabinet and found what he was looking for, some type of surgical knife. "No one cares about you animals, bringing your diseases to wipe us out. Thinking you're better than us."

He stood still, slapped the side of the knife on his palm. "But don't worry. I know people who've a use for you." She retreated to the corner of the room. "You'll still fetch a decent price, after I'm done." He laughed.

She yelled for help, but it was only a whisper. Rolf advanced. "Ever been to the desert?"

The nurse returned. As soon as she saw the scene, she called for help---security, code 9, emergency, code 9---she seemed to be slapping something just outside the door, and then a loud beeping alarm rang.

Rolf walked slowly backwards to the cabinet and returned the knife. He pulled out his notepad and began tapping his fingers furiously.

A team of security guards rushed into the room. Two of them escorted Rolf to safety. As he left the room, Rolf ordered, "Put her down." Three others cornered Kate as if she was a rabid dog. Kate tried to explain, but they didn't listen. One pulled out a guard stick with a glowing red tip. He thrust it toward her.

Only the nurse's intervention saved her. "Stop, don't harm her. All of her tests came back negative. There is absolutely nothing wrong with her. Hold off, hold off. Kate, just sit down, please. Trust me. I'm sorry, but you need to trust me now. Sit down and tell us what happened. Calm down. You have blood all over your hands, and I know it isn't yours. You must understand how this looks. Please, calm down. Think."

Kate sat. "Can I get some clothes? That pig! He grabbed, he hurt me. He ..."

"I know. It will be alright. Just settle down. We'll figure out what happened." The guards also settled and stood waiting. The nurse turned to one of them, "Can you grab her clothes? From detox. Or just grab some spare clothes from storage. Either way. No reason she should be naked. She's clean."

Regis returned. He looked at Kate and must have known what had happened. He couldn't seem to look her in the eyes. She could feel his anger, and his shame. Something in him seemed broken at that moment. He turned and stormed out.

Go. Find Rolf and kill him.

TEN:

COFFEEHOUSE MEMORIES

Mr. Shephard dismissed the teams. He was pleased with himself. He almost wished he could be one of them. It would be exciting. But he had so much more to do. This was only one of five identical competitions he was running for this project, and this was only one of dozens of major R&D competitions he sponsored. The model worked, as his forebears had proven.

He hesitated. Why had he given them the founder's memory? He hadn't planned to do so. Only a select few had ever experienced that memory. Had it been the chippy's little intervention? His genuine confusion or lack of imagination? No, that wasn't the reason. It had been a long time, at least a year, since he'd accessed the memory. He needed it. It reminded him of the path they were on, where it began, and when it took off.

He resumed, but this time he began a few minutes earlier, grinning in anticipation of the Founder's personal history.

***

Jonathan stood at the window with one arm resting on an elevated table, fingers tapping and then caressing a large sleeveless coffee cup. He repeated the pattern. A light, quick touch to gauge followed by a slow, soft rub to confirm. His hand played like a child left alone. His other hand rested in a pocket, on top of his mobile, just in case he was needed. His mind wandered from his past to his present need to go legit.

It began at his loft in Santa Monica, back in 2006. Although the zoo never closed, he had the day off. He was happy to let someone else deal with customer complaints about the slow public Wi-Fi. He'd been watching some crappy porn while passing time and trying to get excited. It just wasn't doing it for him. Same old crap. Bad plot, bad acting, and tons of just plain ugly. He thought about heading over to Josie's place to get the real deal, but it was hot outside, and he was tired. He settled for a nap. He woke and caught the happy ending. Lucky him. He knew he could do better than what he was watching. Heck, he'd done better back in college. Now, that was an exciting thought. He texted Josie: `C'mon over. Now. Urgent.` She texted back: `5 min.` It didn't take much to convince her. They invited over some friends, the good looking fun crew, and had a party—good food and drinks, music and dancing. At 10 pm, they busted it out, their idea. Let's make some porn! Laughs from the crowd. No seriously, and they got to work.

Within a year, he ran his own porn production company. He'd persuaded Jimmy, a college buddy who was a reasonably successful novelist, to write scripts for kicks. He'd persuaded his core group of friends – the dirty dozen as they referred to themselves – to take an intensive three month acting class—

straight, legit acting, the normal stuff. He'd recruited some
college interns to be staffers and production assistants and
instituted a strict "don't touch the interns" rule. He'd been real
busy. The porn business was flooded and cutthroat. He
enjoyed it and did reasonably well. They all did.

Jonathan realized he had made it, in 2010, when he met
with his accountant Bob in an elegant office in downtown Los
Angeles. "Jon, you're pulling in a steady stream of cash,
millions, and you've very little overhead. I'm glad you
followed my advice and paid off your debts." When Jonathan
realized he wasn't leveraged anymore, that his big debts had
been paid off, he had what he would later describe as a genuine
religious experience; he'd say, "I was reborn!," in his best
preacher voice, "No longer an investor of borrowed money, I
am an investor of my own damn money." It was an amazing
feeling, a mixture of accomplishment, pride, power, and
freedom. Sometimes it was hard to believe that he was making
so much dough through advertising networks connected to
his portfolio of web properties, a few subscription services that
provided higher end content and encrypted traffic flows for
the privacy conscious, and experimental multiplayer games.
Who would've thought that Nude Casino would rake in a
quarter million a week? It was almost too easy.

Despite the powerful awakening, he did borrow more, a
lot more money. He had to if he wanted to build a virtual
world. So he gave a pitch to a select group of investors,
wealthy but hungry for more and a need to park money out of
sight. He was happy to be of service.

The most important business pitch of his life took place in a barely furnished conference room in some run-down Los Angeles high rise that hadn't been renovated since the late 1970s. Jonathan couldn't remember exactly where it was, who attended, or even what he was wearing. He remembered what mattered, the critical parts of his pitch:

"No, it's not a game, fellas. It will not be a game. And it isn't going to be a website, alright?" The room was full of chattering monkeys in thousand dollar suits.

"Listen," he insisted. "We're developing a virtual world that people can escape to. Just think of all of those people who just sit in front of the television or browse webpages on their screens so they can find some pictures or videos to watch. Yeah, you know what I'm talking about Green. Can you say boring? The web is already dying as people migrate to mobile. Why are people migrating? They want to move. They want action. They want to play with each other, interact." The room was quiet.

"Well, we're working on a members-only virtual world that will be accessible from any device—desktop or mobile— and when you're in, believe me, you'll be active, inter-fuckin'- active!" The audience leaned in, arms on the table, hands above their heads; it was like church.

"Look, you all know about the live webcam shows that people slobber over. The mere possibility of directing the show, of participating just a little bit with the actress doin' her thing, is all it takes to get 'em going. We're talking about taking that up a few notches, past the next few levels, if you know what I mean. Fully interactive, the highest quality anime avatars that we've been testing for years to make sure people connect with them. I mean, you'd be surprised at how, after a few weeks with moderate use, people start to *feel* what they see and think they've made their avatar do. It's incredible. I know because I've tried. And man, it's amazing and, here's the kicker, what really matters: It's fucking addictive ..."

Jonathan had tried it only once, loved it, and swore to himself to never do it again, and he barely kept that promise. That part of the pitch had been easy; the investors couldn't wait to signup themselves. They were mostly concerned about execution and keeping it secret.

"We've got an incredible team—really interdisciplinary, you know—the computer science geeks mixed in with my content crews and even a behavioral psychologist trained at Princeton with some big shot Nobel Prize winner." They loved the Ivy League cred; it got a few of them nodding in that blueblood rhythm. The Nobel was icing.

"She's been at the forefront of all of this, helping us design the environment and avatar-human interfaces so that people connect and feel what we want them to. Everyone on the team has shares in the project and is fully committed to it and nothing else. Besides, they've all signed the legal crap. We've got 'em. No worrying about defectors. ..."

A withered old skincat wearing a bright red shirt interrupted, "Yeah, fine. But how you going to keep a lid on it? The press, not to mention the government, will ..."

Jonathan jumped in. "It's called the darknet, for a reason, Red. Look, the world won't be accessible to anyone who hasn't been invited and fully vetted. It won't be on the normal Internet, not part of the web, not indexed by Google, not on Facebook, or any of that crap. No, it's members only, and members need to be vetted by our security team. Everything is encrypted, no prying eyes, no gagglers, no cops, no fricken' terrorist or extremist crazies trying to hide and make their plans. Let them play in other worlds, not ours. No, we vet 'em so we know them, and frankly, so we own them if necessary. It certainly will begin as a very exclusive, expensive club, but believe me, the network will grow and if anything, our biggest problem will be keeping up with demand."

They all invested and got even richer, and so did Jonathan. The business thrived. It devoured the next eight years of his life. Fortunately, Anna saved him.

Jonathan let go of the coffee cup and his mobile. He put his hands on the edge of the table, bracing himself. A thin wet film glazed his eyes. He left his hands where they were and recalled the day he decided to change— May 22, 2021.

***

Sitting in his favorite rocking chair on the back porch of his luxurious Saint Helena ranch, Jonathan wondered why he felt rotten, so utterly blah. He thought about all that he had. The ranch, the penthouse condo in San Fran, a second house in Palo Alto, the beach house in San Diego, the cabin in Colorado, and then he lost interest in completing that list. He started another one, this time thinking about the business. He had dumped the production company, but otherwise he still owned all of the porn distribution properties, the web stuff, the advertising network, again, he started to tire of listing stuff, so he jumped to the end, to the big hit, the members-only, off-the-grid, virtual world. It rolled in more money than he knew what to do with. His investors were thrilled. His team was thrilled. Yet here he was, blah.

Was it Anna? How could it be? He was finally serious. Anna was a brilliant artist. He happened upon her work in a small co-op gallery on Valencia Street. She cut through bullshit like no one else. Her techno-urban cityscapes pulled him in and held him, like an almost comprehensible idea that promised to disrupt your settled beliefs. She was much the same. She seduced him first with her art, but her presence was more powerful. She said little but meant much, and often didn't need to say anything at all.

Jonathan loved her, and wanted to do nothing more than sit here with her and watch the sunset. She was in New York visiting with her ailing mother. Maybe he should have gone with her. Her mother only had a few months left. He'd been afraid. He had heard so much about her mother and how much Anna loved her and looked up to her. He worried she'd not approve of him, and then he'd lose Anna. So he stayed away on the pretense that he was needed for work. It was a lie. She didn't know. It didn't matter. He knew what really mattered to Anna. Him. She still loved him.

She'd fallen in love with him without knowing what he did for a living, how he made his fortune. She had thought he was just a wealthy businessman who invested in Internet startups. He told her the truth once he decided that he wanted to spend the rest of his life with her. He had to. He told her how he felt first, almost a down-on-your-knees proposal, and she said she felt the same. They held each other for a long time, and it was the best he felt his entire life. Warm, safe, complete, content in a way that was different—he thought it was something like being held by your mother when you're a baby and at the same time like being that mother, a melding of the two. Something like that. Then he broke it. The feeling, the moment was torn apart by the truth. He should have held it longer. But he wanted to tell her, to open up completely, to confess. He did. She listened intensely, as always. When he was finished, she said, "OK, Jonathan, eres un chico porno virtual? El chico porno virtual, supongo." She paused, and then in a slow, measured tone, she said, "No me gusta eso. Hacer algo diferente, algo bueno." That's it. She said nothing more, and he didn't push. They sat quietly, no longer holding each other, but not distant either. They didn't fight or argue about it. Since then, she occasionally let a look of sad disapproval slip through when she was looking at him. But she said nothing more. She didn't need to.

He would change. He sat on the porch trying to figure out what to do. He couldn't escape the fact that he was the virtual porn guy, VPG as he would call himself until the day he died as a reminder, his reality check. But he could use what he had built to build something else, something different, something legit, something that Anna would support. Again, he constructed a list, this time focusing on the assets that he could repurpose—the people, hardware, software, technology, and heck, even a few behavioral psychologists.

***

Jonathan blinked and two warm droplets slowly inched out of his eyes. They emerged from the outer corners, like mice in mid-morning. He felt them stop, perching on his cheekbones. His hands activated to wipe off the tears, but he held his hands firmly on the edge of the table, and he focused on the minute feeling of perched tear on skin. It was a precarious balancing act, like so many things in life.

Anna married him last year. It was a small family wedding. The happiest moment of his life was exactly when she stepped out from the hallway, to walk down the aisle. He only saw her face, her dark brown eyes found him and she smiled in her knowing way. That moment held all meaning.

Jonathan remembered little else of the wedding ceremony, reception, or late night celebrations. Except, later in the evening, he vowed to Anna and himself that he would do right by her. She answered, "Sé que lo harás," and again granted him her smile.

While he cherished his life with Anna, his marriage vow drove him mad sometimes. He frantically searched for a new path, but his efforts to date had failed miserably. His established properties continued to flourish, especially the darknet world. There were many aspects of that project that were admirable, at least from a technical perspective, and he wondered if there was a way for him to take it legit. Then he caught himself. What the hell? It was on the darknet for a reason!

Snakes and meerkats to fricken' ants. Utterly brilliant.

Who'd have thought to combine Google Glass, self-driving cars, and the motor function management system? That had been brilliant, but then Jonathan realized it was only the beginning.

***

Mr. Shephard braced himself. He'd experienced the Founder's epiphany before. It was pure bliss.

Standing in the San Francisco coffee shop, hands gripping the table, eyes staring out the window but no longer focused on the pedestrians walking like ants, Jonathan saw a glimpse of a future, radically different from the present and yet not so distant. The new Google Glass—its magical combination, its transformation of chaos to order—inspired him. It was one critical seed. But there were others.

Over the past decade, the tech circles buzzed about two other technologies he could leverage. The Internet of Things, as they called it, was a ubiquitous network of sensors, little mini-sensors on everything from toasters to cars to whatever you could attach 'em to, constantly gathering data, and connected to the Internet, or whatever it was that the Internet had become. He lost track of the names. But it was the basic concept he worked with in his mind. Interconnected networks of sensors and data about everything in the environment, ubiquitously integrated into the environment, reconstructing the environment itself—*that was the key.* The other technology he would leverage also had a bunch of buzzwords attached to it, but again, he pulled the concept, and for that, Big Data was all that he needed. Massive amounts of data, massive storage, and massive processing capabilities.

Jonathan knew he would spend years and probably hundreds of millions developing the system. That didn't worry him at all. In this moment, he saw it. He felt it really. His heart and lungs and head filled to the bursting point.

His virtual world didn't need to be consigned to the darknet. No. It didn't need to be virtual, not some disconnected place, some fake cyberspace. That was the biggest mistake. The libertarian wetdream of the 90s. No, he would make real worlds that existed within, alongside, as a part of the world we know. They would come to be the world we know.

***

Mr. Shephard permitted his own emotions to run freely. The memories triggered such euphoria. That moment. That realization of something truly revolutionary through the sheer power of intellect, inspiration, and dream. God spoke to his great-great-great grandfather in that coffee house. Mr. Shephard felt it. It could be true. He liked that truth. Nothing in his life experience or the lives of others that he had experienced compared with that moment.

Yes, God had spoken to his great-great-great grandfather, given him insight and inspiration, and a glimpse of the future where everyone would be connected and working and living together in a cooperative shared environment—a safe and stable heaven. Perhaps God had even spoken to Mr. Shephard through his ancient relative. That also seemed right. He swam in this deep pool for a long time, savoring the feeling of purpose and the power to change the world.

That evening, Mr. Shephard relived the coffeehouse memories again and again.

ELEVEN:

THE GRAND ST. LOUIS

The room they moved her to seemed no different than the holding pen where Rolf had violated her. The only difference Kate could identify was slightly more give in the back cushion of the couch. The bastard had vamoosed, disappeared into thin air. Hospital security had searched the hospital complex and contacted the police, who apparently were now searching for him. Kate suspected he wouldn't be caught. Animals like that have hidden dens and protective packs. One of the nurses had told her as much. "They won't find him. He's got friends; some say he's connected."

Regis had disappeared as well. He hadn't returned to see her, and when she asked about him, no one provided any answers. The two guards were more talkative. Initially, they'd asked her about Rochester and what the bio-mod communities were actually like. Her curt though polite answers stifled their attempts. She was in no mood to chat, not with them.

The beige silky – but not silk – clothes felt insubstantial, which made her uncomfortable. Quick glances reminded her that she was in fact clothed, but the naked feeling was unsettling. It reminded her of a time, the only time, she'd gone skinnydipping as a teenager. She'd been reduced to a floating head, trying to disappear behind waves. They had returned her clothes, but she thought it best to start blending in and so she accepted the nurse's gift, her spare clothes.

Maybe she should head back home, get away from here as soon as possible. It was an idea worth entertaining but only for a few moments. She couldn't quit. No, she'd continue with her research. The holding pen had been hell, but she'd been to hell before, and she'd never let the devils win. What would a meeting with her dad have been like after this trip to hell? What would he say she should do? He'd listen to her, comfort her, offer to help, and ask about her plan. A plan started to form in her head.

She heard a knock at the door. One man and two women, dressed in all white, fancier clothes. Kate couldn't identify what exactly made them nicer than what the others had been wearing. Who cares about their clothes? She had asked to see the hospital CEO or whoever held the top administrative position at the hospital—the person in charge, damn it! Maybe these three would be able to help her.

The man stepped forward. White wavy hair framed his wrinkled face. He had reddish brown skin, and calm brown eyes. Kate was drawn to them. He had a soft smile, not a trace of wickedness. He reminded her of her father, what he might be like if he were born and raised here. She tensed at the thought, steeling herself.

The women flanked him. Each had an air of importance about them. The first had a military look—strong, confident, tall, with shoulders up and chest elevated; she meant business. Her eyes were also blue, but they did not pull, they pushed. The second was the opposite. This soft, motherly older woman looked pained, her shoulders sagging as if she bore Kate's trauma. Yet she wore a smile. Her skin was darker, more like hers. Most remarkable, however, was the woman's height. Kate had never seen an adult under five foot tall.

The guards stood in attention, nodding to each of the three. They seemed to give the first woman an extra degree of respect. Yes, she must be their boss.

"Miss Genet - Doctor Genet, I would like to offer you our deepest apologies, personally and on behalf of this hospital. What happened down there is atrocious, unacceptable obviously, and really unbelievable—I mean, I cannot believe we let this happen. It's just unheard-of around here, and deeply troubling." Kate nodded.

"I should have introduced myself and my colleagues. My name is Doctor Martin. I am the Chief Physician. This is Doctor Reynolds. She heads our Inpatient Psychiatric Unit. And this is Chief Jenks. She's Head of Security."

Jenks stepped forward and half-bowed to Kate. "Doctor Genet, I'm very sorry. This is inexcusable and should never have happened, plain and simple. I will get to the bottom of this." She must have a military background, Kate thought. "Our security protocol was not followed, and Rolf abused his power beyond the pale of what anyone imagined possible. We …"

Kate interrupted, "Hold on. One of the nurses said he wouldn't be found because he was connected, and even in the room, they seemed frightened of him. I mean, are you saying no one had a clue about this monster? I don't believe it for a second. You …"

"Excuse me, Doctor Genet. We'll conduct a thorough investigation. I can tell you that Rolf was known as a very strict leader of a very difficult unit, and, well, he didn't love b-mods because of the risks. He came from Nashville, after all, a few years after the SentaPV outbreak. That much was common knowledge. But …"

"What? SPV has long been eradicated."

"Only for bio-mods, Doctor Genet. Not for us."

"I don't understand. I would have heard of an outbreak in Nashville. It would be major news …"

Doctor Martin interjected, "Doctor Genet, I assure you, it happened, hundreds of people died, and many believe a b-mod carried the virus straight into Nashville General. But we can discuss this later. It is not really germane."

Jenks, who had waited with arms crossed behind her back, resumed. "As I was saying, Rolf was known as a strict leader of a difficult unit. But the attack …" She seemed to soften slightly, unsure what to say, and then she caught herself, straightened up and continued, "It is, ultimately, my responsibility, my fault." Then, in a rapid motion that completely shocked Kate, Jenks stepped forward and kneeled before Kate, bowed her head, put her hand forward and lightly touched the ground just in front of Kate's feet. She held the pose for three seconds and then stood up. "I need to go. But we'll talk." She turned and left. The other two nodded to her as she left, and Kate just sat staring.

Doctor Martin turned back to face Kate. "There will be an investigation so we can figure out how this happened and make sure it never happens again. But I'm not here to discuss any of that. I just want to offer you my assistance. Make sure you are OK and can get settled."

Kate nodded. "I'm not fine, not at all. That bastard." She shook her head and calmed herself with a deep breath. "I'm not fine, but I will be. You're right. I need to get settled. I need sleep. And to be honest, I can't sleep here, in one of these rooms."

"I understand. According to Doctor Gert and nurse Hansen, you are OK physically, nothing that requires further medical attention. You might wish to talk with someone though, to make sure you're ready to leave. Obviously, you've been through a very traumatic experience. Perhaps Doctor Reynolds could be of some assistance to you."

Doctor Reynolds, sagging as if bearing the weight of Kate's experience, was about to say something, but Kate cut her off, "Not today, Doctor. I might take you up on that offer in a few days, but not now." Kate looked at Doctor Martin.

"OK, Kate, if I may call you that."

"I prefer Doctor Genet."

"Doctor Genet, then, let me see what we can do about getting you settled. Where are you staying?"

Kate hesitated and then lied. "I don't have a place to stay yet, Doctor. I arrived last night and came straight to the hospital." No reason to tell him. She'd see what he had to say.

He looked puzzled.

"I didn't know where else to go, really. I don't know anyone here, and didn't think bio-mods would be welcome. So I thought the hospital would be the safest, …" she laughed like an adolescent and shook her head, "the best place to go and find people like me, doctors who care about …"

"Don't worry." He stepped toward Kate and began to extend his left arm, but then he withdrew and continued, "There are two options. First, there is one operating hotel, the Grand St. Louis. It caters to mods basically. There is a decent flow of visitors, mainly for business. My assistant can call and make a reservation for you, if you like. Second, you could squat a vake."

"A what?"

"A Vake. You could move into an empty house. There are plenty of them, and the Housing Department maintains large groups in various sectors of the city. Minimal maintenance, mind you, but good enough so it can be used. Most communities work together and cooperate with the Department to maintain a dozen or so Vakes in their neighborhood. So, if you like, my assistant can set up some vake visits and you can find one that suits you. I should say that this is what most humans do when we travel, not that we travel much. We're familiar with the idea of moving into one of these empty houses. I understand if you might find it odd or unsettling."

"Are they safe? I guess I worry about what I might find, or who might find me."

"Oh, yes, they're safe, Doctor Genet. Safe as one could be anywhere these days. Some neighborhoods are better than others, of course. But I understand your concern, and frankly, the hotel might be your best option. You could always find a vake later. That reminds me, how long do you plan to visit?"

She ignored his question, annoyed with him for asking but also with herself for not having an answer. "I think the hotel is probably my best bet, at least for today. I don't know if I could fall asleep in an abandoned building right now. Too creepy." She half-smiled.

"Understood. Let me go talk with my assistant right away. I'll be back in a few minutes. Doctor Reynolds can keep you company." He left.

"Doctor Genet, do you mind if I sit?" asked Doctor Reynolds.

"No, of course not." Kate marveled at the woman's diminutive stature. Her hands and feet and limbs were so tiny. She seemed frail and weak.

"Thank you." She sat in a chair, smiled, and looked to Kate as if waiting for her to say something.

Wary, weary, not in the mood to talk, Kate just leaned back on the soft cushion.

Reynolds shifted back in her seat as well and breathed out slowly. Then she leaned forward, shoulders raised, and said, "I want you to know that I'm here for you, to talk, to listen, to answer your questions perhaps. Whatever you prefer. I will be honest and not play games, and I'll keep your confidence, as is my professional obligation, but more importantly because it's who I am. Trust takes time, and after today, it may be difficult for you to trust me or anyone else. That's perfectly natural, and OK. Don't let it bog you down. But trust is important, and when you're ready to find and build it, let me know." Another deep breath, and she settled back in her chair with a soft smile.

She didn't say another word. Neither did Kate. Kate welcomed the silence. She wasn't about to open up to this stranger.

***

The hotel was nowhere near the hospital. The PTV took her through the empty streets. The sunlight, even when filtered through the heavily tinted windows of the PTV, seemed incredibly bright. It woke a part of her.

She thought of Adam, but he was a little older. He was no longer a purplish, wrinkled newborn. He was plump with thin wisps of light brown hair, and bright blue eyes. He burp smiled and then grunted at her. She smiled back, reached out her hand to caress his chubby leg, and started to speak, to tell him something.

She woke to a beeping noise. "Arriving, Final destination," a soft voice informed her.

The Grand St. Louis was an elegant, very old building that overlooked a large park. She shifted to manual and drove to the parking garage entrance, a tunnel. Again, she drove around a series of three parallel segments with alternating wind currents and emerged into the underground lot. A wide stairway led up to the hotel lobby.

When she emerged into the lobby, she was astounded. People were walking, talking, gaggling, cavorting. It was active, alive, happening. And there were no unmodified humans in sight.

Kate stood watching. About two-dozen people milled about in the main lobby, and she spotted more activity in an adjoining room, probably a restaurant or bar. She saw bio-mods with dark complexions and sturdy builds. They seemed large and full of life. A few had significant physical modifications, height and musculature. Athletes? No, that made no sense. No reason they'd be here. Soldiers? Possibly. The others were not remarkable. They could be human, although Kate doubted it. Something about the way they moved and spoke with each other seemed exaggerated. It was as if the biochemical interactions among them created an aura that gave them a special vitality, something she'd never noticed before but definitely something she'd not seen since being in St Louis. She was tempted to run over and join in. Would she feel different? Would it refresh her? She puzzled on these questions, and then she noticed their clothes. They were wearing bio-mod clothing. The aura faded, and she wondered whether she'd imagined it.

Talking in small groups, no one seemed to notice her. So she found a spot off to the side of the door she'd just exited and blended into the shadows, or at least, she imagined that was what she was doing. A fly on the wall.

She noticed another group standing together and her heart beat faster. Comp-mods for sure, she thought. They were so different from the bio-mods. Thin and rigid, barely moving, void of vitality. Their heads swiveled. Kate noticed that their mouths were not moving, but she was sure they were communicating with each other somehow. Bunch of bots. Or maybe they were a unit. She didn't know what to think about them, except to wonder why they were here. She froze, fascinated by them. She felt her blood rushing with more fervor, but it was quickly countered with a wave of exhaustion. Should she stay put and observe? Go talk with the bio-mods? Sleep?

Sleep. A human appeared. A young woman came out from an alcove Kate hadn't noticed. "Doctor Genet??

"Yes."

"We have a room for you. I've been waiting for you to arrive. I should have seen you come up from the garage, but I was pulled away to take care of something. I apologize."

"Don't worry about it. I'm fine. Is there a check in?"

"You're checked in already. Don't worry. Before I forget, here, take this." She handed her a small plastic card.

"What's this?"

"Credit. Your employer set it up for you. We don't rely on bits or auto-exchanges. We abandoned those systems, for, uh, security reasons. I'm sure you understand." Kate nodded. "Just use this if you need to purchase anything."

"OK, thanks."

"Let me escort you to your room. Do you need help with your bags?"

"No, I've got this, thank you." She had another bag in the PTV but didn't need it. Tomorrow, she'd have plenty of time.

***

Sleep yanked at her. But she needed a shower. There was only one setting, lukewarm. Still, it felt good on her scalp and neck, running down her back. It took a long while before she picked up the soap, and then it took a long while for her to put it down, only a third of its original size. She tried not to think of Rolf, that bastard had done enough and she did not want him to cause her any more pain, but images of his cruel face flashed in her mind just when she thought she would find a calm respite. She pushed him away with deliberate thoughts of others, Regis, Villa, and her mother and father. She bowed her head for a while and almost dozed off. She barely caught herself.

The room was dark; the bed comfortable. She slept soundly.

Dreams lingered in her mind, struggling to gain a share of her, for an opportunity to live and shape. It was, after all, their calling. Nightmares were particularly powerful lately and had only a thin membrane to cross. Others were simply not in the game. Sexual dreams had long faded to a ghetto, although a slight spark had encouraged a few to begin working up plans. Kate's small dreams of friends and childhood memories were able to squeeze into the limelight here and there, but not tonight. Something held all of them at bay. She would sleep soundly.

***

Kate woke famished. She'd slept for 14 hours. She put on fresh clothes she'd packed. After food, she'd buy some new clothes. She bounded down the three flights of stairs. Off the lobby was a restaurant serving both breakfast and lunch. She ate both. She didn't notice the other patrons until she was almost finished. She chewed on a piece of sweet and sour jerky, looked up, and noticed three men watching her. They appeared to be bio-mods. When her upward glance caught them, they turned away, spoke briefly, and left. A pit in her stomach called out. She was full of food and had drunk three cants of water. But the pit persisted. Were they watching her eat? Was she eating like a pig, cramming the food in? She had been famished. Or was it just that she was the only bio-mod female in St. Louis? Were they watching her just like she had been watching others last night? Curious flies? Something unsettling about the way they'd been looking at her, but she didn't dwell on it.

Her waitress, pretty with little brown dots on her cheeks, told her that she had a few options for getting some more appropriate clothes. Kate could pick up clothes from a shop in the hotel, she could ask for the hotel to send someone to her room to get measured and that person would go out and buy clothes for her, or she could venture outside and go to the distribution center, a massive shopping center downtown. The waitress seemed to think that the last option was not a good idea. Her eyebrows had risen and her tone wavered into a higher pitch when she suggested it. Kate said, "What would you do if you were me?"

"Easy. I'd start with option one and if I didn't find what I like, then option two. The last option really would be my last resort. The center is a pain in general, and it would be worse for you." She turned and walked away before Kate could ask why.

Kate spent the day at the hotel. First, she purchased clothes from the shop. She contemplated going to the distribution center, despite the waitress's warning, but her father's voice crept into her head, "Kate, what's your plan? Think. Don't just do." Her stubbornness faded. The hotel had just what she needed and in a few different shades—white, off-white, cream, beige, and nougat. She couldn't stand the lime greens and dull yellows.

Next, she sat in the lobby. She watched people, and she wrote notes in her notepad about everything that had happened the previous day as well as what she witnessed while sitting there. Writing had a therapeutic power. It relieved her to get it all out, and it forced her to examine the details of what had happened, the sequences of events, the choices she made, and the actions taken by others. When satisfied with her notes, she wanted exercise. She went to the front desk in the alcove and asked about her options. The hotel basement had a large exercise room and a swimming pool.

Kate went to the exercise room with the idea that a long run on a treadmill would be perfect. About fifteen other hotel guests were using the room. She walked past the weights and pulleys and various other equipment, some of which she did not recognize, and she headed for the treadmills. All but one were being used. She stood dumbfounded, staring at the comp-mods running on the other treadmills. Their bodies moved perfectly, in a steady fast-paced run that involved the form of a professional athlete. Arms and legs moved in synchronicity with each other and the treadmill itself. The legs were incredibly well built, thin but muscular, as if they ran a few miles every day. Kate inched toward the front of the machines, trying to be inconspicuous though not trying too hard because she was so distracted. It didn't matter. Their eyes were focused straight ahead on God knows what. They were staring blankly at the wall. Their eyes never shifted; their attention was fixed. They didn't see her. She smiled at the nearest one. No reaction. She waved. Nothing. Bots, my God, they really are just machines, no different than the treadmills. This confirmed something she'd always been told and more or less believed but never really knew. She'd almost hoped to be wrong, hoped that the stories weren't true or at least that they were incomplete. But this was like finding out that Santa Claus didn't exist—as a kid, she always believed him to be a myth, but hoped otherwise. Wouldn't that be awesome!

She no longer felt like running on the last treadmill. She left the exercise room and went to the pool. No one else was swimming. There was no attendant, only a stack of folded white towels on a bench. For a moment, she stood still and wondered whether the comp-mods could swim, how the water would affect them. She imagined one of the bots from the treadmill jumping in. Suddenly, he was convulsing, floating on his back with arms and legs flailing wildly. He didn't say anything, and then she noticed it was eerily silent except for his splashing and the whirring buzz of a giant fly she could not see. She shuddered. Poor bot short-circuited himself. Then she stripped off her outer clothes and dove in. She swam fifty laps, alternating her strokes, and as she fell into a rhythm, she relaxed.

***

She ate in the hotel restaurant and decided to have a drink at the bar afterwards, mainly so she could extend her evening. She sat at the corner of the bar so she could have a decent view, cut down the angles of potential suitors, and have an easy escape route, in case any suitors actually approached her. She was not in the mood. The bartender offered a wide range of drinks, alcoholic as well as the more conventional bio-mod concoctions, ranging from upps to dreamers. She was in St. Louis, so she had a draft beer. It was refreshing.

The patrons were mostly bio-mods. Some humans mixed in. There were no comp-mods at the bar, as far as she could tell. A slow, droning music played in the background. Kate tried to play a guessing game with herself—the challenge was to figure out someone's past based on their appearance and how they interacted with others. Could she figure any of these guys out? She flitted from person to person but found that she was unable to come up with anything interesting that seemed plausible. It was just random guesses, and thus stupid. She was certainly curious. She hadn't expected to see bio-mods in St. Louis. She didn't know anyone who had been here. And here they were, a dozen or two bio-mods hanging out in the hotel bar. They were here on business, not vacation. But what business? Or maybe they had run away, like Villa had mentioned. But why? From what? Why would they have run? Kate worried. What would they think of her? She finished the last third of her beer in an extended gulp, followed by a burp that she barely kept silent. She started to get up and noticed someone watching her. He hid his face behind folded hands and forearms, elbows propped up on a table; something about him seemed familiar. When he noticed that she noticed him, he turned abruptly, stood and left the bar. She sat back down and waited for a few minutes. She did not want to leave right after him. She asked the bartender for a cant of water, and she left when she had finished it.

She ran up the stairs and to her room. The exercise felt good. When she opened the door, she found a small note on the floor. "Tomorrow morning, check out of the hotel. You are not safe. Go to the hospital. Sleep well, but do not open your door for anyone."

TWELVE:

CHANGES

Rolf. It must be him. But why would he bother with her? Why not just move on and let her be? He'd probably send others to do his dirty work, members of his pack, devils like him.

Kate wanted to leave, go down to the lobby, out in the open where other people mingled. Wouldn't she be safer there? There must be security at the hotel. She hadn't noticed them, but that didn't mean they weren't there. Still, it was hard for her to rest assured that the hotel security would help her very much. No, she couldn't rest, assured or otherwise. She was tired and needed to sleep, but the note had electrified her.

She sat down on the ground and stretched her legs and lower back, hands grabbing feet and pulling her down. She took slow, deep breaths and forced herself to calm down. She needed to think, to plan.

Would someone come busting through her door? Not likely. The door was heavy and the combination of mag lock and classic bolt made breaking down the door next to impossible. The only way someone who meant to do her harm could get into her room would be through subterfuge, a casual knock, the pretense of an emergency. She double-checked the locks. Both active. She surveyed the room for other points of entry but found none. The incredibly thick windows were firmly integrated into the walls, serving more as walls than windows; they were highly reflective and only allowed a little light to pass through them, and only from the outside. No one would pass through those windows. It was only the door that she had to worry about.

So Kate worried. Suppose whoever was after her, if in fact anyone was, obtained a key to her door. Then what? She took two chairs from the desk, which was near the window, and moved them closer to the door, outside of its turning radius by a few feet so the light from the hallway wouldn't necessarily reveal them. She set them down on their sides. Obstacles for the bastard. She looked for others. She put all sorts of random crap on the floor of the room in between the entrance and the natural path to the bedroom. Who knew if it would work, but it was better than nothing. She put a few pillows under the sheets in the bed, arranging them to look like a sleeping body curled up. She had cleared out the front closet except for an extra pillow. She turned out all of the lights and sat on the pillow in the closet, waiting and listening.

***

"I told you you'd die bio-bitch." Rolf's black beady eyes held her. He had a thin rod with a red tip pointed at her. She knew what it could do, what he meant to do. Burning heat. Excruciating pain.

"Wait," she pleaded, "please. I don't know why you're here. But …"

He wasn't listening, at least not to her words. He heard something else, her helplessness, her fear. He grinned, wicked.

Kate groped with her hands for something to use, to defend herself from this monster. All she could find was a pillow. She'd cleared everything out. Only a pillow and the dark. She put the pillow in front of her. Not much to hide behind, not much of a shield, but better than nothing. She inched further into the small dark room, trapped. Her mind raced, her heart pounded.

He stood in the doorway. Huge. There was no light. Only the red-hot tip, a lone star burning. He no longer looked human. His face shrouded in darkness, only a bare red glint reflected off his teeth, a thin line of grinning knives. She thought it ironic that they called bio-mods animals and here was this monster, hunting her.

"You're mine." He growled.

Kate compacted into a tight ball, almost shrinking away completely.

His tone shifted, suddenly human, melodious even. "Come out, Kate. We've much to discuss, you and I. I've still got to finish our exam. The mental examination is required for all of you animals."

Kate retreated further into the black hole at the back of the closet. Perhaps she wouldn't be able to escape it, but maybe it would allow her to escape him. A wormhole to another time and place.

"Kate, come out now!" He stepped into the closet and thrust his red-hot poker into her face. It burned a hole straight through the pillow.

She felt the heat from it, the danger. Her hormones went into overdrive and something snapped.

***

Kate was lying down on the bed in the hotel room. She was waiting for him. He was showering, to get ready for her, for their coupling. She wasn't sure it was a good idea to try this again. But she felt she had to give sex another try. She'd done it twice before and it hadn't been good, no, not at all, but it wasn't completely horrible. Her hormones had responded normally, shaped by the pharmacological modifications she'd taken since puberty, but both times, she'd felt overwhelmed by an intense sweeping feeling. She hated the absence of control. Apparently, most people loved it; some said it was like surfing a 100-foot wave. She felt like she was drowning.

Johan seemed alright once she'd given him a chance and gotten to know him. She hadn't been attracted to him at first, but he had grown on her. There was something charming about his smile when he looked at her. Though she wouldn't admit it to herself consciously, she feared she was falling in love with him.

The bathroom door opened slowly. "Kate, I'm coming for you. Kate, my little bio-bitch." Rolf stepped from the bathroom grinning.

No! Not him. This is not right. It was Johan. "Johan?"

He whipped out his thin, dangerous rod. She jumped up, ready to fight. She wasn't wearing any clothes. She didn't notice, but he did. He rushed toward her, and she screamed.

Wake up! Wake up! Please, God, let me wake up.

***

She sat up abruptly in the closet. She did not remember the dreams, although she felt shaken up. She knew she'd struggled, and she vaguely remembered Rolf, a trace of bile in her throat.

Her body ached. She stood and stumbled; her left leg sizzled. She shook it to wake it and exited the closet. The room was a mess, as she had left it. She took a long shower. She closed her eyes and saw room 542. A dream? She felt like she could open her eyes at any point; she still felt the water washing over her. But she didn't open her eyes. She wanted to see him. Nicola, Joseph and Adam were together on the hospital bed. The room was filled with sunlight, as if the walls and ceiling were only thinly there. Suddenly, Kate thought of her own child, a vague thought thrust in her mind that she couldn't make clear, the child of some future or alternative self.

She opened her eyes, refreshed. She dressed, packed up her belongings, and left. The cleaning staff would have a field day trying to figure to what had happened in there. She wasn't coming back, so it didn't matter. She'd go to the hospital.

Thirteen:

Help

"Doctor Genet. Good morning. How can I help you?" The clerk looked ashamed. Did he know what happened with Rolf? Of course, he knew something. They were trying to find Rolf, and the clerk had handed her over to him. But did he know the details?

"Good morning. I would like to meet with Doctor Martin."

"Do you have an appointment?"

"No, I met him yesterday, and he should be expecting me."

"Without an appointment, I doubt he'll be able to see you. He's incredibly busy, booked twelve hours straight. But I can call his assistant and see."

"That would be great, thank you."

"Chief Jenks left a hospital-wide notice that she should be notified when you return. The notice indicates that we should let you know when we signal her. Never seen that before, to be honest."

Kate understood. No surprises. "I'd be happy to meet with her first. Can you let her know and also let Doctor Martin's assistant know that I'd like to come by his office?"

"Sure, will do. Do you want to grab a seat?" He motioned to the waiting room.

Kate nodded and found a seat. No Mr. Salonich. She wondered where he was, whether he was alright.

In a few minutes, the clerk walked over. "Chief Jenks cannot meet right now. She is busy for about an hour but will meet you after that. In the meantime, would you like to go to Doctor Martin's office? His assistant said that you should do so at your earliest convenience."

"That works for me."

The office suite was on the fifth floor. By habit, Kate took the stairs. As she turned the corner of the third floor landing she was startled when she noticed someone coming up the stairs behind her, about one flight below. Had the person come from the second floor or followed her from the first? Fear washed over her, and she bounded up the remaining two flights. She exited the stairwell with a glint of sweat, although she was not breathing heavy. There were plenty of people mulling about the hallway, so she decided to move down the hallway about twenty feet, lean against the wall near an open door where a few people lingered, and watch the stairway door. A moment later, a young man exited. He looked in the other direction first, scanning, and then turned toward her. Before he made the full turn, she stepped through the open door to hide. She found herself on the outside of a small circle of nurses who watched over something, perhaps an operation. Kate caught a glimpse of a patient lying on a bed. But she didn't want to be discovered in the room. So she slowly turned and exited the room, looking to see if the man was still there. He was not.

**

"Doctor Genet, good morning. I'm Doctor Martin's assistant. My name is Gina. He isn't available for a few hours, but if you like, I can schedule a lunch meeting. Would that be alright?" She was probably about the same age as Kate, though she seemed a little more weathered, a few wrinkles around the forehead and eyes appeared with her broad smile. She looked straight at Kate while she spoke and something about the way she did bred trust. Perhaps it was the tone in her voice as well.

Kate nodded, "Sure, that would be fine."

"Alright, will do. He thought you'd be back today or tomorrow. He'll be glad to meet with you. He asked me to show you around the hospital, make some introductions, you know, help you get situated. So if you like, I can do that. I mean, I need to clear a few things, and then …"

"That would be great. But I'm supposed to meet with Chief Jenks in an hour."

"Maybe we could just stay put and grab some coffee. After lunch, I'll show you around the hospital and introduce you to some people that Doctor Martin thought you should meet." She motioned toward a sitting room and started walking in that direction.

"That works. I actually wanted to ask you about the vakes."

"You didn't like the hotel?" Gina said, with a concerned look on her face.

"No, it was alright." Kate hesitated. Should she tell Gina about the note? It seemed premature. "The room was fine, and the restaurant and pool and everything were nice. I just didn't feel right when I was there. This is going to sound odd, but I guess I didn't like being around all those mods." She smiled weakly, unsure about how Gina would react.

Gina laughed abruptly and caught herself. "Sorry."

Kate said with a smile, almost a laugh "It's kinda funny. But to be honest, I felt like there were too many eyes on me. It was a little creepy. Maybe it's just my imagination or something, because of yesterday."

"I understand. But I would've thought you'd feel safe there because of the mods, more of your own kind rather than people who might be prejudiced." She poured a cup of coffee and handed it to Kate.

"I thought that too." Kate shuddered as Rolf crossed her mind. "I wanted to ask you about the vakes. Doctor Martin mentioned them."

"Just so we can talk." Gina walked over to the sitting room door and shut it. "Vakes are another option for housing. How long do you plan to be here?"

"A few weeks. It could be longer, I suppose. We'll see. It depends on how my research goes."

"You could get a vake through the normal process, go to the housing department office, register, and see where they put you. This can be done relatively quickly and you'd have a place in a few days, three at most. They're pretty efficient. There are a ton of vacant houses throughout the city and the vake program is designed to spread people out and keep the stock in decent shape, keep the neighborhoods in decent shape."

"Makes sense."

"Yes, but the thing is, for you, it might not be the best idea."

"What do you mean?"

"Well, a couple of things. First, you need to register. That means creating a public record of where you are. I'm not sure you want to do that with Rolf on the loose. He or his friends could easily track you down. Rumor is that he's connected to the Trinelli family, and you never know what they'll do."

Kate clenched her fists at the mention of Rolf. Her left knuckles still ached. "Why would he surface? Aren't the police after him?"

"I don't know, Doctor Genet. I'll let Chief Jenks and Doctor Martin explain, it's not my call. I'm just saying I wouldn't register. Besides, you don't know where they'll end up assigning you. But you can be sure it won't be in a highly populated neighborhood. They'll put you in one of those places where there are a lot of vakes. Fewer long-term occupants in those neighborhoods. So it's not as safe, if you ask me."

Exasperated, Kate asked: "So what can I do?"

"I'd say you should take the vake in my neighborhood."

"What do you mean? Can I just take it?"

"Technically, you're supposed to register, and go through the process. And they don't take requests. So no, you wouldn't get it. They won't assign people to the last few vakes in populated neighborhoods. They leave it to the people living there to maintain the few leftovers, clean the yard, keep away the rot, and all that. It's in everyone's interest. Then the community can use the vakes when family or guests come to visit, which rarely happens. But it's there, you know, for us to use. You could just be my guest, my cousin or something." Gina smiled. Kate thought of Villa for a second, and she smiled back.

After their coffee talk, Gina took Kate to Chief Jenks. On the way, Gina started to explain the layout of the hospital complex. She seemed out of breath, so Kate slowed her pace. For the most part, the hospital followed a similar plan as the bio-mod hospitals Kate had spent time in, except that there were entire wings missing. Gina would give Kate a more complete tour in the afternoon. So Kate switched topics and asked about security and in particular Chief Jenks.

"Security is tight at the hospital. We've got the old security sensor system in place, with video, audio, chemical, bio, and heat monitors. The triggers go off occasionally and everyone is trained to deal with the HSS protocols—health, safety, and security training is a big deal around here. Then we've got the security personnel, a serious bunch. Many of the guards are militia trained. Chief Jenks is at the top of that pyramid. She's one tough cookie."

"Do you trust her? Would you trust her with your life?"

Gina looked puzzled. "Why? What do you mean? Are you talking about Rolf?"

"No, well, sort of. I was just wondering whether I should tell her where I'll be staying."

"Oh, I don't think she needs to know. Not that she couldn't figure it out, if she followed us, you know, down to the garage and then out."

"Right." They arrive at Jenks's office and parted ways. "I'll come back up to the suite around noon."

***

"We've confirmed your story, Kate. Unfortunately, it may be even worse than we thought."

"What do you mean?"

"It looks like you weren't the first person Rolf molested."

An intense pressure surged behind her eyes and tightened muscles in her neck. Her hands slowly clenched and hurt.

"We can't be sure and are still investigating, but it appears that other women may have been abused by Rolf."

"Recently?"

"Over the past five years. We think you're the first victim to fight back. The others didn't report anything. He must have left them in such fear of reprisal. But we talked to the guards, and they said that when bio-mod women were quarantined, Rolf excused them, reassigned them to another station, just as he did with Regis. He was the guard in the room with you."

"Yeah, I remember him. He didn't want to go."

"Nurses have also come forward since your attack and expressed suspicions. It's really too early to say anything conclusive. As I said, we're investigating. But I'm glad you fought back."

"Me too." She shook her head. "So what now?"

"Rolf is being hunted. We believe he's still here, loose in St. Louis. There are rumors among staff that he is connected to the Trinellis."

"Gina mentioned them."

"It's only a rumor. I can't really believe it, not without more."

"But who are they?"

"They're a powerful criminal organization. Operate across the Midwest, but also have ties on the coasts."

"What do they do? What does Rolf have to do with them?"

"Look, we don't know Rolf is with them. The Trinellis run black markets in everything. We don't know what Rolf might have done for them. Maybe he just secured medical supplies. But he might have fed them people. Human trafficking is a real problem, and the Trinellis trade in mods and humans." Jenks paused and looked at Kate with suddenly intense eyes, like she was sizing her up and doing a calculation. "It is too early to say. We need to conduct our investigation. It's underway."

Kate shook her head. "Where?"

"Where what?," she replied without hiding her frustration.

"Where are the bio-mod women who were quarantined in the past? Are they still here?"

"I don't know. I don't think so." For a moment, she looked like one of the nurses in room 542.

Kate continued. "Where do the Trinellis take them? I mean, the authorities, the police must know something about where they do business."

"Like I said, they're all over. But the trafficking is down South and West mainly." Her tone turned curious. "Why do …"

"The desert?"

"Why do you …"

"Rolf asked if I'd ever been to the desert."

Jenks took a breath. To herself, she muttered, "Maybe he is …," and then she shook her head, regained her rigid pose, and proceeded. "Let's focus on what we know and how we'll keep you safe. Here at the hospital, we've implemented a series of security protocols that all but insure his capture if he sets foot within the complex."

"Including the garage?"

"Yes, without doubt. The biometric systems are tuned to his signature and will immediately alert us of his presence and the guards are armed and will not hesitate to subdue him with whatever means necessary. You are safe here. That I can guarantee. However, I'd like to talk to you about what can and cannot be done off premises."

"Alright."

"A few things you need to keep in mind. First, you are a foreigner in a place where many people fear you and your type. Do not underestimate how important this is. You must appreciate that many humans bear the harsh conditions, the unbearable heat, for a single reason—to stay away from mods. Not everyone, mind you. I'm here because this is where I grew up, and I love my home, my community. I don't fear you or bear you or your kind any ill will. But that is me, and others of course, but not everyone. You must be vigilant and smart about where you go and with whom you associate. Do you understand?"

"Yes."

"Second, Rolf is on the run, but he is a powerful man. He's smart and resourceful, and outside of this hospital, apparently he has friends. The police have been informed and are actively looking for him, but it's hard to say how high a priority his capture will be for them. It isn't like he killed anyone, and again, since you're bio-mod, there is bound to be those in the police force who believe Rolf is being wronged."

"What? That's ridiculous."

"I understand, Kate. But there is no direct proof of what happened in the quarantine room. The video camera in the room was disabled. We're looking into what happened to it. But all we have is your word. The nurse also." Kate's head sagged. Jenks looked in Kate's eyes. "I believe you, I'm on your side, yes?" Kate nodded. "Good. Look, as I was saying, when you leave the hospital, you are at risk. Be careful. Lie low." She handed Kate a small communications device. "You may use this to contact me if you are in danger, here or outside. OK?"

"Yes. Thank you."

"Do you have a rod or something to protect yourself?"

"No. I took self-defense classes, but I don't …"

"I didn't think so. I wasn't sure whether to tell you this or not, but I've assigned someone to you, someone with a special interest in protecting you, a debt. He will shadow you and protect you to the best of his ability. His life is yours. Let's hope you keep both."

Fourteen:

Neighbors

Doctor Martin sat behind his desk, looking at her with a worn, sad face. He tried to hide it. But she saw through his mask. The glances away from her face, the way he chewed on the corner of his bottom lip, from the inside of his mouth but in a way you could barely see from the outside. Should she comfort him? Say it wasn't his fault? It wouldn't help, and besides, her gut told her mouth to stay shut. Just wait. Let him tell you what's on his mind, what he's done for you, to make amends. He wants to make it up to you in whatever way he could, and frankly, he's the chief. If there was anyone she wanted, that she needed, to be on her side it was him. Just let him do it himself.

"Sorry I couldn't meet you this morning, but my schedule is completely outside my control. I couldn't make it happen without letting something else slip. You understand, I hope."

She nodded. "Of course." It was her turn to bite, just pinning her lips shut with her front teeth pressed into her lower lip.

"Gina tells me you had a meeting with Chief Jenks. I trust she informed you about our efforts to track down Rolf and our cooperation with the police."

She nodded.

"I really can't believe it. I have known him for years and, yes, he was a bit of a …" A quick gnaw. "Well, he had strong views on how things should be done, from a security perspective. He was really worried about bio-mods bringing something we just couldn't handle, something worse than SentaPV. I'm sure you can appreciate that. But I never thought he was capable of such grotesque behavior." His eyes met hers, directly without wavering. He finally found the courage.

For a moment, she lost hers and looked away. Tears gathered but did not flow. She met his gaze. Blood rushed to her face; it was red with anguish turned to anger.

Martin winced, bit his full lower lip, holding it tight like a dog toy, but he did not break eye contact. Then he said, "Kate, I will do anything I can. We all agree. But I want you to know that I, I personally take responsibility." Eyes held firm. "In my hospital, on my watch. I hired Rolf, gave him considerable latitude, his power to hurt you." He shook his head and breathed deeply.

Kate settled. She wiped her eyes. The emotions subsided. What just happened? She hadn't expected to react this way. Her plan for the meeting with Doctor Martin was simple: keep quiet, let him talk, and generally look like a sympathetic victim. Her emotional reaction was unexpected. She almost spoke, but didn't. Let him talk Kate.

He waited a moment and then continued, "I want to do what I can to help you with your research. Tell me about it."

She told him everything. She had decided to do so earlier. It was the best way.

He listened intently but seemed puzzled. He didn't say much, other than to state the obvious, that allergies seemed an unlikely cause of death for bio-mod infants. "You have my support and that means the full support of this hospital in doing your research. I can give you an official title, Visiting Faculty Researcher, and with that, a reasonable level of clearance. You'll have access to the areas where observation is permitted."

Pretty much like her observer role at Mass General, except that she didn't nearly have the same level of clearance that Biomen had provided.

"Gina will arrange for you to spend some time in the maternity ward and to meet with our allergists. I suggest that you observe and get to know people for a week or two before asking too many questions. I probably don't need to say this, but I ask that you respect patient privacy and our medical staff's discretion."

"Of course. Thank you. I appreciate the help." Though everything hadn't gone exactly as planned, she couldn't have hoped for a better outcome.

***

Kate had to learn to blend in. The color of her skin turned out to be less of a distinguishing feature than she'd thought. She was in control and could avoid the dead giveaways. It just took a little work. Speech and stories, those were the keys. There were so many turns of speech that she took for granted. The only thing she could do was listen to Gina's advice, listen to her own speech, and listen to others. It was hard. Kate had always been a bit of a talker, and it was difficult to let others take the lead so she could listen and watch what she said. Anxiety would creep into her chest as she held back. Oh, how badly she wanted to just jump in, to explain how she saw things, how a task should be done, to use and show her talents. Yet she accepted the challenge of keeping quiet while others blathered on.

They'd spent the first few nights at Gina's house, making plans for her move into the vake and working on stories. They tried a couple, initially sticking somewhat close to the truth. Kate was a bio-mod who rejected her culture and wanted to get back to her roots. Not bad, but Gina worried that word of a female bio-mod might spread. They settled on passing her off as human when outside of the hospital. Gina's cousin Kate from Chicago come down to do some research at the hospital. Keep it simple. Never say more than necessary, but have backstory to satisfy anyone who asked for more. Most wouldn't. But it was those who did that you had to worry about most.

Gina helped with clothing and other aspects of her appearance that might tip someone off. The most difficult had been cutting most of her long brown hair. It had hung below her shoulders, but Gina insisted that very few humans kept such length because of the heat. Kate hadn't noticed, but it was obvious once she began to pay attention to it. Gina cut the hair. When finished, she smiled and said, "Shit, I think this could backfire."

"What do you mean? What did you do?" Her friend Alissa had once cut her hair too short, made her look like a younger boy. She'd been able to fool Alissa's older brother and his friends. But she was only 11. Now, she wouldn't be able to disguise her gender.

"Kate, your emerald green eyes look even more beautiful. My goodness. You're going to be attractin' men with them."

Kate smiled. No, not a disguise.

"You want to move in tomorrow night? I'm off work Saturdays, and so we could get it cleaned up during the day and get the moving done at night. I have some stuff in my basement that I'd like you to have, old furniture and whatnot."

"Sure, that would be great. Thanks so much. You know, I'm not sure why you're doing all this for me, but I want you to know I really appreciate it."

"Like I said, I know what he did." She cringed and wouldn't say his name. "It's not right. I know it's hard after, too. You fought him off, and that's good, that probably helped. I'm glad you did. But still, it's hard, I know." Gina looked down at the floor, hiding her face from Kate. Kate knew tears were coming. She stepped toward Gina, and put her hands on her shoulders. "It's alright. It's alright. We'll be alright." She pulled Gina toward her and hugged her, letting Gina rest her face on Kate's shoulder. In the moment, Kate felt strong. The image of her fighting off Rolf came to mind, and a sense of pride arose from within. And then she realized that Gina had not been able to fight off whoever attacked her. They both wept, holding each other for support.

***

It was brutally hot. At least 120 degrees, Kate guessed. The walk from Gina's to the vake, her new home, was short, only a block and half. But five minutes outside brought sweat galore. No one else was outside. Kate noticed a few people looking out from a second story bay window. She smiled and waved. They waved back. It was a mother with two children, a boy and a girl. Gina waved. "You'll love the Davies. Super nice family. John is probably working today. I'm surprised they're not napping. It's just after noon." The mother waved a final goodbye and closed the thick paneled blinds. "Steph might come over tonight for dinner. She wanted to meet you."

The vake didn't look like a vake, at least not from the sidewalk. The front yard looked the same as most of the others in the neighborhood; it was covered with some type of gravel and a creeping groundcover. Nothing that Kate recognized, but apparently it worked. Obviously, someone took care of it; even the bushes were pruned. "You sure this is the right house?"

Gina smiled. "Yes, of course. Look, eleven." She pointed to the front door, marked with wooden numerals.

"It looks occupied."

"Like I said, we all take care of it. The vakes are a community resource, and our responsibility. And now it's yours!"

She walked up the steps and opened the front door. "C'mon. We've work to do. The inside gets less attention, a structural check once a year and a cleaning once every other month. After you."

Kate almost gagged when she stepped in. It was hot, maybe a little cooler than outside, but there was no breeze, and the air was heavy. She felt wool cloaked by it. Her heart sped up as her breathing slowed. Not panic, but something close to that. Suffocating slowly.

"It's nice, right? Kate?"

"Oh, yes, definitely." She squeezed out like a mouse under a door. "Just adjusting to the air."

"Yeah, it's a little heavy, musty. You know, no one has actually lived in this house for at least a decade. It's been a while. So the VAC system has been out of commission, and there is more dust and whatnot than we can possibly get rid of in the occasional cleaning, and of course, not everyone takes their cleaning turn as serious as they should. But we'll take care of that. Right? That's why we're here."

"Sure, of course. I'm alright now. Just takes a second to get used to the air, that's all."

The three-bedroom house was more than she needed. So after a quick tour, they decided to focus their efforts on the first floor, the basement, and one of the bedrooms upstairs. They opened the windows throughout the house to let the fresh air in, and they spent the afternoon cleaning, working side by side, room by room. By 4, they were exhausted and satisfied. They lay down on the cold tile floor in the basement with a rolled towel under their heads. Heavenly. Kate slept.

***

Kate sat up. A soft padding noise, followed by a creak in the wood floors, a sudden stop, then a slow resumption of the soft padding. She listened to the pattern. Was it mice? Really big mice? A dog perhaps? She realized that she hadn't seen an animal, other than birds, since she'd arrived in St. Louis. Maybe they hid in houses, in vakes. Pad, creak, stop. "Shhh."

Someone was moving around upstairs. Kate nudged Gina. "There's someone upstairs." She whispered. Gina shook her head to clear the nap fog, and listened. Pad, pad, pad, … creak, stop. Giggle.

"Tracy! Bobby! Down here. What're you up to up there?" Startled, Kate looked at Gina. "It's the kids. They wanted to come meet you. That's all."

A young girl bounded down the stairs. A slightly younger boy followed. Ten and eight, Kate guessed.

"Tracy! Bobby! I told you to wait on the porch." A voice yelled from upstairs. "Gina, you here? We brought dinner and drinks."

"Down in the basement, Steph. We'll come up. Hey kids, this is my cousin, Kate. The one I told you about. She's moving into the vake. Your new neighbor."

Each kid reached out a hand to Kate, offering to help her stand up. Kate smiled and accepted their offer. Not much help, in fact, holding their hands made getting up more difficult because if she actually pulled on them, they'd come down sooner than she'd go up. So she folded one leg under her and mostly got up on her own that way, but still pulling a little to make them feel useful. They smiled and tugged hard. "Thank you, Tracy. Thank you, Bobby. Pleased to meet you."

The temperature outside had dropped substantially, and the breeze filled the house with fresh, evening air. They ate cold soup and sandwiches, and got to know each other. Kate stuck to her story and let the family do most of the talking. John joined them around eight. He welcomed her warmly. A few other neighbors joined over the next few hours, and by midnight, a dozen adults sat on the front porch sipping cheap Canadian wine while the children played capture the flag across a few yards and in the street. Kate had never experienced anything like it. An utterly relaxing, remarkably satisfying feeling of simple acceptance. They asked her questions politely and tried to get to know her, but the focus was mostly on her future and only occasionally about her past. Her story was sufficient. Perhaps the story wasn't even necessary, she thought while someone poured her another glass of wine, but only for a moment.

***

She woke after noon. The mat Gina gave her to sleep on was damp. Her clothes wet with sweat. It smelled almost sweet, like candy laced with salt. Thrumming in her head commanded, but what? What were her orders? What was she to do? Like the ringing bell in the hospital, it demanded attention, announced something bad.

Water, she needed water. She had drunk warm wine until three or four in the morning. People kept bringing more. Her new neighbors welcomed her with wine in some sort of ritual. They talked all night, simple acceptance without 1000 questions. It had been perfect. They brought wine in bottles and jugs, and some food too, cheeses, flatbreads, and dried meats. Most of it came from up North where crops still grew. No one brought water.

She tried to retrace the end of the evening. The drums beating in her head refused to allow it. No, not until she gave them what they wanted. Water. She closed her eyes and lay down on her back, rubbed her temples. Alright, find water, that was all that mattered. She tried the faucets. Nothing. Not a drip. She looked in the kitchen. There was a refrigeration box, but she knew it didn't work without power. Still, maybe someone left water in there. She looked and found a few bottles of wine and some leftover food, but no water.

With a sigh that hurt, she closed her eyes tight and pled to the gods that the monkeys lay off the drums. She pulled out a hunk of cheese and an open bottle of wine. A glass or two would calm them, give her some peace.

"I wouldn't."

Startled, Kate turned toward the unfamiliar, soft male voice. Instant dizziness, head pounding pain, and vertigo hit her. She stumbled.

"Whoa. You're not doing well, are ya? Look here, grab a seat."

The man grabbed a chair and pushed it toward her. He was somewhat older and dressed in silky tan clothes with a hat and boots that looked to be made from a fine mesh unlike anything she'd seen before. The hat had wispy flaps, almost a veil, that draped down but had been pulled back to the sides. Beneath the hat, curly blond hair and light blue eyes.

"I'm sorry to barge in like this, but the front door was open. Not a good idea during the day. Lets the hot air in. You want to trap the cool night air. Doors and windows shut tightly around 5 in the morning and keep 'em shut until sunset."

Kate raised her eyebrows a little. Her head pounded, and she groaned.

"Sorry, didn't mean to lecture ya. You probably know all of this. I find the routines fascinating."

Kate stood dumbfounded. She nodded slightly, interested to hear what he might say about the local routines.

"I didn't make it last night. I wanted to come by, but I got caught up with something, some work." He hesitated and then went on. "They did it for me when I first arrived, wow, almost a year ago." He shook his head in disbelief. "Be forewarned, they'll do it again. There'll be more welcoming parties. You're the new member of the community and that's a reason to celebrate and get to know you."

Kate nodded slowly and smiled. Encouraged, he kept talking.

"I didn't bring wine, which is the real custom, you know, or sometimes food. No, I brought ya something much more important." He smiled, waiting for a reaction from her, a reaction she was too hungover to give. She slumped a little in her chair, and just looked at him with eyebrows slightly raised.

"Just a moment." He went to the front room and returned with a large jug. It looked like the wine jugs people had brought last night. Something stronger?

"Water, my dear, water." He smiled big as she stood up. "Let me put it up here and then you can use this little spout" He looked for a glass, saw a used wine cup, and went to grab it. Kate was already on her knees, mouth beneath the spout, chugging. Ahhh, let the monkey drummers choke on this. The drumming didn't stop, but she felt a little better.

"Thank you, um, I'm not sure I caught your name. I'm Kate." Glug, glug, ahhh.

"Conlin. My name is Conlin. Pleased to meet ya, Kate."

"Thank you for this. I really needed it. Last night was a long one. Too much wine."

"Yeah, I know. I been there. This jug will last ya a day or two. You can refill it at most people's houses, use their water tap." She nodded; he continued. "I can always refill it. Just let me know. I'm just down the block, four houses and across the street."

She smiled. "How do I get a well tap?"

He perked up, excited to explain. "I bet you have one already. Most houses do. Mine did. There's an aquifer that runs off one of the rivers, and it can be reached with a well tap, but you need to have your pumping and san systems running." He spoke quickly.

"San system?"

"Sanitation. Yeah, all the houses in this area were built around the same time with stand-alone systems. Really all over the Midwest. The self-reliance movement in the 60s and 70s. 'Get off the grid' was the rallying cry, ya know."

His smile faded. Kate must've looked puzzled. "I have no idea what you're talking about." She admitted.

"Sorry. My work gets the better of me sometimes. I study climate adaptation. I'm an anthropologist, and so this is a research interest of mine. What matters is you need to get your system up and running. To do that you need power. Water, sanitation, and your comp-sys depend on it."

She barely shook her heavy head. He was impressive. Who would've thought unmodified humans would do this sort of research? An anthropologist? She tilted her head, as if contemplating a complex problem. Who supported his research? The research could be quite interesting, but who would pay him to do it? Perhaps a university? A few beats of the drum in her head brought her back to reality. Thrum, thrum. She took a long drink, attached to the spout like a nipple.

Conlin stood watching. Was he studying her? What held his attention? He seemed fixated on something. Maybe Gina was right. Her eyes were pulling him. She looked away.

"To get power, do I need to tap into the grid? That would defeat the purpose, right? Self-reliance would be an illusion."

He nodded a few times. "Yeah, Kate, exactly. It would be an illusion, that's an interesting way to put it." His gaze fixed on the wall, his mind obviously wandering.

Kate laughed aloud.

He returned. "What's so funny?" he asked.

"Nothing. Sorry. You get distracted like me, on tangents, that's all."

"I guess I do." He smiled. "The houses have self-reliant power generators too. Solar systems, panels, slow heat induction batteries, and iso-batteries for storage. The whole system is integrated into the house, the building materials even, as I understand it."

The systems must've been designed as a response to the rapid warming and huge taxes levied on all fossil fuels. The bio-mods relied heavily on a distributed network of nuclear plants and a more conventional distribution grid. Biomen had major investments in both, she'd heard.

"Have ya tried to boot your system?"

"Turn it on?"

"Yeah."

"Yes, we did, at least I think so. Gina and I were down in the basement control room yesterday, and she showed me the panels. We flipped the switches, but nothing happened."

"Show me?"

She hesitated for a moment and then took him to the basement. Her head thrummed lightly, only a flash of caution as they descended. She didn't sense any danger and a quick look at Conlin confirmed that she could take care of herself if need be.

He examined the panel. "Everything looks fine, but you need to leave the solars on. This switch needs to be left on, like this." He showed her the position.

"Alight, will do. How long till it starts working?"

"Technically, it should work right away, but you won't know it until it has stored enough energy to boot up. That's how I think it works. I'm not an engineer." He shrugged. She did too.

"Thanks. We'll see what happens. How long do you think until we have to wait?"

"Give it a day it two." He stepped toward the stairs. "I've got to go." He walked upstairs; she followed. "If ya like, I'll stop by Tuesday evening. See if it's up and runnin'." He hesitated at the door.

"That would be great. Thanks again for the water." He left and shut the door firmly behind him.

What an interesting anthropologist, with his mesh boots and hat. She laughed. Her headache commanded, more water! She drank until her stomach was full. Then she began cleaning and making a list of the people she'd met the night before, the things she'd need for the house, and the things she'd learned about humans.

FIFTEEN:

CONLIN

Kate met Gina at her house for breakfast, but she really wanted a shower. Her systems hadn't come on yet, and she'd developed what seemed like a second skin. She felt gross.

"You're early," Gina said. "Coffee?"

"Sure, but can I hop in your shower?" Pleasantries would have to wait.

"Of course. Your water's not flowing?"

"No." Kate shook her head. "No power, no water. Should I have someone come fix it? Or do I need to, I don't know, have someone from the housing department turn it on from their central office?"

"No, it should work on its own. We don't want to involve them."

"Well, I'll give the solars another day or two to boot up."

"To what?"

"Boot up, get going?"

"OK." Gina looked confused, but only for a moment. "There are towels in the bathroom."

Kate nodded and went upstairs. The luke warm water and mild soap washed away days of sweat, dust, and grime. She was quick, worried about using too much precious water. When she returned to the kitchen, Gina stepped back in surprise.

"Wow, that was quick. You forget something?"

"No, I didn't want to waste water."

Gina laughed, stopped about to say something, and laughed again uncontrollably while shaking her head in disbelief. "Thanks for that, Kate. But it's alright. Besides the water we drink, pulled straight from the tap in the ground, all of the water gets recycled and reused continuously. The san system is incredible. It's got tech that rivals what we've got in the hospital, you know."

Kate smiled. "Next time, I'll linger then."

They sat for a simple breakfast of granola and dried berries.

"Kate, why did you risk coming here?"

"To find out about allergic reactions in newborns, like I told you."

"I understand. But why do you care so much? You said the reaction was incredibly rare, like one in twenty thousand, right?"

"Yes, that's right."

"We struggle with so many more serious problems on a regular basis. Every day, people die from heat stroke, viruses we can't get a handle on quickly enough, diseases we don't understand. My god, I could go on and on. We've seen tons of preemies just because of severe dehydration, and the complications for the babies and mothers …." Gina turned her head away from Kate to look out the window for a moment. "It seems like such a luxury to worry about such a rare death."

"I guess it is, or it would be. But it's not just the rare death."

Gina turned back, her face curious. "What do you mean?"

"I'm not sure, but there's more to it. It's like the Lillypad Lurker."

Gina shook her head, "I've no idea what that is."

"Oh, never mind. Like the tip of an iceberg."

"No, tell me, what's the Lillypad Lurker?"

"It's from a kid's story my mother used to read to me, about a behemoth that hid within still ponds, covered with Lillypads. Frogs and insects would land on the pads and be caught, and in the story, this kid almost gets eaten when she wanders too close, entranced by a white Lilly."

Gina tilted her head, "OK. I don't see the point."

"Well, the moral of the story was to look beneath the surface of things, you know, beneath Lillypads lie hidden behemoths." Gina shrugged. "And so I've always thought of scientific mysteries as lurking behemoths, things we've failed to see because we've accepted conventional wisdom. The truth, really, the truth is often covered in Lillypads."

"Are you saying you think allergies are a cover? A lie? That, uh, the hospital or, no, it'd have to be all of them, or Biomen ..."

"No, that's not what I meant." Kate tilted her head back and rolled her eyes shut for a moment. She opened them with an audible outbreath. "I need to think, but that's not what I meant. Not something deliberate or deceptive." She paused again rubbing thumbs against fingers. "Something about an allergic reaction seems wrong, and accepting it's an allergic reaction without investigating also seems wrong. Compounded error."

"I'm confused. You do or don't think it was an allergic reaction that killed the infant?"

"Adam." Kate corrected. "No, I mean yes, I think it probably was." She shook her head, her eyebrows tight. "Well, I'm not sure. I'm confused too. I've had two possibilities in mind. First, it could've been an allergic reaction, as the doctors said, in which case, we need to know more about it because there could be broader implications for bio-mods. What if we think we've modded out allergies but haven't? It could be something to do with the drug cocktail, could be genetic, could be environmental. We've stopped paying attention to allergies, Gina. It's been decades. That seems crazy to me. My supervisor agreed. That's why he authorized my visit."

Gina nodded, opened her lips as if she was about to say something, but then closed them.

"Second possibility is it could've been something else altogether, something no one bothered to research because the deaths are so rare. You know, allergic reaction is a plausible explanation given the symptoms, so it's not worth the trouble to investigate further. But again, this seems crazy to me! So shortsighted."

"A Lillypad, I guess. But what's the behemoth?"

Kate smiled, "I don't know. No one's looked. But, Jesus Gina, you've added a third possibility. I suppose the lurking behemoth could be even worse, something more nefarious, like in the story."

"Seems farfetched." Gina stated without conviction.

"I agree."

They both were silent for a minute. Should she explain how her quest was more personal? How Adam's death had affected her? They'd already opened up a canister. Better hold off, save it for another time.

Gina broke the silence. "What's it like then at your hospitals? In the bio-mod community?"

"We focus much more on what you might call prospective medicine. It is a luxury, as you put it." It wasn't something they could be faulted for, but why did she feel guilty? Kate shrugged her shoulders. "It's central to who we are, the society we've built. Bio-modification over generations has been the means for getting there."

Gina just nodded.

"In the hospitals, we manage people's health and help them plan and achieve what they want for themselves and their children. Much of what doctors, nurses, and other medical professionals do is forward looking and not reactive." Kate had never thought about it this way; she'd just taken it for granted. "We're so fortunate," she mumbled. "Of course, there are emergencies, accidents, and so on. The ER is active."

"You know, I've never quite believed what people say about bio-mods. That you're depraved, that you've destroyed the natural order of things. That you're really no different than the comp-mods."

"What do you mean?" Her neck tensed, and she tilted her head to the right in a stretch.

"Many people here fear you both. They assume the worst. There's almost a religious aspect to it, a belief in human purity, and the idea that technological manipulation is just the snake in another guise."

The implication that bio-mods were in the same category as the comp-mods riled Kate. "But we relentlessly play Darwin's Game." She almost pleaded, but she caught herself and her tone hardened. "We've never modified the rules. Evolution governs. We improve the players, but within natural limits. We remain human. We're definitely human." Did she sound too defensive? Must have. Gina's face had fallen flat. Kate relaxed the tension in her body. "The comp-mods though, I'm not so sure. They've constructed a different game altogether. Their actions are automated, like machines."

Gina shook her head. "No, I don't agree. They're different, sure, but they still seem human, like you and me."

"You've met comp-mods?"

"Yeah, sure. I've seen a few come through the hospital." She hesitated. "I didn't really get to know them. But from what I could tell, they weren't fundamentally different from you or me."

Kate thought of the comp-mods on the treadmill and shuddered.

***

Having settled in, Kate scheduled observations at the maternity ward. She wasn't sure about it anymore. What did she hope to learn watching deliveries or seeing nurses care for newborns? They didn't use the Biomen cocktail or even have basic gen mods. They might have allergies in general, but nothing related to the drug cocktail. Part of her warmed. Just observe. Enjoy the babies and families.

She walked in unafraid. It was slow. Only a few nurses working, and no doctor in sight. The nurses welcomed Kate and showed her around. It was more or less the same as every other maternity ward she'd seen. She didn't say anything about her research; she just indicated that she was there to observe, to learn techniques, and by no means to evaluate or judge. Just learn. They seemed to accept her. The day passed slowly.

***

Conlin returned with another jug of water. He wore his odd mesh hat and boots. "Up and running yet?" he asked.

"No. Still nothing."

He frowned. The sun had almost set. "Maybe I should check out yer solars and see if they're even …"

"No, you don't need to do that," she insisted.

"But it might be as simple as a broken panel or disconnected conduit. I'm no expert, but I've a decent idea of how these things work. It's an early adaptation technology, after all. Emission-free, independent, sustainable power generation. That and the whole self-reliant system approach to dwellings was really the big jump post-rapid-warming." He paused. She nodded. "Anyway, I've studied the tech for a while, even tinkered with my own when I got here."

"Alright, but be careful. How will you get up there?"

He feigned a look of astonishment. "Uh, a ladder." He held the look for a few seconds and then laughed. "You might have one in your garage and, if not, I've one at my place."

She ignored his slight snarkiness. "I'm going to make a salad for dinner. Would you like to join me?"

"Sure, that'd be nice. I'll get started."

Each spent an hour or so working on the task at hand. Kate cut up vegetables she'd picked up with Gina and mixed in grated dry cheese for flavor. Simple and delicious.

Why was she so comfortable with Conlin? He was intriguing alright. Smart and odd, and he helped her without cause or reason. He probably felt sorry for her since she was a newcomer like him. He knew what she was going through. But she had invited him to dinner, and even when they first met, she'd taken him in the basement to check the control panel without worrying about being alone with him.

How odd? He was attractive in a way, but he wasn't her type, whatever that was. She laughed. She didn't feel an attraction. Quite the opposite. She felt comfortable.

"Kate, come here." He yelled from outside. "Kate."

She went out and looked up. He was at the top of the ladder holding something that glinted in the dwindling sunlight. "This here, it's the induction driver. I think it's broken. Something musta hit it hard because it's gotta crack as big as yer finger. Maybe a tree branch or something.

Anyhow, we need to get ya a new one." He started down the ladder. She grabbed the bottom to steady it. "Thanks. Here ya go." She looked at the thick plastic piece. It was translucent and she could see grooves and wires within it, far below the surface. She hadn't seen anything like it before.

"Where can we get a replacement?"

"Easy. Another vake." He smiled like an imp.

They ate dinner inside with all of the windows open and talked for hours. She asked him what he'd learned over the past year. Conlin told her about their neighbors, who he trusted most, and where to shop for groceries. But mostly, he talked about his research on what folks did in St. Louis to deal with the intense heat. He'd been up North before and was thinking about going further South where it was even hotter. She asked him many questions but said little about herself. He didn't ask her much; he seemed to understand that she didn't want to talk about herself, that she wasn't ready.

Around midnight, they realized the time. "Kate, thank you for the salad, cheese, and wine, and the company. I've got to be going. It's late." As he exited, he asked, "You mind if I take this?" He turned and walked away with the induction driver.

The next day on the way to work, Gina asked Kate about her evening and why she hadn't come over for dinner. Kate only said that she was tired and decided to eat and go to bed early.

Conlin returned Friday evening. He brought dried meat, cheese, and hard bread. He asked Kate to let him refill her water jug. She had planned to go next door, but she let him do it. He seemed to like helping her, and it would give her some time to clean up. She found it odd that he didn't even think to ask whether she was free or interested in spending the evening together. He just assumed. Not that she had other plans or didn't welcome his company. She was happy to spend another night talking with him. But how did he know? Shouldn't he ask?

Conlin brought the water and a concerned look on his face. His forehead creased in three neat rows.

"What's wrong?" she asked.

"Not sure. But I had an odd feeling when I was coming out of my house, like I was being watched, and when I was walking over I had it a second time. So I turned suddenly. I actually counted to three in my head and then twisted 180, and I swear I saw someone dart behind a building, Steph's house."

Kate nodded, but apparently she didn't look surprised or concerned enough.

"Kate, do ya know something?"

"No, not really." Puzzled, she spoke mostly to herself. "It's possible they're watching me."

"What? Who's watching you? Why?"

"It's a long story. But, tell me, what did the person look like? A young man?"

"I think so. I couldn't really see much. Dark clothes. He moved quickly."

"Just one person?"

"That's all I saw." His voice wavered, and his eyes focused on her intensely.

"Conlin, don't worry. I think this guy is like my guardian angel, just watching to make sure I'm safe. That's all."

"Safe from what? From who?"

"No reason that I can explain, not right now. Trust me. I'll tell you some other time, perhaps, but let's just forget it. Agreed?" Her tone sharpened at the end, as her green eyes pleaded.

He conceded. "Alright, if you say so. Let's go inside. It's still too hot."

They went to the basement, sat on the cold floor, and poured some wine. They sat in silence for a few minutes, and then Conlin said, "So I'll tell ya what I found today."

***

"Are you crazy? You can't just steal it. Can you? Just take it? Aren't there laws?" Kate started to stand up but then plopped back down.

"Well, sure, you're right that it's not legal to take building materials and whatnot from vakes, but people have cleaned out much of the valuable stuff as needed. It's customary to use vakes as a warehouse to store things of value that someone in the community might need at some point."

"Like furniture, utensils, tools, and so on?"

"Yes, exactly. Taking that stuff is legal. But taking a door off the hinges isn't."

"Which is exactly what you want to do."

"Yeah, I suppose it is. The induction drive may be more like a door than a chair."

They both laughed. What an absurd game they seemed to be playing. Door versus chair, but what about a painting on the wall or window blinds?

"What do the laws actually say?"

"Who knows?" He laughed. "No one actually reads the laws, except some stiff in the Housing Department."

"Fair enough. But I'm trying to imagine how the law would even distinguish between things that could be removed and things that were part of the dwelling."

"A silly game, if you ask me. Necessity dictates that we find you an induction driver, plain and simple."

"Is it safe? Can you just walk in and grab one without getting caught?"

"I hope so. I wouldn't want to have to explain myself to the people in that community. They wouldn't be happy."

"How will you do it?"

"During the afternoon. No one will be outside, and everyone will have blinds down and curtains closed."

"Yeah, but you'll fry." She imagined him up on a ladder, leaned against the side of a white house. Sweat covered his face, which was colored a bright red.

"I'll be fine." He smiled at her. She relaxed. "You need your system up and running."

"Conlin, why? Why me?"

"I don't know. I can't keep lugging water over here, and Kate, dare I say, that a shower would be a good idea, you know." He smiled sheepishly.

"You don't like my stink?" She laughed, and so did he.

Again, they chatted until midnight, and he left.

Sixteen:

The Reverse Turing Test

Saturday evening was another welcoming party. About fifteen neighbors came over with wine, food, and water. Gina introduced her to everyone. Again, it was a very informal affair. Kate enjoyed herself. A few asked about her power system, and she only said that it should be up soon.

Afterwards, she played the evening back in her head. Why hadn't Conlin stopped by? Maybe he'd had enough of her, or maybe he didn't know about the party.

***

Wednesday evening, Colin stumbled up Kate's front walk. He was a mess. His nose had grown considerably, red and bulging. One eye was forced closed by the swelling; it was a disgusting purple. Kate ran to him.

"How was work today?" Despite apparent effort, his voice was weak, a dog's whimper.

"Are you alright?" She replied. "We should get you to the hospital."

"No, I'm alright. I'm fine."

"You're not." Like a parent, she ignored his lie. Why do men act like children when they're hurt? "I can see that. Conlin, look at me." He'd been avoiding eye contact, looking off to the side, but he did as he was told. Then in a soften voice, she asked, "What happened?"

"Let's go inside. I need water. You got some left?"

"Yes. Come on." She held the door open extra wide as if he might hurt himself even more if he didn't clear it. He stumbled in.

"Your leg. You're limping badly." She grabbed him from the side and held him up.

He headed toward the basement. "Can we sit down there for a bit? Cool off."

"Sure. I'll help you down." Like a three-legged crab, they shuffled down the stairs. Conlin groaned once when he stepped lightly on his left leg. "Your knee?" Kate asked.

"Yes. I twisted while running from them."

"From who? Conlin. What happened?"

"I'll tell you in a second. But first can you get me some water? I'm in dire need."

Kate bounded up the stairs and was back in a minute with a full cant. He drank all of it, stopping for only three short breaths. She took it and refilled it. He had settled on her mat, left leg elevated on a pillow, back against the wall. He sipped. "Thank you, Kate. I needed that."

She sat on the mat next to him and waited. Despite her anxiety, it was surprisingly easy for her to just wait. The practice had paid off.

"So, how was work today? Did you learn anything?" He smiled, expecting a reaction from her. And he got one.

"What? C'mon Conlin. Work was fine. Nothing new or exciting, although I'll get to meet with an allergist at the end of the week."

"An allergist? Why? What does that have to do with the maternity ward?"

"Nothing. Don't change the subject. What happened to you? You're in bad shape."

"No, I'm not. I'm great. Never better." She noticed blood in the interstices of his mesh hat. It reminded her of Salonich. Was he delusional? Heat stroke?

"Conlin?"

"Look." He reached into a large pocket of his pack and pulled out an induction driver. He handed it to her, and she inspected it. It looked exactly like hers except no crack. It was a new one, or at least, not her broken one. She smiled, and then she looked at him and frowned. "I'll put it in tomorrow, assuming you can wait one more night?"

He smiled and looked grotesque, at least on his left side where the closed eye bulged even more and looked ready to burst like a rotten fruit. Yet she didn't turn away or feel repulsed. She put her hand to his face, softly caressing his cheek. She was surprised by the sudden attraction. It was unlike her attraction to others in the past, and she wasn't quite sure what to do. It was not lust, though it wasn't fully distinct from lust. No, it was a desire to touch and caress in a way that softened his pain. She just wanted him to feel good, better.

He melted at her touch, closing his other eye, shoulders slumping, head leaning into her hand, and let out a slow, deep exhalation. She slid closer to him, on his right side, putting her back against the wall. She put a pillow in her lap, and she gently pulled him toward her and rested his head on it. With care, she pulled off his mesh hat, his curly blond hair popped out, matted down with sweat and a little blood. She began to slowly comb it with her fingers, softly caressing him, trying to relieve his pain. Another slow, deep exhalation and he slept.

Kate sat as still as she could while he slept. Her mind raced, imagining what had happened to Conlin. Probably residents from the neighborhood where he stole the driver. He'd been seen, ran, and got caught and beaten. But what if it was Rolf or one of his wolves? She shook her head. Rolf wouldn't go after Conlin. There was no reason. He was after biomods. But who understood the minds of brutes?

Kate pushed the thoughts away. No use worrying. He'd tell her when he woke. Conlin's slow breathing settled her. She mimicked his breathing, timing her ins and outs with his. It reminded her of the relaxation techniques her father taught her as a teenager. "Just relax, Kate. Breathe in deeply, hold it for a moment before letting it all out, every bit you can without pushing. Repeat and let your mind clear. When you're settled, you can think."

She went over lists in her head. She planned, as best she could. Her mind was clear, but she held Conlin and continued to stroke his head, and while this made her quite happy, it also introduced static, pleasurable in an intimate way, but also disruptive.

She doubted that spending time in the maternity ward would be of much help in figuring out what happened to Adam. The nurses she'd spoken with had not seen sudden deaths in newborns—deaths, yes, but nothing that happened so rapidly and might be diagnosed as an allergic reaction. Still, Kate wouldn't give up the opportunity to observe the maternity ward. She was surprised by the thought that it evoked a similar feeling as what she felt now, holding Conlin. No, she wouldn't give it up, not yet. She'd give it a few more weeks, at least. But her best bet would be to talk to the allergists.

How would she explain to Conlin her slip about allergists? He'd noticed, and he would pester her about it. He was like her in that way—a researcher, driven to answer questions. Once he had the scent, it would be hard to lose him. Maybe she should tell him everything. He might have ideas about how she could discover the truth. It would be nice to lift the burden of secrecy, to remove the broken glass she tiptoed around. She trusted him. She knew that. Heck, look at us, she thought, lying in the basement alone.

Kate noticed odd markings above Conlin's ears. Small tattoos and metallic engravings that looked like the mesh from his hat, as if the hat had been pressed so tightly against the skin that it left a mark. Perhaps that's why she hadn't noticed them. But now she looked more carefully, inspecting them, and she realized that they were something different, something permanent. She slid her fingers from his temple over his ear, letting her fingertips touch the markings. It was surprisingly smooth. She expected grooves or indentations, but she felt none.

Despite Kate's incredible intellect, the realization was glacial.

Conlin was a comp-mod.

Her mind wandered.

***

"You get the robots, and I'll be colonists," Beth insisted. They were setting up a battlefield in Beth's backyard. The bushes on the side of the deck were Earth, and across the pebbled path, which was space, was a grass field they called the space colonies. One side of the field was the comp-mod colony, and the other was the bio-mods.

"No, that's not fair. I don't want to be them. They're yours, and you know them, so you can be them," Kate replied.

"We'll take turns."

"Or we could both be the colonists and once we set up the robots we can just fight them together," Kate figured.

"Yeah, that's a good idea."

They set up the robot defenses, forming them into a hub and spoke network with a central hub being the big grey rock, which they called AI Command. Though formidable and very well coordinated, the robots were ultimately defeated soundly by the colonists. Kate suggested that all the colonists needed to do was drop a water bomb on AI Command and the whole system would collapse. She'd seen it in a vid. Beth agreed with glee.

***

Otto: "I'm confused. What's the difference between the Turing Test and the Reverse Turing Test? I don't see how we're supposed to apply them to machines and people. The whole lecture was incomprehensible."

Joanna: "Did you do the reading? I didn't think so. Look, let me give it a shot. The conventional Turing test focuses on a machine. That's the subject of the test. You have to determine whether the machine is indistinguishable from a human being. You start with the machine and ask whether it can fool the observer into thinking it's a human. Right?" He looked at them for affirmation.

Kate and Otto nodded.

Joanna: "In a sense, the Turing test established the objective for machine designers. Can we make a sentient machine that could pass as a human? Of course, this hasn't been done. It's impossible, at least, so long as the tester is sophisticated."

"Right, Joanna. We get it. I think Otto is confused about the reverse test. Right, Otto?"

Otto: "Yes, that's right."

Kate: "Me too."

Joanna: "Sure, alright. The idea is to switch the subject being tested. So make a human being the subject, and test whether the human being is distinguishable from a machine.

The context within which the test applies is important."

Kate: "What do you mean?"

Joanna: "Well, you're testing human beings and the technologies that shape them and their behavior. The basic question is whether the technological environment is somehow making humans behave like machines. It's a centuries-old question. But the early comp-mod technologies were really what drove the development of the test by humanist philosophers. Anyway, the question the prof asked us to answer is whether or not comp-mods pass the reverse Turing test."

Otto: "So are comp-mods human beings? That's the question? I mean, of course, they are, right? Does anyone think they're not humans?"

Kate: "I don't. I'm not sure it's that easy. They may be humans, in the sense that they descended from humans and have human genes and whatnot. But it depends on how you define human, doesn't it? I think the test is supposed to force us to ask that question, really. Sure, they're human in the basic biological sense, but you could say the same thing about the test subject, the machine, when you apply the regular Turing test. Right? It's always a machine. But that's not the point. The point is asking whether it's a machine that is indistinguishable from a human being because of its behavior."

Joanna: "Right. So for the reverse, when humans are the subject ..."

Kate: "The question is whether the humans have become indistinguishable from machines. Are they merely things?"

Otto: "I don't know. I've never met one. How the hell are we supposed to apply the test?"

Joanna: "We don't. It's a thought experiment, an exercise."

Kate: "I've always imagined they're like robots, with implanted chips, networked into that massive comp-system, taking orders, you know, fully automated. I don't know for sure. How can we?"

***

They were one with the treadmills and each other, running in unison, a machination of moving arms and legs, with heads and torsos mostly still. It was like a puppet show, with life-size automated mannequins. But it was their eyes, those vacant stares that demanded her attention. She tried to focus on their ears, to zoom in on the space just above the ears, but whenever she got close, she was pulled back to their lifeless eyes.

***

Kate shook her head to gather her wits and looked at Conlin's sleeping face. Eyes closed, but not dead. No, his eyes were never vacant, never dead. His eyes always shone with life, and since she'd met him, he'd been so kind. She smiled as she recalled their dinners alone, talking and laughing. For a moment, she felt guilty for questioning his humanity. He couldn't be a comp-mod. She kissed his forehead.

Kate fell asleep relieved.

Seventeen:

Jackie

Mr. Shephard halted in the middle of his sixth reliving of the Founder's coffeehouse memories to fully digest an urgent message.

> Operative report received. Agent returning home soon. Specs obtained and downloaded. Physical delivery in one or two weeks.

Mr. Shephard summoned the full report, which did not contain any additional relevant information. The senior intelligence official had culled well. Mr. Shephard wished the agent had been able to send the specs, but he understood the risk. Physical delivery eliminated the risk of detection and interference before the communication was completed. Of course, physical delivery also maximized the agent's value and minimized his personal risk.

Mr. Shephard decided to ramp down. Instead of another cycling through the coffeehouse memories, which was pure pleasure, he'd follow his grandfather's advice and relive the hard work, what came next—the building of the comp-sys, the regulatory battles, and the deal. All of this would keep him grounded, as it had done for his father, and his predecessors—

just like his great-great-great-grandfather's nickname, VPG, had reminded him of where it all came from, how it was built. "God touched down on earth and had a human son," his father had often said when he was a child, "and likewise you must always touch down, keep your feet planted, your roots intact. You understand Jackie?" Mr. Shephard teared up at this brief memory of his father. He was the only person who had ever called him Jackie, his true name. Well, that wasn't entirely true. According to his father, his mother had called him Jackie when he was an infant, but she passed away, and he had no memories of her.

Mr. Shephard selected a short sequence of memories to touch down. Not a full ride because he had things to do. He had to follow up on the message. He'd meet with the senior intelligence official, and then he'd meet with the system engineers who would work with the specs to design an overlay network that the unmodifieds wouldn't know existed. But first, he'd touch down.

***

Jonathan sat in his favorite rocking chair on his front porch in Napa, making plans. Capital, labor, technology, organization, and freedom. Jonathan needed all of these things to succeed. He had vision. He knew he could and ultimately would succeed. He'd change the world. He'd rebuild it. He had loads of money, and he had no problem getting more. He'd excelled in attracting investors in the past and this opportunity would be too good for the big fish to pass up. The next three were also familiar assets that he'd successfully acquired in the past, and he knew he'd be able to acquire now. He'd use his own headhunter firm, which more closely resembled the CIA's than any commercial firms. They'd compete for the best with the CIA, and Silicon Valley and China too. Jonathan would recruit within his darknet world, pulling the very best hackers who loved the challenges they found there; he'd offer them the opportunity to hack reality itself, surely that would pull some of them. He already had a stable of scientists and engineers that rivaled some of the best tech companies. He'd leverage them and their connections. No, labor wouldn't be an obstacle. Technology and organization wouldn't be difficult to acquire. These were built assets. He had them already, and he'd simply build more of what he needed. Capital and labor were the inputs he needed to build these things. *But freedom!* Freedom to operate, now that was more difficult to obtain. Anna drove him to change, to operate openly, legitimately. This was his life's work. He'd do this for her. But God knew, he'd struggled throughout his life to find freedom in the light of day.

***

To create freedom to operate, he met with the forsaken, his lawyers. Jonathan stood at the head of a large oak table, surrounded by suits. He asked, "Will they sign? We've got them cornered. I don't see how they can't."

Schrag, the short, balding man in a grey pinstripe, replied, "Absolutely. Our portfolio covers most of their territory. We've got broad patents that arguably cover most of the core networking architecture and data management protocols that they've been using for almost five years. We've got 'em. No doubt about it. The downside to litigation is just astronomical for them."

"All of 'em?"

"As you suggested in the first strategy session, we're pursuing the cross licensing agreements in series, with each of them separately." Jonathan nodded, left hand moving in small circles while the right pressed oak. "And yes, we should get most of them, all of them in time. We've one or two minor holdouts." Jonathan frowned and stopped moving his hand. "But we've got the big fish. Google cross-licensed everything we need. That's the biggest, of course. And we fought them on all the reach-throughs. They have no hooks in us going forward. We've the freedom you wanted, sir, freedom to operate." Jonathan stared at a dark crease just above Schrag's eyes, refusing to drop his gaze any lower even as Schrag tilted his head back and lifted his chin. Schrag cleared his throat and noted, "At least with respect to the big boys. You never know what small fry will pop up, right?" He smiled.

Jonathan gave him his due, a quick smile— Jonathan occasionally referred to Schrag as a small fry with attitude. "And our insurance against that risk?"

"Our huge portfolio, for one thing. We've built a decent safety net if any surprises pop up and they're actually practicing entities. We'll shut 'em down unless they sign a deal like the ones we've been executing. Plus, we let the word slip out that the best deals are now on the table. We won't be nice to stragglers."

"What about the trolls? The small fries who aren't practicing entities, who don't do anything but try to hold people up. Or worse, those damn aggregators who just buy up the small fries and fuck with everyone."

"We've a few insurance policies. First, preemptive acquisitions. We've been buying up small fries that come to our attention for strategic reasons. Beside those we buy for technological promise. We've bought thousands of them. They're in our portfolio, mainly because of the potential risk they'd otherwise pose to our business. The analytics program we developed is quite remarkable, actually. It's like a huge trawling net, spotting acquisition targets early, well before aggregators are interested." He paused to see if anyone had questions. None. "Finally, we're members of a few defensive portfolio clubs. One club actively polices filings at the Patent and Trademark Office and fights to invalidate or prevent issuance of patents to non-members. Another just acquires patents and cross-licenses among members. All of that covers 99.5% and the .5% that remains, well, we've got to rely on the old methods."

"So we're shielded, full freedom to operate then?"

"Sir, it's cost tens of billions, but yes, as soon as we execute the cross licensing agreements, full freedom to operate, at least with respect to patents. And we've preserved much of the company's offensive potential."

"Freedom to operate, Schrag! Do we have it or not?" The thunderclap startled everyone in the room, except Schrag.

"Patents are the first stage, remember. The private side. The public side, the regulators, that's the second stage. We've got to deal with DC and to a lesser degree, the states. We've got a plan, but it's complicated, many moving parts, lots of wheels to grease. So no, we don't have freedom to operate. Not yet."

Eighteen:

Progress

Kate's stomach grumbled. They woke. It was late. Conlin sat up slowly, looked at Kate's face, in her eyes, and smiled. "Thank you. I needed that." He lingered. She waited, expecting him to go on, to explain what he was thinking and feeling, or even what had happened.

Instead, he suddenly shifted, and stiffened, maybe having doubts about what he'd been about to say. "I should be going, but I'll return tomorrow and put the driver in. Get your systems running, at last."

Kate stood. Her body was stiff, neck, shoulders, and legs like winter tree branches. She fought her instinct to follow Conlin's shift in mood, to stiffen. "Conlin, you don't have to."

"I do. I need to. Look, I'm fine." He stood up and remarkably seemed much better. The water and cooler air must have helped. He put his hat on. "I'll take this with me since you'll probably be at work when I stop by." He put the driver in his pack. He smiled. He wasn't cold, no, the warmth was still there. He softened some with his smile.

They walked upstairs. "Do you want some food?"

"No, thank you. I'd love to stay and eat, and talk. But I can't. I need to go home and check on some things before I go to sleep. You understand?" He almost pleaded.

"Yes, of course. You look better, although still a mess. We should go to the hospital."

"No, I don't think so. I'll be fine."

"Can I help you tomorrow? Let's put the driver in tomorrow evening. At least, I can hold the ladder." She smiled.

"I think it would be best if I did it in the late morning while everyone is off at work. Then the systems will have time to boot up. By the time you're home, you'll be up and running."

"If you say so. Dinner tomorrow, then? At least, I can make you dinner."

"Deal."

***

"Gina, I don't know how he got beat up or who did it. But he didn't want to go to the hospital." Kate whispered even though they were alone in Gina's PTV, on their way to the hospital.

"I'm not surprised. He's also new. So it makes sense. He probably wandered into the wrong neighborhood and ran into some locals."

"He wouldn't want me to say anything, so maybe you could swing by tonight around eight, you know, like it was unplanned. He's coming over for dinner, probably around seven."

"Really?" She was incredulous. "The two of you?"

"Yeah, we're friends. It's just dinner. We talk a lot. I guess it's 'cause we're new."

"Uh, huh." Eyebrows raised and pushed together.

"Plus, we're both research scientists. I suppose we get along 'cause of that too."

Gina perked up and interrupted with urgency in her voice. "Does he know about your research? The allergies? That you're a bio-mod?"

"No, I've stuck to the story. Tightly. As far as he knows, we're both just ordinary humans."

"Right. OK." Gina kept nodding, her brain apparently processing, perhaps planning what she'd say that evening. Still a little dazed, she said, "Well, sure, I'll stop by around eight. I'll bring a jug of water, you know, and just act like it was a random stop-over."

"Perfect."

"I'll see what I can do about checking out his injuries. Maybe he'll let me, maybe he won't. I'm not going to push."

"Of course not. Just do what you can. Thanks, Gina."

"Are you meeting with the allergists soon? I thought that was today."

"Yes, Doctor Rakoff at noon, and then next week, probably Wednesday, I'll meet with Doctor Christians."

***

Doctor Rakoff was an older man with white hair to match his white silky clothes. Wrinkles marked the years, and by the number of them on his brow alone, Kate guessed he was in his eighties. Despite his age, he moved about like a rabbit on adrens.

They met in his office. He was standing at the door to welcome her and did not sit still for more than a minute throughout their discussion, even though he directed her to sit in the comfortable chair near his desk. The room smelled like tea and sweat, and the aroma was oddly soothing.

"Pleasure, Doctor Genet. You're looking to figure some puzzle 'bout allergies you folks haven't modded out. Right?" He spoke like he moved.

"Yes, Doctor ..."

"Well, you're lucky. I'm the senior allergist here." He stood next to her and placed his hand on the side of her chair, for a moment, and then he hopped behind the desk. "I've got Doctor Christians by a year. Ha!"

"Well, uh, thank you for meeting with me."

"My pleasure. Now, you talk to Doctor Christians. She knows a few things I don't, but only a few." He smiled, reminding Kate of a ripened Fredric. He rounded the desk and was coming back towards her. "She pays attention to rare stuff, especially rare immunologic disorders that affect children. I focus on common allergies, stuff that impacts the most people. I diagnose, treat and manage common allergies, asthma and primary immunodeficiency disease, which're usually genetic." He stopped, seemed to consider reaching out again for her chair, but swiftly turned back and went behind his desk. His constant movement was distracting, almost dizzying to watch.

"Well, I am a geneticist, and until recently, I thought we modded them all out. To be honest, that's why I'm here."

"Why don't you tell me what happened then?" He sat, but only for a minute.

She retold and relived Adam's birth and death. She felt Adam's pull, though she kept that to herself, and she felt her guts drop and heart stop when she spoke of his death. She didn't describe this either, but it must have showed. Rakoff rushed to her—or maybe he just hopped superfast—and put his hand on her shoulder.

"It's alright, Doctor Genet. I've been there. It's the price we pay as doctors, as medical professionals. Death and life are our currency."

Kate nodded, not comforted but regaining her balance. "What I don't understand is the diagnosis, the explanation for what happened. Doctor Schmidt, Fredric, everyone seems to accept the conclusion that a rare allergic reaction caused the death. But frankly, I don't see how that can be right. It doesn't add up, and when I couldn't find answers back in Boston or Rochester, I decided to come here."

"What was the explanation exactly? You haven't really given me any details. Do you have a copy of the medical report or autopsy?" He leaned on his desk and then slid onto it, seated with wiry legs dangling.

"No, I couldn't, patient confidentiality. You understand. I was there. I saw what happened, the discoloring, the sudden change. His heart stopped. He stopped breathing. All at once." Her heart raced.

"I understand." He slowed a little bit. "We can work from there, with the symptoms. I'd like official paperwork, the medical explanation, that's all. Your employer couldn't get you access to the paperwork? That's surprising, at least from what I've heard about Biomen. I thought they owned the hospitals."

"No, that's not true. They're separate."

"OK. Look, some symptoms are consistent with an extreme allergic reaction. Anaphylaxis, of course, is a very serious allergic reaction, rapid in onset, and it can cause death. An immunologic reaction to something in the drug cocktail could trigger it. I suspect you've seen this in clinical studies." He was still sitting, more or less till, except his fingers danced on his thighs.

"Well, no, I don't think so. That's one of the oddities. It only occurs in the field." Rakoff nodded, his lips closed tightly. She continued. "There's a rare incidence of these sudden infant mortalities shortly after administration of the cocktail."

"OK. Allergic reaction is a plausible explanation. But I'm confused. There is a treatment that has worked for over a century—you give an injection of epinephrine, basically, adrenaline."

"But there wasn't time. It was so rapid."

"Now that's puzzling. Anaphylactic shock may involve systemic vasodilation that causes low blood pressure, which you can detect and treat, as I suggested." He breathed out heavily. "I've never heard of shock that led to instantaneous system failure like you've described. The infant changed color all over?" He sat still and looked at her intensely.

"Yes."

"Did he puff around the eyes or elsewhere?"

"No, not at all."

Quietly, almost to himself more than Kate, he said, "His heart stopped. Did the doctors conclude that he suffered from cardiac arrhythmias, abnormal electrical activity in the heart?" Kate nodded but he wasn't looking at her. "This would be distinct from the anaphylactic shock, although maybe they could be related." He hopped off his desk and began pacing, apparently deep in thought.

After a minute or two, he stopped and said, "It could be an allergic reaction. I'd have to see the paperwork, to know more before I could be of much help. Otherwise, it's just speculation. I've never seen or heard of anything that involves the same symptoms in an infant or adult. But frankly, we don't use your drug cocktail. It's likely something to do with that. We've plenty of allergies to deal with, but nothing I can think of resembles the reaction you've described. Maybe Doctor Christians will have more."

"I appreciate your time." She started to turn toward the door when he slapped his hand on his desk.

"You know, what comes to mind, Kate, is poison. There are a number of poisons that cause systemic shock and failure. Poisons of this sort affect most people the same way, and so we don't think of them as allergens. Although, sometimes the treatment is the same. Allergens are like poisons for certain populations. It's as if your drug cocktail is a poison for a very small population."

"I'm not sure it's fair to call it a poison, doctor."

"Not what I meant. Not the point. Point is the symptoms match. Possibly, this is a different way to understand the cause and evaluate treatment options. That's all."

"I understand. This is very helpful."

"I'm sorry, but I've got another meeting."

"Thank you for your time and knowledge, Doctor Rakoff."

***

Her vake looked the same from the outside, but once inside, Kate could feel the difference. The air was less humid and easier to breathe. The ventilation system had removed water and dust! Her systems were up and running. Thrilled, she ran to the waterspout in the kitchen and turned it on. She heard a rustling, the pipes breathing, sucking. Water flowed, and she drank it straight from the faucet. Cold, fresh water pumped from an aquifer deep underground. She looked for the light pad on the wall and tapped it. Cold, dim lights from above and a strip that ran the perimeter of the room. She tapped the pad again and they got a little brighter. She tapped once more and they went off.

She wandered the house, exploring an entirely different place filled with gadgetry to make one's life simpler, only some of which she recognized. She went upstairs to the computer room that she'd only been in once before. There were screens on most surfaces, the walls, ceiling, desktop. It was always tricky to figure out a new system, a system configured by and for someone else. The technological systems built by humans, probably decades ago, were quite different from the systems she used back home, not completely foreign but unfamiliar.

She walked to the wall near the front of the house and touched the screen. A menu displayed; she said "security," and a new menu displayed. She said "perimeter video," and the walls around the room displayed a 360-degree panorama view of the area outside her house. She adjusted the zoom, the angles, and played for a while. At first, it was neat but it quickly became boring. No one to watch. Everyone was at work or inside their homes waiting for the sun to set and the temperatures to drop. But her senses adjusted the more she played with the system and she caught movement that had been right under her nose. Birds. She sat watching two birds pecking at the dirt under one of the tough shrubs on the eastern side of the house. She felt so sneaky, so powerful, just watching them. A fly on the wall.

Two flashing red lights caught her attention. One was on the screen on the wall displaying the front yard. She turned to it and saw Conlin walking up to the house. A slight limp still, but otherwise he looked much better. She smiled. An uneasy discomfort crept within her stomach. She turned quickly to the other red light, but it had stopped flashing. She scanned the display but saw no one in the backyard.

Conlin rapped on the front door. She didn't want to leave, worried that she might miss something. Eyes focused on the backyard screen, she slowly backed out of the room, and then she turned and bounded down the stairs.

"C'mon in. The house is so different, thanks to you. I am in your debt."

"No, Kate. Never. Was the least I could do."

"For what?"

"Just for being here. It's not about paying back debts. Simple gifts, that's all. You've given me many. Your company, to say the least."

"Alright, just come in and grab a seat. We can stay on the first floor. It's comfortable. Still a little warm, but cooling down, and the air is clean."

"Yeah, it is. Look, here, this panel. You can adjust the temperature, if ya like, if you want to move off the default settings. They're set to minimize the work done by the systems and the differentials between inside and out."

"I was just upstairs in the computer room. Playing with the security cameras. It's interesting." She laughed. "I was mesmerized by the birds. You know, you rarely see them outside. They hide when people are out. I could just sit up there and watch them."

"Yes, I do that too. At night, you'll see other critters come out." He smiled.

She remembered the second red light and asked, "Can you set it up to record? Or to give you a warning?"

"Yes, absolutely. It's easy to do. In the security settings, there are options. I can show you."

They went upstairs. The room displayed panoramic views. Conlin asked her permission to touch the screen, she nodded, and he went to work. It was amazing how quickly and effortlessly he manipulated the various menus, submenus, and different screens that flashed in front and in a 180 degree arc around him. His injuries almost disappeared as he moved like a bio-mod athlete. Her jaw slowly dropped.

"There. You're configured. Video recording with playback anywhere in the house. Just swipe like this"--he drew a circle in the air and poked a finger through the middle, a small screen opened just beyond his finger--"and you can access the video from the menu. You can also remotely view the real-time displays." He watched to make sure she had it. Kate had already swiped and poked. He grabbed the air where his screen displayed and it disappeared. She did the same with the same result. "I've also set the security system on lock and warn. It will lock all doors and windows immediately upon sensing anyone within five meters of the house, and then if you're here, a screen will display for you. You can then decide what to do, admit or lock down and target."

"Have you ever had to ..."

"No."

"I need to play around up here some to find out what else I can do."

"I can show you."

"No, not right now. I've got to finish making dinner. Do you want a glass of wine?"

***

They sat at the table in the kitchen and ate a simple meal of vegetable salad, bean salad, and crusty bread with soft cheese. Kate was excited to actually cook something, some hot food, but she hadn't purchased the ingredients. She hadn't been sure that the power would be on so soon. But it was, and they were celebrating.

"Your face looks terrible, you know." He tried to look offended, which Kate understood only from slight shifts around his right eye and the right corner of his mouth. "Well, not generally, I mean, the bruising, the injuries to your face look really bad. Does it hurt?"

"No, I'm fine. I barely feel anything, seriously, the left side of my face is a mystery to me." He turned his head to the left, as if trying to look at his own face but disappointed that he couldn't.

Kate laughed. "Stop that. You'll get dizzy. How about your leg? Was it hard today, getting up the ladder? I wish I could have helped."

"Now that was a pain. My leg throbs still, whenever I put pressure on it, and climbing up the ladder wasn't easy. I tried once, only once, to step up with my left leg, and God, pain shot through like lightning."

Kate winced. "I'm really very grateful that you did all of this for me. You're a true friend." She reached out and softly touched his right cheek. They both lingered, looking into each other's eyes. Then Kate pulled back slowly, and said "But you haven't told me what happened, how you got the driver, and how you got so badly injured."

"Not so badly. It's not so bad."

"Conlin."

"Well, it's not that exciting. I took my PTV down south to a neighborhood with tons of vakes. I thought it would be easy to find an induction driver that wasn't being used and was in good shape, and I figured no one would be around. And besides, if they were, they wouldn't really care, you know, because there are so many vakes. I thought I would look like just another person scouting for a new place. People do it all the time."

"Right. But you don't look like just another person."

"What do you mean?"

"I don't know. Since I've met you, I thought you looked a little different. I think it's the mesh hat and boots."

"These, really? I got these up north, in Canada. Lightweight, blocks sunlight and UV and everything, but lets heat out to keep you cool. Not many people have them down here, but I didn't think it made me stand out. Didn't even think of that. Crap."

"You're the only person I've seen wearing that mesh."

"No, really? I've seen others. I guess that explains why they came over to see what I was doing."

"What happened?"

"I scouted the neighborhood for about fifteen minutes, driving around to see if anyone was around, any PTVs in driveways, or any other signs. When I was satisfied that no one was around, I parked in the driveway of an old house that was a vake."

"How could you tell?"

"No systems running. A house that hasn't had its systems running for a long while in this heat shows signs. I wasn't 100% until I got close and took a look at the windows, the dust on the inside pane and blinds. So then I got my ladder and set it against the side of the house, climbed up slowly, and removed the induction driver. I replaced it with your old one, thank goodness. Otherwise, I might not have gotten out of there."

"What do you mean?"

"I told one of them to go up the ladder and look at the driver with a crack, and that confirmed my story, that I was a technician from the housing department checking out the solar system that showed a sign of potential malfunction. I talked fast enough that they wouldn't completely understand what I was saying, but slow enough that they caught the gist of it. It worked."

"Wait, back up. Who were you talking to?"

"Bunch a locals; they snuck up on me while I was up the ladder working on putting your driver in. There were five of 'em, I think, maybe six. Young guys probably working one of the alternating shifts as apprentices. I should've thought of that. Not many of them in our neighborhood, but in the lower class neighborhoods, it's much more common." Conlin sank in his seat, closed his eyes, and went on:

They stood at the bottom of the ladder. One of them said: "Hey, man, whachya doing up there? You messin' wit' one of our houses."

"No, let me explain." I said, "Can I finish this first? I'm just checking on the solar system. It's my assignment."

Another one, probably their leader, said, "Yeah, guess so, but you better hurry yer ass up. It's friggen hot and you got us standin' here, waitin' on you. We ain't goin' nowhere."

I finished up, and came down. As soon as my foot touched the ground, my left foot, then the kid, he was really only a kid, he kicked me. It was vicious. Hit my left knee from the outside, and my leg buckled and I fell hard in a clump on the dry, hard-packed dirt.

Three of them laughed, the pimply kid who kicked me stood over me glaring with an evil look, and the leader, a thin wiry guy in his twenties, walked over and kicked me in the face. "What da fuck you doin' on one of our houses? No notice you was comin' so no problem with us defendin' our vakes. That's how it goes, mister. Sorry boutchyer luck." Another kick kept me down and might have knocked me out for a minute or two. Next thing I know there's a guy climbing the ladder, the kid has his foot on my chest, and the leader is looking in my PTV.

"Look," I quickly said, "I was told this morning to check out the solar system. Someone might be moving in and records indicate it wasn't running. I think that driver's cracked. That's it. Needs a new driver."

The guy on the ladder had stopped to listen. He went to the top. "What's a driver?"

The kid pressed his foot down. "What's a driver, man?"

"It's the thick plastic block wedged in between the two panels. You can see wires running inside it. To the left a little when you're up ..."

"I see it."

"Be careful. It'll take some effort to slide out and I almost fell back when I tried." The foot on his chest lightened.

"Yeah, I see it. It's cracked. Let me see if I can ..."

"Wait," I yelled, "someone hold the ladder."

One of the loafers walked over and held it.

"Yeah, here it is." He pulled out your old driver, wobbling on the ladder. If the other one hadn't held the ladder, he'd a fell. "Should I bring it down or put it back?"

"Bring it down," some of them yelled, but the leader shouted, "Just put it back. I don't want you guys messin' with it. This's a good house and we got someone comin', which is good. We need 'em. So we want that system workin' good. You," he pointed at me, "you gonna get it up and runnin'?"

"Yes, of course," I replied, "that's my job."

"Yeah, but you know, affer we roughed you up, you still comin' back?" I nodded; he continued. "We'll keep you safe when you come back. You know. We didn't know who you was, up on one of our houses. We gotta look out."

"I understand. Really I do." I meant it, and it probably showed. I hadn't thought they'd be there, but I knew that neighborhoods like this relied on local watches. They had to. The kid didn't have to kick me so hard; that probably triggered the rest. They probably wouldn't have touched me if the kid hadn't gone violento. "I'll be back with a working driver,

probably in a week or two. They're not easy to find anymore,
but I think they have 'em in the warehouse near the river."

They let me go, almost as if we were now friends, like I'd
been initiated. You know, I almost want to steal another
working driver and return to them.

Conlin smiled. He made it sound less frightening than
she'd imagined, but regardless, it was for her. She was
responsible for his suffering. Kate felt awful. Smiling made
him look a little better, but his left eye remained hidden
between puffs of purple and yellow. Still, he seemed happy and
so she smiled back. They nibbled on what remained of their
dinner, mainly the crusty bread, and sipped wine in silence.

Kate and Conlin were sitting in the front room listening
to music when Gina arrived. Kate had been so happy to
discover the stereo system and virtually unlimited collection
of music; nothing from the past eighty to one hundred years,
but that didn't matter to Kate. She selected Chopin and let the
system go from there. They sat on, or better, sank in, plush
chairs with their legs on small supports and their feet dangling
a little, waving about to accompany the music like soundless
bells.

A little screen appeared in front of Kate. It displayed her
front yard and centered on Gina, who was walking up to the
front door. To the right of the display were options for her--
Admit, Monitor, Threat Check Scan, and Target. She quickly
selected Admit. What would happen if she slipped and
selected Target? Would Gina have been neutralized with a
dart? Kate shook her head at the thought.

"Who's that?" asked Conlin. "A visitor?"

"Gina. Looks like she brought water. Wait until she sees my systems are running." Kate smiled and jumped out of the chair. She opened the door and welcomed Gina.

"Hi Kate. I thought you might need some more water. But I see you've got the system up and running at last. Excellent! I'm so happy for you. Have you tried the pump? You must have." She walked in and hugged Kate. "Oh, hi there, Conlin. Nice to see you. Don't get up."

"Hi Gina. Good evening. I've been trying to get up, but this chair, it just sucks you in. It's a trap, I think." He smiled, and so did Gina and Kate.

"Let me grab you a glass of wine?" Kate asked Gina. She headed to the kitchen.

"Sure. I'll get myself trapped too." She sunk into one of the chairs. "I love these things. Sometimes I fall asleep in mine."

"Me too," said Conlin.

"I hope you don't mind if I say so, but you look awful. Your face is, well, are you alright? What happened?"

"Long story, but basically, I got roughed up by some locals in a neighborhood down south a ways. It looks worse than it is, really. I'm fine."

"You never know with head trauma. Did you go to the hospital yet?"

"No, you know," he tilted his head when he looked at her and she nodded, "I will if it gets worse. But I haven't and don't plan to unless I need to."

"What were you doing?" She looked to see if Kate was returning; she wasn't. Kate watched and listened from a small screen she'd called up in the kitchen. "Was it your research?"

"No. That never presents trouble. Actually, I stole something, for Kate."

"You did what?"

He laughed. "Her solar system wasn't working because she didn't have a working driver. I got one from a vake in a neighborhood where there are plenty. I ran into a few locals, kids really. It worked out fine in the end."

"Did you hurt anyone?"

"Not too badly. Just broke a few arms and legs." He maintained a straight face for a few seconds and then laughed. "No, of course not. Look at me. I couldn't hurt a fly. I talked my way out of it. They weren't too bad actually, just protecting their neighborhood."

"Well, you sure are a great neighbor to Kate." Gina suggested.

Conlin shrugged and looked down. "I guess."

Gina smiled satisfaction, as if she'd solved a puzzle. "I should look at your injuries to make sure they're healing properly. It's up to you."

"Sure. That'd be fine."

Kate shut the screen and returned with Gina's glass of wine. Gina got up from her chair and went to Conlin to take a closer look at his eye. "You get punched directly?" she asked.

"No, kicked."

"Aaah," Gina shook her head. "It looks okay, but I wish you would've told me earlier. I could've gotten you a cold pack, or given it to Kate. But now, it wouldn't be much help. I'll send one tomorrow anyway. Is that it? A kick to the head?" Gina was good at this, pretending she didn't know more.

"No, I fell and injured my knee, my left knee. It still hurts to walk on, if I put too much pressure on it. But now, while I'm sitting, it's fine."

Gina looked uncertain about whether to go further with her examination.

Kate intervened. "Why don't you show her, Conlin? Get up for a minute." She looked at him, eyebrows raised, lips pursed.

"Fine. Your house, you're in charge." He smiled and then winced as he pulled himself out of the chair to a standing position. Kate and Gina offered to help, each extending a hand, but he managed. He stood for a moment waiting for instructions and when none arrived, he began to walk around the room in a circle, counterclockwise, with his left leg taking the smaller inner circle. It was oddly humorous to watch; all three grinned and then started laughing.

"You're limping, alright. It's hard to tell how bad it is. Sit back down and pull up your pant leg," she said with authority.

He obeyed. He loosened the fastener at his ankle and slid the loose cloth up to mid-thigh. The swelling was much worse than Kate expected. His knee looked like an alien head, colored like his bruised eye. Gina showed no surprise, her face calm and unimpressed. She put her hands just above his bruised, swollen flesh and looked at him, "Do you mind?" He shook his head. She massaged the knee and surrounding leg, as if checking to make sure everything was in its proper place, all the while looking at Conlin's face to see how he reacted. He remained stoic.

Gina asked, "So it only hurts when you stand or put pressure on it?"

"Right," he responded.

"Probably just banged up 'n bruised. Doesn't look to be broken. But you never know. You could have a small fracture or something else. You could come into the hospital to have it imaged and examined. Even a custom support would help with the healing." Conlin shook his head. Gina continued as if she expected his answer. "If not, stay off it for at least a week. I'll see about getting you some crutches. They may be hard to come by though."

"Will do." He looked at her for a moment, waiting for her eyes to settle on his. "Thank you, Gina. I appreciate your care."

She smiled. "My pleasure, my friend." She turned to Kate. "Another glass of wine?"

"Sure. My goodness, I didn't even see you drink the first glass."

The three relaxed in chairs, drinking wine, and listening to Chopin.

Nineteen:

The Grizzly

Kate woke late, her head throbbing. Too much wine, not enough water. She was in her comfy chair, suspended and light, except for the ton of bricks that throbbed. She shook her head to clear the morning fog, and quickly regretted it. Take it slow. She glanced at Gina and Conlin. Both were still sleeping in their chairs. The music still played softly.

It was already 10. She woke Gina, who needed to get to work. Gina propelled her body out of the chair and skipped to the door. "Thanks, Kate. I'm going to run home and get ready. Leave my house in 20 minutes?"

"Sure. You think I should wake him?" Gina shrugged. "I'll let him sleep." After Gina left, Kate stood over Conlin for a minute, smiling. She kissed his forehead and went upstairs to shower and get ready.

***

Kate met Gina at her PTV. The two hopped in. Gina gave the PTV instructions, and they both closed their eyes to squeeze in 15 minutes of sleep. The PTV took the usual route.

Kate hadn't slept well and couldn't sleep now. She'd never been a napper. She thought about Adam for a moment, and then her thoughts turned to Conlin and his crazy story. He'd been surprisingly nonchalant about getting beat up so badly. He probably would've wanted to go back, steal those kids a new driver. She smiled, keeping her eyes closed. Maybe a short nap would be possible.

The PTV screeched and shuddered violently. Kate and Gina woke abruptly. A PTV in front of them had stopped, and there were two large CTVs, commercial transport vehicles, on each side of their PTV so it had nowhere to go to avoid a collision. It had braked and stopped without crashing, as it was designed to do in such an emergency. Kate breathed a sigh of relief. But it was short-lived. She looked ahead and saw Rolf and two other men exit the stopped PTV.

"Gina, Gina. We've got to go. Back up. Get it to reverse." Her heart pumped furiously. Kate looked behind her and saw another PTV, pull up behind and stop. There was no escape. Rolf had her trapped again. A ferocious energy surged through her veins.

Gina woke from her stupor. "Security systems. Activate full lock down. Signal police."

Kate heard the PTV locks activate. She fumbled in her pack to pull out the communication device Jenks had given her. She pressed the red button, released it, and pressed it again, hoping it worked.

Rolf was a bear, not a wolf as she'd previously thought. He was tall, broad shouldered and menacing in a way that made

Kate think of a brown grizzly, so different from the black bear she'd seen in upstate New York. Her stomach ached as he lumbered from his PTV toward hers, grinning knives. He wore baggy light brown clothes that made him look even bigger as he walked. Two smaller men in fine clothes walked beside him.

A side door of each CTV opened. Three men jumped out carrying large metal arms of some sort, a mechanical device. Kate immediately understood. They would rip the doors off their PTV easily. Rolf had planned this. He must have. He must have waited for the right opportunity. Her mind raced, looking for some defense. She turned to Gina, who seemed dazed, slow to fully process what was happening.

"Gina, it's Rolf. He is here for me. I don't think they know you're in here. Can you crawl in the trunk? Can you get back there? Hide? Gina!"

Gina shook her head. "Rolf. Yes, I see him. What is he doing here?"

"Gina. Snap out of it. Crawl in the back and hide in the trunk. Can you do that? They can't see us in here because of the windows. But you only have a minute before they tear off the doors."

"Yes, there is the thing in the middle of the backseat. It slides." She started to climb back, but slowly.

Kate shoved her. "Go on Gina. Quickly!"

Gina just made it when the three men on the right attached the mechanical arm and began to yank the door off the PTV. She slid the cushion back in place as the door popped off. Kate put her back firmly against the seat, pulled her legs into her body and held them there, stomach and leg muscles tense like loaded springs, and she waited. The three men stepped aside as Rolf approached.

"Kate, my little bio-bitch. I told you I'd get the naked truth. I will. You've screwed up my life, and man, I'm going to screw yours and your friend's too. Ever been to Vegas? They like your type out there and pay well for it too." He stood near the door. "C'mon out, Kate, or Doctor Genet if you prefer. Let's have a chat. We've business to discuss."

"Leave me alone, Rolf. The police are on their way. You better run back to your hole in the ground."

He growled, bent down and grabbed at her with his huge paws. "C'mon, bitch. Let's go. It'll only be worse for you if you struggle. You will learn to obey."

"Fine," she conceded. She reached a hand forward as if asking for his assistance in getting up and out of the PTV. He went for it with his right hand. She launched her body, feet first, pushing off her back into him. He swiped at her, but too late. Her feet landed squarely on his face, again busting his nose and causing his blood to flow. He fell back and roared. "Grab her," he yelled, his voice muffled. The two men at his side approached the PTV cautiously. They stooped and feinted a sudden attempt to grab her. She kicked out and missed them entirely. They each grabbed a leg and roughly pulled her out of the PTV. She held on to the seat at first, but it was no good. So she let herself slide out. She screamed in pain. Her lower back scraped the ripped metal, opening her up, just missing her spine. The two men did not stop their pulling. They slowly dragged her toward Rolf's PTV.

Rolf yelled, "Find the other one. There's another woman in the PTV. Normal human, but still worth something in Vegas or Atlanta." The men turned back to the PTV and looked in from each side.

Kate watched in horror, everything upside down. "Leave her alone. Please." Everyone ignored her. Then she saw someone else, a man in light clothes sneaking toward Gina's PTV. He crept up behind the men on the right side of the PTV. One had gone in. The sneaking man was bent over slightly, so the men on the other side wouldn't see him. He had something in his hand. She saw a flash of red and he plunged it into each of the men standing outside the PTV on the right side. The others noticed the two go down. Alerted, the three on the other side rounded the car quickly. "Hey, we got someone here. He took out Anthony and Giovanni." Rolf turned around, and the two dragging Kate let go of her legs and rushed back to the PTV. Rolf walked back slowly, apparently confident that the five thugs could handle whoever was there. The man in the car shouted, "I think the other woman is in the trunk." Everyone ignored him.

The five men surrounded the sneaking man who no longer tried to hide. He stood a bit taller, although still somewhat crouched in a fighting position. Both hands held weapons with red tips. The other men also pulled out weapons. The five quickly dispatched the one. They were trained fighters as well. Only one of them sustained an injury from a swipe of the fire stick. Two of the thugs held the man down against the front of the PTV. Kate recognized him.

Rolf approached and laughed when he saw the man's face. "Regis? What're you doing? You're protecting this scum? This infected bio-scum? You were one of mine." He shook his head, feigning disappointment. "But no longer." He turned away, back toward Kate and grinned at her. "Kill him, slowly. What is it your family does to traitors? The Trinelli flaying, right?" His wickedness was thick in the air, a taint. "That's what he deserves."

One of the thugs pulled out a long knife.

***

Kate couldn't believe her eyes. Three hulking men in grey suits walked past the PTV behind Gina's. Their pace steady. Their hands empty. They were much larger than any of the thugs, perhaps a head taller than Rolf. Their shoulders double the width of an ordinary person. These were bio-mods without a doubt, and Kate knew how they'd been modified--extreme physical mods of the sort reserved for security forces. Were these enforcers working with Rolf? She shuddered at the thought.

Rolf saw them. "What do you monsters want?" The Trinellis took a defensive position in front of Rolf, Regis and Kate. The Trinelli in Gina's PTV stepped out of the side door at that moment. "I think she is in the back." He gasped when he saw the three men. In a motion so quick that it was difficult to completely register visually, one of bio-mods grabbed him by the neck, lifted him off the ground, and threw him into the open door of the CTV. It was gruesome, like a bird smashing into a windshield, splattering flesh and blood while crushing bones and cracking glass.

The Trinellis brandished their weapons and charged. Rolf backed away.

The three bio-men made quick work of the five Trinellis. They were much too fast. The Trinellis tried to take advantage of their numbers and weapons, but the fight was over within two minutes.

Kate and Regis laid on the ground for a moment, unsure what to do or who these men were.

Rolf's PTV left the scene in a hurry.

"Where is your friend?" one of the men asked.

"In the trunk, hiding," Kate replied.

"You should get to the hospital. All three of you. He'll be back with more of them. He's with the Trinelli family, and they won't let this go. Return to Rochester as soon as possible. It's not safe for you here."

The three men turned and left. Kate got up and tried to run after them, but her back hurt too badly. She called out, "Wait. Who are you? Did Biomen send you?"

One called back, "Just return home, Doctor Genet."

TWENTY:

ROBERT FLYNN

Besides the coffeehouse memories, Mr. Shephard most enjoyed Jonathan's meetings with the mysterious Robert Flynn. Freedom to operate was elusive but necessary, and Flynn was critical to Jonathan's salvation.

***

Jonathan showed the letter to the suit, Schrag.

> Dear Mr. Jonathan Shephard,
>
> It is my pleasure to invite you to attend an exclusive seminar I will be hosting at the Greenbrier. The topic is simple: Don't Regulate Me or I'll Capture You. You will appreciate the sweet irony, no doubt.
>
> The seminar will take place on Saturday, June 28th. I have taken the liberty of reserving a suite for you for a few days, Thursday to Sunday. Feel free to extend your stay as you wish. It is a wonderful place, and it is my treat.

I look forward to meeting you.

Best wishes,

Robert Flynn

"Who is this guy?," Jonathan asked.

"A lobbyist in Washington, DC. One of the best, maybe the best. This is a good opportunity."

"Really? A seminar at the Greenbrier, the hotel with the bunker below that was supposed to be where Congress would hide in the event of a nuclear attack, right?"

"Right. We need to get ahead of the regulators in DC. Right now, that is probably the biggest risk to you, to your plans. The DOJ is already itching to do an investigation into our patent dealings, frame the whole thing as an antitrust concern."

"What do you mean? Are we under investigation?"

"They've been talking to competitors. I've been getting feedback from my insiders. They're definitely nosing around, building the base facts to support a more detailed investigation. We're monitoring the situation and playing some of the standard defenses. You know, I've got a well-connected think tank working the trade press, and we've been cooperating as necessary with the senior DOJ official on some other matters to build the relationship. But I have to say, as you know, this is just the tip of the iceberg. You know we'll have to manage a dozen or more different fronts in DC alone, and then there's the states and the EU. It's a lot."

"That's why I hired you and your entire team. That's why I bought your firm. You were the best. Now you're mine. And your job, your only job, is to maintain my freedom to operate."

"I understand. And Rob Flynn can help. A lot. He is the best lobbyist in DC. His client list is a trade secret. But from what I've heard, it's the very top of the food chain."

"If it's critical to the mission, then by all means, go to the seminar."

"I can't. He didn't invite me. That's not how he does it. He chooses his clients very carefully. And to my knowledge, he deals with them directly. I don't think they'd let me in the door."

"That's ridiculous. I've more important things to do than run off to West Virginia for a seminar. Besides, there are plenty of lobbyists in DC. The city is frickin swimming with those carrion feeders."

"I disagree. There are tons of lobbyists, no doubt. But none like Rob Flynn. My advice is that you should go and see what he has to say."

***

White Sulphur Springs, West Virginia. June 2025.

Just outside White Sulphur Springs, West Virginia, Jonathan's driver announced that they would arrive at the Greenbrier in 10 minutes. Ten seconds later, Jonathan got the message:

> Tell driver to take next road on right. Go three miles and then left on the unmarked dirt road. Go two and half miles and stop near fence. RF

Jonathan followed the directions, as did the driver. He grew curious. When they arrived at the destination, he got another message:

> Take your bags out and set them on the large rock with the flat top. Then dismiss driver. RF. PS. Don't worry, you're safe. Just precautions to keep our meeting beneath the radar.

Again, Jonathan complied. He wasn't worried for his safety. He'd left enough mouse droppings, and Rob Flynn must have known that. No, he wasn't worried. He was pissed and slightly intrigued. After the driver left, taking the car to a nearby hotel to wait until called upon, another message arrived:

> The fence is not armed. Come through, follow the path, find the green door, and follow the winding tunnel. There will be lights after 30 yards.

Jonathan did not hesitate. Once he had determined to go ahead with it, he plowed ahead. The green door was a bit difficult to locate, as it was concealed well within a clump of large bushes with small red berries, and it blended somewhat into the moss covered terrain, and mostly because it was horizontal rather than vertical, providing access to a ladder and the barely lit tunnel 30 yards below.

When Jonathan opened the green door, he received his last message:

Excellent. There will be no further messages.
We'll meet in less than five minutes. Just take
the tunnel to your immediate left when you
reach the bottom of the ladder. RF

Jonathan complied. He wondered what this Flynn would
be like. He had thought initially he would be a typical suit with
that extra flair of someone who made a living kissing ass and
brokering deals, never getting their hands dirty or investing
anything of their own or taking any risks. But a different image
settled in as he walked down the dimly lit tunnel. He thought
he'd be an ex-marine or navy seal. He'd have some military or
intelligence background.

They met in a T-junction, where his tunnel ended. A tall
man in dark clothes stood waiting. He wore black jeans, black
boots, a dark grey shirt barely visible at the neck, and a black
jacket. He even wore a black cap. A bohemian ninja, Jonathan
thought. His bright white smile, that news anchor smile, was a
beacon, a lone star radiating all on its own. Walking toward
the junction, it was the smile that Jonathan locked his sights
on.

"Excellent, welcome," he said in a soft, raspy voice.
"Pardon the precautions, but it's best to remain under the
radar, now and forever, right?" He laughed to himself. "Follow
me."

Completely surprised that this was the person he was here
to see, Jonathan followed the odd man. They walked in silence
for a few minutes down a dimly lit corridor, no longer a tunnel
but more of a proper hallway with concrete walls. At the end,
another green door. Rob tapped away at a keypad and opened

the door. They were in an incredibly lavish sitting room. Ornate furniture, 18th century artwork, a glass chandelier. Jonathan felt like Alice in Wonderland.

"Here we are!" Flynn announced, marking the moment with another radiant smile and a wave of his left hand. "I need to attend to matters. The presentation is in three hours." A lovely young woman appeared. Where had she come from? "Denise will show you to your suite and get you settled. I'll see you shortly. Tootaloo." He slid away before Jonathan even noticed.

Jonathan couldn't believe he'd left so abruptly. No glad-handing or ass-kissing. He missed it, in a way, and yet he never liked that crap anyway and was impressed that it had been dispensed with.

"Good afternoon," Denise breathed, "can I show you to your rooms?" Her clothes were loose and silky, but they caressed her as she moved, intimating at what one might do and feel. Jonathan shook his head, cleared the thought. He'd never cheat and really wasn't interested--been there hundreds of times and it was ultimately shallow compared to what he had with Anna. Denise intended to mesmerize and was good at it, but he was beyond her reach.

"Yes, of course. Thank you, Denise."

***

The suite was exquisite. Two bedrooms, an open kitchen and dining room, a huge lounging room, a hot tub, and more. Jonathan didn't care much about it. It was a place to rest and work. He didn't plan on anything else.

On the desk, there was another letter.

> Dear Mr. Shephard,
>
> Welcome to Greenbrier. You are in a special wing of the grand hotel. It is reserved for special meetings and not open to the public. For your privacy and that of the other participants, I ask that you kindly stay within this wing and keep its existence private. There is a more formal agreement for you to read and sign in the folder below. I am sure you understand, given the nature of our meeting. Rest assured that everything you might need or want is available in this wing--just pick up the telephone and ask.
>
> At 4 p.m., we will meet in the conference room, down the hall, third door on the right.
>
> Best wishes,
>
> Robert Flynn

***

Jonathan entered the conference room at 3:56. Denise waited just inside the door. "Welcome. We have a seat reserved for you in the second row. I'll show you." She took his hand and bid him to follow. He did. The room was dim, with lights lining the walkways. It was a small theatre. The seats were large sofas really with short tables in front of them. Food and drink were set out on silver trays on each table. There were probably five rows of three, and the other seats were filled with other businessmen. Jonathan did not see any women, except Denise and others like her who were working. All of the guests appeared to be old white men. He couldn't be sure, though, because it was hard to see and Denise ushered him to his seat quickly. The spacing of the sofas and the lighting of the room made it impossible to see the other participants from where he sat. He focused on the stage, as apparently he was supposed to.

A large screen slowly illuminated.

WELCOME

Movement on stage. A person. Must be Flynn making his way to the small podium that also slowly illuminated, emerging from the dark. Yes, it was him. Jonathan noticed his bright, white teeth and that unearthly smile.

The word on the screen slowly faded. It was replaced with:

DON'T REGULATE ME
OR
I'LL CAPTURE YOU

That was it, for a minute or two. Flynn stood at the podium. The screen remained the same. Jonathan sat and wondered when the show was going to begin. Maybe there were some stragglers, arriving late, and Flynn decided to give them another minute or two.

Five minutes passed, with nothing more. No stragglers. Jonathan poured himself a glass of water, drank it in three large gulps. He waited. He almost yawned, but at that moment, when he was on the cusp, Flynn spoke.

"Alright, folks. The message is simple. You've read it. You've digested it. You've begun to wonder if there is more to it. And I'm here to tell you that there isn't. This is it. Read it again. Digest it. Understand it. And be ready to commit to it fully."

He stopped and waited. Another minute passed. Jonathan started to fidget.

"DON'T REGULATE ME." A thunderous roar that didn't deafen but instead reverberated throughout the body. "Or." A soft, calm note played on a reed instrument, probably an oboe. "I'LL CAPTURE YOU." Deep, booming thunder again. Suddenly, incredibly bright light flashed throughout the room; for a moment, it was more difficult to see the other people in the room than it had been when it was dark. The light sizzled; the air was hot and smelled of ozone. Flynn had their attention. Jonathan and the others sat with their eyes wide open, not sure whether this was pure theatre or something more.

Then, in the voice of an evangelist, Flynn continued, "I want you to understand these simple words, to internalize them. They are more than a mere slogan, more than mere strategy. This must become your abiding truth. Your unwavering commitment. It will save you, and your legacy, from the corruption of government and everyone else who would poison your plans, your visions." He paused and looked at Jonathan; Flynn's dark eyes intense and focused, pulled at

Jonathan, straightening his neck while drawing his undivided attention.

"I know your visions. I know them very well." His voice grew louder as he spoke, building in intensity but maintaining a slow, steady pace. "You are powerful men, with powerful ideas, with visions for the future, for a world that will be better for everyone and for you and yours too." A slight pause, more pulling, there seemed to be no light in the room except a channel of light from Jonathan to Flynn and the screen that floated behind him.

"DON'T REGULATE ME. Or. I'LL CAPTURE YOU." Flynn boomed. "Say it." He calmly commanded.

They did. Jonathan did, and somehow he knew that everyone else in the room did, although he did not hear anyone else. This must be what it's like to be at one of those churches with the booming ministers who sweep you up in the flurry. Kind of a rush. I must remember this. I can do this too.

Flynn continued. "It's our strategy. You will each face the same sets of pressures, obstacles, and enemies, and the key to your survival is to be the fittest, to crush the competition. You already know, NO ONE can compete directly with you, not with YOUR IDEAS, not with YOUR TECHNOLOGY. They cannot compete fairly, plain and simple." He paused.

"Instead, they want to kneecap you, using government as the shotgun." A shotgun went off and an image of his mangled legs flashed in his head, accompanied by a slice of sharp pain. A split-second of agony. Jonathan shuddered. Fuckin' A.

"Don't let them. We won't let them. We'll fight together, and I have a plan, don't you worry. You know it already." He paused, again staring intensely at Jonathan.

"The key is to fight government regulation—government's too damn big, I tell you—don't regulate me, say it!" They did. Jonathan said it loudly, and he heard a chorus of others.

"AMEN!" Flynn looked possessed, ecstatic and full of energy.

Then he calmed. "You must understand that it will come eventually--yes, regulation will come. It always does, always has, since the dawn of civilization. But when it does, it must be, it will be *your* regulation—you will own it, you understand. You capture them, the regulators, sure, of course, but also the process, the ideas, the people, and the public. We capture it, and we shape it, not your weak-kneed competitors or the sanctimonious public interest organizations that are really in their pockets anyway. No, you'll be in the driver seat the whole time, and I am your GPS, your Glass, your Genie in the bottle."

A reddish light began to illuminate the stage. Flynn stood still and smiled. He turned to the screen as if to pay homage, and then back to the audience. "Understanding, accepting and committing to this simple strategy is what I ask of you today. I will meet with each of you to discuss our arrangements and plans for the near term and next five years. But now, I would like you to enjoy yourselves. I have paired you with another person who you must know. Go eat and drink with them, and enjoy the rest of the evening's events." He nodded and then turned and walked out the back.

Jonathan turned his head and noticed Denise standing to his side. "Good evening," she said. "Can I escort you to the cocktail reception? There is someone you must meet."

Twenty-One:

Gallows Storm

The trip to the hospital in Regis's PTV took five minutes, but it felt like an hour. Kate's back screamed in agony, blood still flowing from little rips and a deep gash. Regis was in worse shape, sprawled across the back seat silent and motionless. Gina was fine.

Gina obtained authorization to instruct Regis's PTV. An emergency override of some sort gave her the power to control the vehicle but, more impressive to Kate, it also gave the vehicle priority on the roadway, like an Emergency Transport Vehicle.

Once on their way, Gina said, "Rolf is working with the Trinellis. They're bad news. He must have been planning that for a while, and just waiting for the right time. The bastard. Must have been our late start, not as many people on the road this late in the morning." Kate just nodded. She wanted to ask about the Trinellis, but she didn't have the energy. It didn't matter. It wasn't difficult to figure out. Traffickers. She was more curious about the three bio-mod men who rescued them. Who were they? Had they been watching her the whole time?

***

Chief Jenks was waiting for them, arms crossed, back straight, face calm. She went to Regis first and upon seeing him, ordered the emergency nurses to get him on a gurney and into the hospital. She whispered something to him, for a moment looking like an old woman, a mother. Then she turned to Gina and Kate. "Kate, I received your signal and dispatched a team. They tracked your signal as they approached the scene, but you were on the move by the time they got there. So they followed you back here. Are you injured?"

Kate nodded and turned to reveal her shredded lower back. Jenks yelled for assistance. In a minute, Kate was on her way to the emergency room. Jenks walked alongside her and said, "We'll talk as soon as you can. You're safe here. The hospital is safe. Don't worry."

"I won't. Thank you," Kate replied, as the nurses swept her away.

***

An older male doctor Kate didn't recognize stood near her bed when she woke. Kate smiled weakly. She was tired. He smiled and said, "Hello. I'm Doctor Joseph. Gina asked that I look in on you."

She sighed and let out, "Nice to meet you. Thanks."

He continued, "You're fine, Doctor Genet. We stitched you up. There was a nasty scrape, not too deep though, and one slice that needed stitches and glue. Given your healing rate, you'll be back to normal in a few days." He knew she was a bio-mod? She supposed that most of the hospital knew.

"What about Regis, the other person who came to the hospital with Gina"

"He is in critical condition. He needs time. It will be a few weeks at least. We'll see." He hesitated, and then said, "There is a police officer aching to get in here to speak with you. I'd rather have Chief Jenks here before you talk to him and maybe even during your chat. So, why don't you rest a bit more? Close your eyes and rest. Don't call for the nurses or get up to go to the bathroom or anything, if you can manage. I'll get Chief Jenks. OK?"

"Sure. I'll go back to sleep." She drifted.

***

Jenks was there, waiting. "Kate?"

"Yes, hi Chief. How long have I, uh, what time is it?"

"It's only four in the afternoon. You slept a few hours. Are you fine to talk now? We can be brief, but I wanted to talk with you before the police officer outside comes in. He's been waiting all day. He seems fine. I looked into him, to make sure, and well, he checks out with guys I trust in the force. But, still, I want to hear your story first, and if you like, I'll stay while he questions you."

"That would be good. Have you spoken with Gina? She was there too."

"Yes, she filled me in as best she could. But there's a gap. She was in the trunk. And besides, it's best to confirm and get the different angles on the event." She was anxious, wanted to know about Regis, what happened to him.

"Sure. From the beginning?"

"Yes, go ahead. Tell me from the beginning."

Kate told Jenks everything that happened from the moment she woke up. Jenks just listened.

"Who is Conlin?"

"My friend, a good friend. Oh, my god, he's alone back at my house."

"Message him. Tell him to stay indoors with the security fully armed. He'll be fine. Besides, I don't think they'd go after him. He's of no value to them, certainly no market value. Besides, too risky, too much exposure."

Kate sent him a short message: Stay inside, full security armed. It's not safe. Kate

Kate wanted to say more; she wanted to leave and go find him, make sure he was safe. But she knew she couldn't. Jenks watched Kate like a scientist, observing, as if the expressions on Kate's face or the way that she tapped her message revealed deep insights or usable data. Kate didn't mind. She'd be doing the same thing if their positions were reversed.

"Kate, I don't think you can stay here."

"In the hospital?"

"No, the hospital is safe. I mean in St. Louis. It isn't safe. Regis, he can't protect you. And I can't assign others. I can't do much to help you outside of the hospital. I'm embarrassed to say, but this morning proves it. I'm sorry."

"It's not your fault. Rolf. He planned it, and he had help from the Trinellis."

"And he was patient. Had he rushed in to the hospital, or even in your neighborhood, he would have been caught by us or the police. But he waited for his opportunity to strike. And now that half a dozen Trinellis are dead, it's escalated beyond Rolf, though I'm sure he's plotting. He's one of those conniving, vindictive Alpha dogs." The last bit was more to herself than to Kate.

Kate took a deep breath. "I understand."

"You should leave tonight, tomorrow night at the latest. They won't expect you to go so quickly, and they'll expect you to leave during the day. So you do the opposite of what they expect. Can you do that?"

"I don't know. I haven't finished my research. I need to talk with Doctor Christians, the allergist. I haven't really figured much out yet."

"Meet with her today. I'll talk with her. She'll come see you, after the police officer. OK?" When Kate did not respond immediately, she continued, "Look, this is difficult. You've been attacked by a monster, twice on my watch, and I am responsible. I understand what you're going through and why you might want to stay. You got away twice and maybe, just maybe, you could do it again if you had to. But you won't. Those three bio-mod security men you mentioned, who, by the way, you will not mention to anyone else, you can't count on them to save you again. And though it pains me to admit it, you can't count on me. I don't want it to happen again. You must leave. Go home where you're safe. The Trinellis can't reach you there."

"But what about Gina and Regis? Conlin?"

"Kate, they'll be fine when you leave. Gina is not a target of any interest. I don't know this Conlin, but I suspect he's even further off their radar screen. Regis, well he probably is in danger; he'll be hunted because he killed Trinellis, two of them according to you. I'll keep Regis hidden and safe from them. That I can promise you."

"OK,' Kate conceded. She was surprised by how much the idea of leaving depressed her. It hurt worse than the pain searing in her back. Duller but deeper. She felt as if it threatened to push her over some emotional edge. Though she knew her home better than anywhere else, it seemed so filled with uncertainty and doubt. A frantic anxiety welled up inside her at the thought of leaving. She liked living here. She had made good friends. That realization, that she could leave her life in Rochester behind and be happy living in this human community, pulled her away from her present reality. She was dazed, distracted by the idea.

"Kate? Kate? Are you listening to me?" Jenks put her hand on Kate's shoulder. "Kate, the officer is going to come in and ask a few questions. I'll stick around."

Kate returned. "Sure, no problem." Kate repeated the story to the officer, leaving out the details about the three bio-mod men. She described them as three large, dangerous looking men. When the officer asked for more details, she said she hadn't seen more since she was injured and lying on the ground.

After the officer left, Jenks nodded to Kate, "Good job. I'll talk with Doctor Christians. She'll come by soon." As she left, Gina entered.

"Kate, my god, you alright? They told me you were fine, but I wasn't sure." She rushed to Kate and hugged her gently. "Oh, Kate. I'm so glad to see you. I was so scared. You saved me. You got me in the back, out of their way."

"I'm so glad you're here and that you're OK." She pulled Gina in, tightening the embrace. "Gina, I'm going to miss you."

"What do you mean you're going to miss me?" Her face lost color, saddened and frightened.

"Jenks said I need to leave tonight or tomorrow night. It's the only way to keep safe, and I don't want to put anyone else in danger. You and Conlin, especially." Kate started to cry, tears slowly forming and breath harder to come by. At first, Kate only whimpered as if holding something back; Gina held her and only said "it's OK." Kate gasped once, and then she let go of whatever she held back, sobbing fully and uncontrollably. After a minute or two, the storm subsided, and she settled into a lullaby-like whimper.

As if on cue, Conlin messaged: What's wrong? Are you OK? I'm at my house, locked and loaded. Waiting for you. Conlin. She smiled and the clouds broke. Her emotions suddenly under control, she started to plan.

***

Later that evening, she recounted the day's events for Conlin. He reminded her of Jenks as he listened. No questions, just intense concentration while gathering facts and impressions and processing the information. His expression shifted only once, when she mentioned the three bio-mod men. She had not filtered anything this time, and Conlin's face contorted— eyebrows up, nostrils flared, lips curled in as if to keep his teeth from chattering—when she said the gargantuan men obviously had security forces bio-modifications. He knew something was amiss. Kate had decided to tell him everything. She was leaving, and he deserved to know it all. So she did. She backtracked, and began with the maternity ward and Adam. She cycled back to earlier parts of her life, to her family, to her studies and career, but only as necessary to provide context or explain details. When her story reached St. Louis and Conlin, she didn't hold anything back.

She told him how he made her curious, how he made her comfortable, and finally how he made her realize that she could fall in love with someone, and to her surprise, that she could fall in love with a human. "I didn't think I could feel this way about anyone. I'm so relaxed and happy when I'm with you. It's like we're in our own little world, and I don't ever want to leave it. But, ..." Tears returned, only wetting her eyes, as she ended, "I'm sorry, Conlin, but it's true. I love you. I can't believe that I know this now, when I have to leave. I'm so sorry."

He was obviously shocked. His eyes focused on hers, his expression compassionate. She knew he cared for her, but this was too much. She worried that he would think of her differently. What did he think of bio-mods? They'd never discussed it; she'd steered clear of such conversations. He couldn't think of her as Rolf did with that extreme contempt. She knew that wasn't in him. But did he think less of her? Did he think of her as something less than human? He continued to sit and look at her, but he did not say anything. She knew he was thinking, processing everything she'd just told him, but her patience was thin.

"Conlin? Say something, please. What are you thinking? I'm sorry. I'm so sorry." He continued to look at her, his eyes focused on her face. He was disappointed and perhaps even scared. "Look, I should probably go." She started to turn, to leave, hoping he would stop her. He did not. He just sat there.

She left the sitting room, went to the front door, and pulled it open. It didn't open, however. It was locked, and there was no way she could unlock it. Conlin had activated the full lockdown after she'd entered the house. She turned back toward the sitting room. He stood in the archway between the room and hallway, his body contorting to fill the space. He stretched his arms high, clutched the moulding with golden hands and white knuckles, and he spread his legs to complete the X with his feet flat on the floor. He leaned forward a little into the hallway, arching his back slightly, stretching his muscles taut, on the verge of an elastic snap.

He was smiling.

"Kate, you can't leave. I'm sorry, but I can't let ya go."

***

"So you're a bio-mod. I had no idea. I thought you were from Chicago. I don't know how ... I mean, you're not what I expected. You're not a monster, that's for sure." He stood in the archway still, but he slumped a bit as if losing strength.

"Conlin, are you alright?"

"Just processing all of this. It's too much to handle, really, a gallows storm, you know. I need a few minutes to think."

"What? What did you just say? A gallowstrom?" An odd expression she thought she might have heard once before but couldn't place.

"A gallows storm. Technically, it's an extreme flood of data that overwhelms the core processing power of an individual that's been disconnected from the comp-sys. Hung out alone in a flood storm. I'm not really suffering from one. My core is perfectly fine. But really, it's an expression we use when we're completely unprepared for something or just painfully overwhelmed with grief. "

"We? Who?" Kate almost shouted, surprising herself.

"Comp-mods, Kate. I'm a comp-mod. I thought you figured it out already, when you cared for me, when you removed my cap. The markings above my ears. I thought you knew."

Kate's legs buckled. "I thought about it, for a minute, you know. But I didn't think you could be, you don't have that dead stare." She stumbled forward.

"Kate!" He ran toward her and caught her, holding her up with his arms under hers. "Kate, why don't we go back and sit down. I don't know if it will help, but I want ya to know something." He squeezed her a little, forcing her to tilt her head up and to listen carefully. "I love you too."

She looked up at him, at his face, and then into his eyes. She ignored the first revelation -- that he was a comp-mod -- and relished the second. He loved her. In the moment, they only cared about who they were and how they felt about each other; for that moment, they seemed to forget what they were. She felt comfortable in his arms, and she liked the way he felt in hers. She raised her head up further, so her eyes were level with his and so her lips were nearly touching his. She waited while their breath mingled and their eyes connected in an embrace. His eyes were full of life and dreams, full of her. They were never dead. She kissed him fully.

They stood kissing for a minute or two, but reality came crashing in when a small screen materialized. It displayed Gina, walking up the front walk. Conlin released Kate and quickly ran his fingers along the menus on the right and bottom of the screen. Additional screens popped up alongside the first, displaying a number of different perspectives of the front and back yard, the street, and the neighbor's yards. Assured that no one else was nearby, Conlin admitted Gina. The three retired to the sitting room to talk.

"I brought you your clothes and everything I could grab from your house."

"What? You went in. They could have been waiting."

"Jenks brought me there. She thought it would be best to clean out the vake so there was no trace that you'd been there and no way for them to figure out where you'd go. I told her there wasn't much, but her teams went through it all. Well, they're still there. Jenks told me to gather what you'd need, and then she snuck me out the back and through John's yard. She is keeping an eye out. There are police driving around as well. I think we're safe for tonight."

"Thanks, Gina." She smiled at her. Then she realized, "I still need to get my PTV."

"You can take mine. It might help. They wouldn't know you're inside." Conlin said. He looked at her briefly and then turned to Gina. "Are ya alright, Gina? Kate said ya hid in the trunk. That was smart."

"Yes, I'm fine. It was her idea, you know. Anyway, I'm tired and a little scared. Jenks says they'll only be hunting you, Kate, that I don't have anything to worry about. I'm not sure I believe it, but what can I do?" She looked at Kate with wet, tired eyes. "You know, I don't want you to go."

"Me either, but I have to. I can't stay. You'll both be in danger. It's not just Rolf. The Trinellis too."

"I know. Where will you go? Rochester?" Gina asked.

"Yes, that's my best option. It'll be good to see my parents, get back to my lab, and everything." She stopped for a moment, lips clenched, fingers twitching. "It's just so disappointing. Obviously the two run ins with Rolf were absolute hell, that's worse than disappointing." Again, she stopped and fidgeted. Conlin and Gina watched her and waited. "I know this is going to sound crazy, but I can't help it. That's not what's on my mind, what's bothering me. I feel so frustrated because I failed. I didn't make any progress with my research. I still don't know anything about the allergic reactions in infants, what happened to Adam. I met with Doctor Christians today, and she didn't have any new information or insight. Like Doctor Martins, she found allergies in bio-mod infants surprising, and she couldn't connect the symptoms Adam experienced with anything she'd seen or knew about." Kate shook her head. "All I've learned is that the humans don't worry much about allergic reactions when delivering babies." A thought crossed her mind: What would she say in a report for Biomen? Saying anything more than that, anything more about the humans generally somehow seemed like a betrayal, even though she had no idea what she would say.

"Kate?" Conlin said.

"So I'm really in the same place as where I started. I feel like, if only I could stay here"

"You can't, Kate." Conlin said. "I don't know anything about allergies, but I do know that people out to kill ya is more than enough of a reason to head home. And I hate to say it because I don't want ya to leave either."

"He's right, Kate, and you know it. You've got to leave before the Trinellis ..."

"I know," Kate murmured.

"You might not have the answer you're looking for, a complete explanation, but it's something to know that, us unmodified humans, we don't have a similar allergic reaction as infants, right? Doesn't that confirm that the infant reaction has something to do with the drug cocktail? The modifications?"

"Well, yes and no. It tells me something, as you said. But I don't know that it confirms some connection to the drug cocktail. We don't have a single occurrence in clinical trials with the drug cocktail, over many years and many, many trials." Kate wondered whether she'd really seen all of the data. Maybe there'd been a cover up or lost data. She massaged her temples, but it didn't help. "I don't know. I'll have to think about it. Today has been so crazy. You know, I don't know why my research creeps up in my head when there are more immediate and more important things to think about. It's just I expected Doctor Christians would have some answer."

Conlin stood. "Kate. Take a deep breath. You've been through a lot, and you're upset about a lot of things." She complied, taking a few deep breaths. He went on. "Gina is right, though. You learned something, and you'll have to be content with that, at least for now. Maybe we can open up a communication channel so you can talk with the doctors here. But for now, we've more pressing issues."

Kate sighed. "I know. But I don't want to leave you two." She began crying again. Conlin and Gina went to comfort her. Conlin, who had already been standing, got there first, but he waited for Gina. The two of them knelt before Kate, and she moved forward to embrace them. All three held each other tightly.

***

Room 542. The beeping was deep and furious, and the flashing red light pervaded the room, making it a freakish nightclub. The thrumming pushed everyone to move more quickly in an awful frantic dance, while the red lights somehow exaggerated everyone's facial expressions. Fredric and the nurses moved about the room in a manner that almost seemed coordinated. Nicola and Joseph were untouched by all of this. Their panic and confusion seemed normal, real, unadorned by the accents of a dream. They were in the eye of it. The red light did not touch Adam. He was calm, and he stared at Kate, drawing her attention away from the rest. His death came swiftly, suddenly in a flash. Kate felt it again, felt her heart stop.

The dream moved at its own pace, as if alive and intent on communicating something to Kate. She recognized this only vaguely in her subconscious, a curious tickle. With Adam's death, the beeping faded to continuous ringing, and time slowed. The coordinated dance gave way to a blurring of broken people and discordant noises and emotions. Except for Joseph. Joseph was clear to Kate. He was distinct from the rest. In the eye, in her eye. For a moment, a sliver of her subconscious had deja vu--wasn't this a dream from before? The dream shook free from the idea, that brief restraint, and Kate saw and heard Joseph above the fray. The chaos of the dream dissipated fully, as Kate focused on Joseph. His head dropped into his hands, and he sobbed as he shook his head. "No," he sputtered in a low, guttural moan. She felt his heartache. He muttered to himself, "Oh, Adam, I'm caught in a gallows storm. I don't understand. How could this happen?

Why?" Again, a sliver of her subconscious had deja vu, and it persisted; the dream lingered letting it fester. Joseph still muttering, "It's all my fault. I know we shouldn't have done this."

***

Kate woke. She recalled the dream, accepted its veracity, and fell into deep thought.

***

Conlin slept to her left, and Gina to her right. Once again, and one last time, together. They had decided to wait one day. Jenks had thought it would be fine, maybe better if it gave Kate a chance to rest and make sure her back injury was healing as expected. But she would have to leave tonight.

The pain in her back had receded. She looked at her two friends, an unmodified human woman and a comp-mod man. What a scene. Never would she have imagined that she could be lying in bed with an unmodified or a comp-mod, much less both! And she was sure that they probably felt the same way.

She'd had a faint idea of what unmodifieds would be like. She knew they were civilized and had sophisticated technologies, but somehow her understanding that bio-mods had evolved substantially beyond normal humans left her with a distorted impression that ignored much of what they were. Like most bio-mods, she had thought of them as relics from the past, a living reminder of what bio-mods had been long ago, where they had started. But they weren't really. They weren't primitive, inferior, or relics. They were just human. Kate smiled.

Comp-mods, on the other hand, were no longer part of humanity. She had always thought of comp-mods as something other than human, machines really. Like those drones on the treadmill. They'd lost their humanity when they let computer chips run their bodies and process their thoughts. The merging of man and machine left the human side wanting, she'd thought, a terrible tragedy but also a living reminder to bio-mods of the perils of pursuing perfection, of hubris. She remembered a line from a university lecture that had always stuck with her, "They'd abandoned Darwin's game, and it cost them their souls."

But apparently, this wasn't true either. They were still human, at least some of them were. Conlin was. She loved him deeply, and he loved her, and Kate knew he was no machine. His soul was not lost. He'd been more human, more compassionate and comforting and real to her than anyone else. She looked at him and shook her head slowly; she was in love with a comp-mod.

***

When the two woke, Kate was going through her things and repacking. Gina seemed refreshed. Conlin did not. He looked exhausted, worn. He walked straight to Kate and hugged her. "Breakfast?" he asked.

The three sat and ate a simple meal. Kate broke the silence. "Conlin, what was it you said yesterday when you're disconnected or something? A gallup?"

"A gallows storm."

"Yes. You said it was an expression you used."

"Right. Well, it has two meanings, one technical and one, it's just something I say when I'm really surprised and overwhelmed. Why do you ask?"

"Well, is it something just you say?"

"No, not really. It's a comp-mod expression. Lots of people use it. I mean, I think so, at least. I never really thought about it."

"Have you ever heard anyone else use it? Someone who isn't a comp-mod?"

"Huh? What are you getting at Kate? I am a comp-mod, if that's what you're struggling with."

"No, that's not it. I understand that, and yes, that is something I'm struggling with and want to talk about too. But no, what I'm wondering is whether only comp-mods would use the expression, you know, refer to a gallows storm when overwhelmed."

"If that's what you're asking, then yes, it's a comp-mod expression. I can't imagine a human or bio-mod ever using it. It wouldn't make sense. But why do you ask?"

Kate didn't respond; she was lost in thought.

"Kate?" Conlin asked.

Gina, who had been listening while cleaning up, perked up. "Kate, you alright?"

Kate returned. "What? Yes, I'm fine. Look, I know why Adam died."

Conlin and Gina looked surprised and doubtful, perhaps worried that Kate was losing it.

"Joseph, Adam's father, he was a comp-mod."

"What?" Gina said. "What does that have to do with a gallows storm?" Conlin said.

Kate tilted her head back a little and pursed her lips, as if pondering what to say. Then she said, "Just after Adam died, and the hospital room was utter chaos, Joseph said he was afflicted by a gallows storm."

"Really?" Gina said, as Conlin said, "Are you sure?"

"Yes, I'm sure. I had a dream last night."

"A dream," Gina and Conlin said at the same time.

"Yes, a vivid dream. I have them often. Many biomods do. Dreams allow us to recall sensory perceptions, memories. A dream can tell me something, focus my attention on something I witnessed but failed to notice. Not all of the time, of course. But this time, last night, well, I know. I was recalling details from the hospital. Joseph said, 'Oh, my dear Adam, a gallows storm afflicts me. I don't understand. How could this happen?' I remember it distinctly. It was so clear."

"In the dream or your memory of the hospital room? I'm confused. I don't know how you can be so sure." Gina said. "Even when a dream sticks in my head after I wake up, I can barely remember any details."

"Kate, I just used the expression yesterday. And so it popped up in your dream. That makes sense. But it's a completely different thing to say that this Joseph actually said it a few months ago in the hospital room."

"Gina, Conlin, trust me. I understand what you're saying, your reservations. I do. But I also know what I know. It's crystal clear, I'm sure of it. Yes, I agree that your use of the expression probably prompted something, triggered the recollection. But I was in the room. I did hear what Joseph said. I just didn't notice it at the time. It was just background noise at the time." Kate hesitated to see if they had anything to say, and after a moment resumed. "So the dream showed me a memory. Of course, it had fact and fiction, you know. There was no dancing in the hospital room, but there was in my dream last night." Gina and Conlin looked even more concerned and doubtful. Kate continued. "That was fiction, sure. But the facts were crystal clear and meant for me to see, to remember and comprehend." She waited a moment. "I'm 100% confident, but I can see that you're not. We can go over this forever and not get anywhere. So let's not bother."

"Alright?" Gina said, wondering what was coming next. Conlin raised his eyebrows and half-smiled.

"Besides, Joseph was different. He was a little off. I noticed it, heck, even Fredric noticed. But we had no reason to pay any attention to it. Fredric asked me something, like did I think he was weird." Kate paused, looking up for a moment, and then continued. "The biochemical feedback too. He didn't have any that I can remember. Not something you'd necessarily pick up on in a packed room. But it's probably part of why he seemed off to both me and Fredric."

Gina and Conlin said nothing, but they looked less doubtful.

"Suppose I'm right, then. Just think about it. The rare infant deaths in bio-mod hospitals are from mixed couples, a bio-mod and comp-mod couple, or perhaps comp-mod couples, though I'm doubtful there are many of those. They don't show up in the clinical trials because no comp-mod would ever participate. I mean, comp-mods in bio-mod territory would hide the fact that they're comp-mods, right? I hate to say it, but the social pressure would be overwhelming. The idea of a mixed couple is unheard of, complete taboo, and you can only imagine what people would say about the child of a mixed couple. So any mixed couples would have to pretend to be pure bio-mod for their own sake and the baby's. No one would think that the baby would be in danger. Why would they? But if that's what's going on, maybe the drug cocktail is like a poison, like Doctor Rakoff said."

"I don't know, Kate," Gina said.

Conlin remained silent, his smile gone.

"If I'm right, if this is what is happening, then it could be avoided. Right? I mean, if mixed couples know that their infants will die, then they won't hide the fact that they're mixed; they won't agree to use the cocktail. If I'm right, we've got to prove it."

"What if the hospitals know already? The allergy explanation could be some kind of cover up." Gina asked.

"No. I don't think so. How would they know? I observed the intakes. Nothing blatant indicated that Joseph was a comp-mod. He had a whole bio-mod history somehow. We went over it, his records, everything. I don't know how he got all of that. So someone knows and helped them hide the truth and pretend to be bio-mods. But I don't think it's the hospital. That doesn't make sense to me."

"So what's your plan?" Gina asked.

"I don't know yet. I don't have one. Go back to Boston, I guess, and see if Nicola and Joseph would talk with me. I'm not sure I'd want to approach them without more, though."

"Come with me to San Francisco," Conlin said abruptly. "You won't find any mixed couples here in St. Louis, but maybe you will out there. My sister works in a hospital. Maybe we can get you in there to continue your research, see how mixed couples fare, assuming there are some. A natural experiment, I suppose."

"But you live here."

"I need to go back anyway. I've reports to deliver, and I need to check on my house, see my sister. Besides, I'd like you to come." He smiled.

"But I'm a bio-mod, Conlin. I'd be ostracized, seen as an animal or worse a monster, right?"

"No, not by everyone. But look, you could easily pass as a human, a human from St. Louis actually, coming to San Francisco to learn about comp-mod maternity wards and see if some of the best practices might be useful for human hospitals. A perfectly plausible and acceptable cover, I think."

"I'm not sure. I mean, I'd love to go with you."

"Trust me, you'll love the *Sōmen*."

"What?" Kate asked with a hint of annoyance.

"They're noodles. You'll love them, definitely worth the trip." He smiled. "OK, seriously, it'll give you time to think, and an opportunity to do some more field research. If there are mixed couples on the East Coast, there are mixed couples on the West Coast, right? It's a curious thing in its own right. How do these couples meet in the first place? Where? I would have thought we were the first." With that slip, he stopped.

"I'll come with you, Conlin."

Tears wet Gina's eyes. "You're welcome to come too, Gina," Conlin said.

Gina laughed, "I'd love to, but I can't. My life is here. I'll miss both of you."

Twenty-Two:

Stories

Conlin's PTV was unremarkable from the outside. It looked no different from Kate's and blended well on the streets of St Louis. But it was different on the inside. That was evident from the moment they began their road trip. Conlin didn't give it instructions. It just went, all on its own.

"Where is it taking us?" Kate asked, her voice quivering like a string instrument.

"What do ya mean? The PTV?"

"Yes." She paused for a second and took a breath. Then, in a calm voice, she continued, "We haven't had a chance to pre-program our route or anything, and we haven't given it instructions."

Conlin smiled and then explained, "I did." He tapped the side of his head between his temple and ear. "I instructed the PTV to take us to my home in San Francisco, and after a brief back-and-forth on possible routes, I selected the northern scenic route. It also happens to be the safest. We have to avoid Nevada. So when we hit Salt Lake City, we'll head north into Idaho. When we ..."

Kate just stared at him. She understood immediately but acceptance came more slowly. Her body tightened as instinct pushed for caution. She noticed that Conlin remained perfectly calm, unaware of her struggle, and she thought of Johan. She shook her head.

He continued. "Ya know we could visit Portland. We'll be quite close. It's a wonderful city, and I have friends there. What do ya think?"

Kate shrugged her shoulders.

"We've got plenty of time to decide. For now, let's just stick with San Fran. I should get home first, talk to my sister."

"Sure." Kate responded. The reality of where she was heading and with whom settled in her mind. She relaxed.

***

Target heading West, probably going to San Francisco.

WHAT? WHY? THAT DOESN'T MAKE SENSE.

[silence]

EXPLAIN.

We have no idea. We told her to return home. But she left her PTV at her house. She was hiding with a friend, a man. He may be a comp-mod.

WHAT? THAT DOESN'T MAKE SENSE. WHAT WAS HE DOING THERE? WHY WOULD SHE HIDE WITH HIM?

We aren't sure. They spent time together. Check the logs we sent. He spent a lot of time at her house. He set up her solar panel system. We believe they are friends.

ARE THEY TRAVELING TOGETHER?

We believe so.

FOLLOW THEM. CONTINUE TO REPORT. MAKE SURE SHE STAYS ALIVE.

How far?

WHAT DO YOU MEAN?

How far should we go into comp-mod territory?

AS FAR AS NECESSARY. ALL THE WAY.

Sir, it will be impossible to be discreet. We will be detected and detained. We don't have authorization ...

OK, FINE. FOLLOW AS FAR AS YOU CAN WITHOUT BEING CAUGHT. REPORT HOURLY. WE'LL ARRANGE FOR A MORE DISCREET OPTION IN CALIFORNIA.

Svart looked at his two hulking partners. "We'll continue as far as we can. But they'll get a local spook for Cali."

***

"Why don't I pretend to be a comp-mod? I'm not so different from you. Sure, you're a little quirky." She smiled at him. "But I don't see why should I be an outsider?"

He laughed. "Because you are, and there's no hiding it Kate. No one would believe that you're a comp-mod. It would be obvious because you have no visible comp-mods." He motioned to the marks above his ears and then he lowered the collar of his shirt to reveal a glistening red dot, almost like an eye, at the base of his neck. Then, to drive the point home, he got very close to her and stared deeply into her eyes. At first, she felt attraction building within her and from him; she felt his attention. But then Kate noticed something different in his eyes, a thin film or gloss or something. It was barely noticeable and probably impossible to see without his effort to show her.

Conlin pulled back and said, "Besides the visible markers that any comp-mod would spot easily, the more immediate and important reason you couldn't possibly pass for a comp-mod is that you couldn't join the community, the comp-sys network. You'll be marked as incompatible as soon as you're in range. People will try to commune with ya and will know right away that you can't."

Kate hadn't been serious about pretending to be comp-mod. She was just contemplating the possibility, playing around with the idea of pretending to be the opposite of who or what she was. She no longer felt playful. She was depressed and a little scared.

Conlin went on. "But you certainly could pass as a human. I mean, you fooled me." He smiled. "No one would think twice about your inability to connect. In fact, they'll be curious about you and welcome you. Comp-mods don't really look down on humans exactly. They're remnants of a revered past, sort of. Backwards, but not degenerate."

"So bio-mods are degenerate?"

"No, don't be silly. I'm just explaining how comp-mods in general might think, not how I think. OK?"

"Sure. But why would comp-mods think we're degenerate at all? Is that what you're taught?"

"I suppose so. When the twenty-first century modification crises were taught in school, in modern history, I guess, the Eastern push for biomodification is what caused the U.S. to breakup. Pure hubris, tampering with humanity rather than allowing nature to run its course. That was the message. Of course, even as kids, we knew it was economics and politics too. The merger of the genomic and pharmaceutical companies concentrated power. They reengineered people, optimized laborers, took control of them, and the result, at least as it was described in school, was not pretty."

"How so? What do you mean?" She fought the anxiety and anger that tussled in her gut.

"Well, I'm sure you can imagine. Monstrosities of all sorts, physical behemoths without brains, …" Kate thought of the three bio-mod enforcers who rescued her; they seemed reasonably bright. "… bestial hybrids, devilishly beautiful clones. The key, of course, was the lifelong addiction to the drug cocktails. Bio-mods lost their free will and became slaves to their baser instincts and desires, and of course, to Biomen."

"Such bullshit! It's propaganda, plain and simple."

"Yeah, I guess so. But it also comes up in the vids too. Popular entertainment."

"Do I break the mold, then?"

"No, not really. I'm hoping you're one of those devilishly beautiful clones and that you'll invite your sisters to join us." They laughed and kissed.

"Your story from St. Louis is perfect. Just stick to it. We just need to explain why you're coming to San Francisco, and that probably follows naturally from what you've already been saying. My sister, Sophia, can probably get ya access to the maternity wards if you pretend to be human, but definitely not otherwise."

***

Joseph and Nicola got comfortable under the sheets, still feeling good about their lovemaking.

"I miss Adam so badly, Joseph, but, forgive me for saying this, I, I think it was a mistake. We shouldn't have tried. Adam's death was a cruel reminder that we shouldn't be together. We're not supposed to bring a baby into this world."

"Don't say that, Nicola. Don't say that. You don't mean it. I know you don't. It was a random thing, you know, an allergic reaction, like the doctor said."

"It was anything but random, Joseph. And no I don't believe them. They have no clue. They don't really know about us. And so how could they possibly explain what happened to Adam? They couldn't. You saw their confusion. Even the next day, after they'd had time to figure it out, they were still confused."

"Yes, but that doesn't mean it wasn't an allergic reaction."

"To what? The Biomen cocktail, right? The pharmacological modifications meant for pure bio-mod infants."

"So you think I killed him?"

"What?"

"You think it's my fault. It was my comp-mod genes."

"I don't know. I mean, it has something to with that probably. I don't think it's your fault though. Not at all. We just shouldn't have tried to have a baby. It won't work."

"You don't know that. It could have been a random allergic reaction. Maybe we shouldn't have modded him, you know, given him the drug cocktail."

"I suppose. But we knew there was some risk. We fought about whether we should have a baby, and you know, how we'd fool everyone so he could fit in. We lied. We had to. I understand that. I agreed to it. But we paid the price. Adam paid the price."

"I don't think so. It was random. I'd try again someday."

"No, Joseph. Never. I want to spend my life with you. I love you, and you know that, but you cannot ask me to go through that again. We're not meant to have children."

"How can you say that? I don't understand. We're not meant to. Who says?"

Nicola just sat there, looking at him, unsure about what to say. She knew he was getting upset and that it would be best to let him get it all out, let him vent.

He went on. "Nicola, there's nothing wrong with us, nothing at all. When we met in Toronto, I knew there was something between us, that we were meant to be together. That feeling fueled me then and has to this day. I don't mind hiding and pretending because I do it with and for you. We've proven that it's OK for a bio-mod and comp-mod to be together if they love each other. Just because our respective societies view each other as sub-human doesn't mean that we are, or that God sees us that way. We can have children, if we want to. We're capable of it. Adam lived, damn it. He was alive. He was perfect. You saw it, right?" Joseph was crying.

So was Nicola. "Yes, he was."

They cried together for a few minutes.

Joseph whimpered, "But maybe it is my fault. Maybe you're right."

"That's not what I meant."

"Maybe we should have told the doctors the truth. If they knew I was a comp-mod, maybe they could have done something."

"No, Joseph. We did what we had to do to for Adam. What could we do? If we told the truth, the hospital might have refused us. Adam would have been rejected from the bio-mod community, and that wouldn't do. A child needs to belong."

TWENTY-THREE:

FRIENDS

Denise glided next to Jonathan, cradling his hand as she led him out of the meeting room and to the reception. The Greenbrier was charming, and this special wing was decorated lavishly with original artwork that Jonathan didn't recognize but nonetheless appreciated. Nineteenth century American paintings portrayed small town America in exquisite detail. He wondered if someone had purchased all of the masterpieces from that time and assembled them here. He'd not seen their like anywhere else.

The reception was like hundreds that Jonathan had attended. Standard fare: top shelf everything from hors d'oeuvres to champagne. He was surprised when Denise grabbed two full champagne glasses, handed him one, and said, "Congratulations. You will change the world." They clinked their glasses and sipped. She smiled and then said, "Ah, there is Mr. Duardo." She set her glass down on the tray of a steward passing by, took Jonathan's hand, and guided him to Mr. Duardo, who also had a beautiful woman guiding him.

The two women made eye contact with each other, nodded, and then simply let go of the men they guided, stepped back, and faded into the crowd.

"Ah, well, I suppose we're supposed to meet," Duardo said with a strong Brooklyn accent. "My name's Don Duardo."

"Pleased to meet you, Mr. Duardo."

"Call me Donduardo. You know, people just blend it, Donduardo, been doin' it since I was a kid."

"Sure, Donduardo." Jonathan made sure he said it correctly and smiled when Donduardo nodded. "My pleasure. My name is Jonathan Shephard. What do you say we grab a drink from the bar?"

They walked over to the bar. "How about two dry martinis?" asked the bartender, an older man with a thin white mustache. "Sure," they both said. He had already started making them. After he put the drinks on the bar in front of them, the bartender moved to the opposite end of the bar, leaving them alone. Jonathan thought it odd that they had a decent amount of privacy at a bar with almost two-dozen people.

Jonathan and Donduardo exchanged the conventional pleasantries, and Jonathan learned that Donduardo grew up in Queens, loved the Jersey Shore, and hated Washington DC. When Jonathan asked him why he hated DC, the conversation got interesting.

***

"No, I'm telling you the absolute truth. I was a very successful heroin dealer. I don't do that shit anymore, but it is my past and it is what drove me to do what I now do, you understand."

"Which is what exactly?" Jonathan asked. He understood. Donduardo's story was similar enough to his own.

"I do a bunch of things. But the big money maker and DC headacher is synthetic heroin."

"Really? How'd you get into that?"

"Back in 2012 or so, I started thinking about going legit. I had parked tons of money in legit businesses and was getting tired of dealing with the cops and the bosses, paying off everybody, worrying about who was going to shoot me in the head. So I said to myself, now's the time to make a change, and you know, I did. I went to school, Penn State, and got my BS in biochemical engineering. Only took two and half years. While I was there, I cozied up with the graduate students, especially the foreign ones. Most of them are working for me now. Over the past decade, I put a ton of money into R&D, biochem mostly. The big breakthrough was in 2020 when we developed a synthetic heroin compound that brings the pleasure but avoids the pain. Probably the biggest breakthrough was the addiction snap."

"The what?"

"Addiction snap, that's what I call it. We snapped the link, the biological and biochemical link that leads to physiological addiction. People absolutely fall in love with it, don't get me wrong. They want it more than anything else, which is good for business, I tell ya. Sure, that can lead to behavioral addiction, but so can all sorts of things that are perfectly legal.

The key for our product is that there's no physiological dependence."

"I see."

"So, we're legit; my biotech company is legit. We've got a bunch of other drugs in development too, and we've got a state of the art genomics facility. To be honest, that's where the future is. We've got some of the best. The stable of scientists we recruited makes all the difference. And it helps that the synthetic heroin is fueling our stock price."

"What did you do with your old business?"

"For the first few years we had a few foreign subs secretly running drugs we were testing in the black markets and out of the country. It kept some money flowing. Always through backchannels and untraceable. That we were real careful about."

"Is that what's got DC focused on you?"

"No, not at all. It's the FDA. We got a stream of patents on our drugs. Getting FDA approval to market them is a major pain in the ass. Plus those assholes over at the DEA are fighting tooth and nail against our product, say it's listed as a controlled substance and cannot be delisted even by the FDA. We've got lawyers working on the FDA and the Attorney General's office."

"So you can't distribute legally in the US?"

"No, not yet. We make it and sell it abroad though. And it's only a matter of time here. Honestly, the product is just too good, and without the risk of addiction and abuse, it's really just politics holding things up. Guess that's why I'm here."

"Don't regulate Donduardo, or he'll friggen capture you, right?"

"You got it. Man, I think we got half of them captured already. Many of those bastards on the hill are using our product already. Don't ask me how they get it, but they do. It's the other half we've got to nail."

The two men became close friends that evening, swapping stories of their storied pasts and their plans for the future. Both lamented the obstacles they faced, and both agreed that they'd give Rob Flynn a shot.

TWENTY-FOUR:

THE VACANT EYES OF GHOSTS

Kate felt so alone walking the streets of San Francisco. The city was so different from Boston and Rochester. It was beautiful in many ways. Nature touched the city; it was shaped by the bay and hills as much as the builders. She loved the way that it took advantage of the sun. The light seemed to reflect off surfaces differently, making the buildings shine and, at times, almost shift. When she tried to catch a shift, however, it escaped her. She dismissed it as the product of some building material that absorbed and reflected different wavelengths of light, some type of advanced solar energy system that the comp-mods relied on. She knew they'd invested heavily in such technologies, but that was all she knew. She didn't pay it much attention. There were other stranger distractions.

She walked alone down the busy streets. She was a ghost. Transparent, invisible. No one saw her, or at least, no one noticed her. Everyone was on autopilot. It was a city of robot toys marching to a beat only God heard. It was maddening to Kate. She said, "Hello," to no one in particular, a word to the crowd. A little louder, she said, "Hello, my name in Kate." No one heard her. Had she actually spoken? Was it just a thought she'd voiced in her own head? She sympathized with the proverbial tree falling in the forest. She spoke; it fell. That was reality, plain and simple. The observations of others were icing on the cake, luxuries perhaps, but necessary.

She stopped walking and stood in the middle of a walkway, watching the PTVs move on the street and the robots marching on the walkway like slower cousins. She spun in a circle and shouted, "I'm a whirlwind!" Nothing. No one stopped, no one acknowledged her. She was a ghost. A feeling of power and freedom arose within her only to be challenged by an equally strong feeling of dread, emptiness, and sadness.

No, she insisted, she was not the ghost. They were. She was alive without a doubt. They were dead. If they couldn't see or hear her or the beautiful city, the wonderful environment, if they couldn't feel the warmth of the sun or the wind breathing on them, they were truly lost. She was frightened at the thought of being so alone in this city of ghosts, and yet she knew there was nothing to fear since they did not even know she was there. She truly was free and thus safe, but to do what, to what end? Observing this alien world was something, she thought, but not enough.

Conlin. She wanted him.

Conlin was not like them. Yet this was his home. How could it be? He wasn't dead like them. He was nothing like them. He was full of life. She looked into the crowd of robots approaching and called to him, "Conlin, where are you? I need you." Desperation crept into her heart as she felt a deep need for him to come and revive her, to pull her from this terrible dream, to bring her home.

He did not arrive, despite her pleas. The robots routed around her. Was she no more than an inanimate obstacle, a rock in the stream? What would happen if she built a dam? Would they overflow into the street? She walked in a line across the walkway, cutting against the traffic flow. Remarkably, they routed around her with perfect precision, never missing a beat and not giving her any other acknowledgement.

She tried harder to get their attention. "Hey, hey you!" she called to one man while waving at him. Nothing. She made a sudden windmill motion with her arms in the direction of others, and they simply routed around her. Should she reach out and touch someone? Just as she was about to do so, she changed her mind, worried about the consequences. What would they do? She might interrupt the whole computer program and if the worker bees were disturbed, what would the Queen do? Send in the guards? She sat on a bench and wondered if anyone ever stopped to sit there. She was the only one on the bench, and as she looked down the street at other benches along the sidewalk, she noticed that they were all empty. She shuddered and wondered why they had benches at all.

***

Kate returned to Conlin's house. It was a small brown house on 11th Street in the Richmond District. Kate had run a medium pace most of the way, no longer paying attention to the place or its strange machines. The exercise would clear her mind, and besides, she needed it after spending two weeks recovering from her back injury. It was still sore, but not disabling.

She slowed at the end of the block and walked toward Conlin's house. When she reached his neighbor's yard, she saw Conlin standing with an incredibly pretty woman. She was almost golden, with long reddish gold hair and glistening brownish gold skin. Conlin and the woman were touching each other's shoulders with their hands, an intimate connection. Kate began to sweat and breathed more rapidly, her guts churned, and her muscles that had been tired from running re-energized. Despite the jealousy raging within her, she held back. Were they arguing? Kate couldn't hear what they were saying. Were they were even talking aloud?

The woman turned abruptly to leave, and she turned suddenly toward Kate as if she had sensed her without seeing her. She looked directly at Kate, initially puzzled and then with a fierce intensity. She held the look for just a moment, shook her head, and walked away.

Conlin looked distraught, but when he sensed Kate and looked directly at her, to her relief, his face brightened. He rushed to her. "Come inside. I'm so glad to see ya."

Kate followed him in the house without a word. Once inside, she asked, "Who was the woman? I take it that wasn't your sister?"

"No," he laughed, "that's not Sophia. They're nothing alike. That was Ayana, a friend. We got together every once in a while." He hesitated, raised his hands in front of his chest as if about to clench them together in prayer, something Kate hadn't seen in years, but instead he held them steady a few inches apart like he was holding an invisible book. "She knew I was back and was hoping to celebrate. I declined."

"She seemed pretty upset."

"At first, she thought you might join us. She liked the idea actually. Suppose I did too, just a little." He grinned. "I tried to explain that you weren't comp-mod, and it wouldn't ..." He clasped his hands together. "Well, that set her off. When she sensed you and then saw you, she understood. She sent as much. To be honest, I think she was jealous." His smile broadened into a guilty, lustful, and quite attractive smile.

Kate did not return the smile, however. Her jealousy subsided rapidly and took with it most of her energy, leaving her tired and a bit shaken from her day's adventure. She muttered, "How did she sense me?"

"The comp-sys. Sensors in ..."

"Right, OK."

His smile disappeared and his face softened with concern. "So where have you been? Are ya alright?"

Kate told him about her day in a positive, upbeat tone, as if she had been a tourist on vacation, but she couldn't keep up the façade. Suddenly, she broke down crying and told him that she was lost – not geographically, she had known where she was – but she felt like she was in someone else's terrible dream, like she was suddenly dropped on an alien planet, no one would talk to her, no one could see her, it was like everyone was in a trance, robots, zombies, aliens, whatever.

Conlin pulled her to him and held her tight. "Let's sit and have some tea. I'll try to explain." Kate agreed and collapsed onto his sofa. "Everyone you saw today, they were mobiling. Basically, it's kind of a transport mode. I think it's amazing, actually. Whenever I'm away, I really notice how much time it saves and how much exercise ..."

"I don't understand, Conlin. You're like a PTV?"

"Sort of, it does use some of the same technology, actually. Let's see. What happens is the comp-sys takes care of basic navigation and transportation functions while the person is doing something else."

Kate interrupted: "What else? They couldn't see or hear me."

"Kate, their conscious minds were focused elsewhere, on other functions or tasks. There are a lot of things you can do you know. You've only so much time and attention to devote to various things."

"What things?"

"They could've been talking to others on the network, watching a vid, working on research, on solving a complex problem, or just being elsewhere." He paused. Kate still looked doubtful. "Look, Kate, when going from home to work or to the store or wherever, people can choose to delegate rudimentary processes or tasks to the comp-sys so they can do more important, more productive or more enjoyable higher level activities."

Kate interrupted abruptly, "You have a choice?"

"Yes, of course."

"But no one saw me. Not a single person. No one chose the real world."

"What do you mean?"

"Conlin, you live in such a beautiful city, such natural beauty, wonderful architecture, the streets themselves. I honestly don't see what could be more important than seeing the sky, the world you travel in, seeing other people."

"You don't understand because you're a bio-mod."

Kate pulled away from him. "What is that supposed to mean? I'm not smart enough to comprehend the idea that all of those comp-mod drones are either working for the Queen Bee or off in some LaLaLand of fairy tale make-believe rather than living in this world?"

"Huh? No, that is definitely not what I meant. You're smart, just not a comp-mod. You don't experience what we experience. You're right that we tend to delegate. We don't choose to do it ourselves, to navigate and so on. We can, I assure you. We have the choice. But we don't exercise it. We don't need to or want to, I guess. There are just better things to do with our minds. It's hard to explain."

Kate shrugged. "I suppose it would save a lot of time. From a research perspective, more time to learn and think."

"Exactly."

She shook her head. "I'm still not buying it. They moved like machines, together, like networked PTVs."

He looked surprised. "What's wrong with that?"

"Just drones, being controlled."

"Am I just a drone?" Conlin asked.

"No, you're different."

"No, I'm not, Kate." His voice was clear, and his tone adamant, but he was calm and not loud. "I'm like them; they're like me. We're comp-mods, and we have these things in us," he pointed to the marks above his ears, "and the comp-sys provides us with opportunities, and we tend to take advantage of them, me included. But I'm not a drone, and neither is my sister, or even Ayana."

"What do you feel now?" Kate had shifted her tone to sound more like her father. Calm and slow.

"Huh? What do you mean?"

In the same tone, she asked, "Are you on the comp-sys? Are you doing other things right now?"

"No. I mean, yes, I'm connected to the comp-sys but only in a very light, sort of passive way. I'm not engaged."

"Why not? I mean, do you want to be?"

"No. Why do you ask?"

"Why not? Is it pulling you? Tempting you?"

"There isn't a Queen. We're not bees, Kate. There is no 'it' to pull or tempt me."

"Of course there is." She hesitated and then explained. "The comp-sys, or the, how did you put it, the opportunities it provides to do higher level things. Surely there are higher level things to do than talking with me, right?"

"Ah, I see what you're getting at. No, I'm not pulled or tempted. But I see your point. And yes, to be honest, there are opportunities. I could engage and do all sorts of things, ranging from working on my reports to participating in a massive sporting event. I could meet with friends and family and thousands of others and do all sorts of things. But none of it compares with this, nothing rivals, being with you."

Her face lit up. "That's why you're different, Conlin." She'd come full circle. "The others, the other comp-mods wouldn't make the same choice, right? They wouldn't even understand it, especially if they knew I was a bio-mod." She stepped closer to him.

"I guess I am different because I do love you." He brushed her hair back with his left hand, looked in her eyes, and smiled. "But I don't think that makes me unique. I think others could and would and probably do make this choice. Isn't that what started you on this quest, what brought us together? Wasn't it two others like us?"

Kate pictured Nicola touching her nose to Adam's nose while Joseph stood close smiling. "Yes, it was."

***

California wine was much better. Kate enjoyed her second glass after dinner. Conlin sat next to her on the sofa. They had not spoken much during dinner. Kate had thanked Conlin for putting it together while she showered. He had explained how most of the food had been grown locally. But that was all. They ate without talking, still drained from their earlier conversation.

Kate wasn't satisfied. Talking with Conlin should've changed her outlook, but it hadn't, at least not substantially. It was nice to know that they had choices, but she couldn't get beyond the fact that they didn't really seem to choose. One must have the will to exercise autonomy, and so their apparent autonomy seemed illusory.

At least she was with him. She nudged closer to Conlin as they sipped their wine. "Ayana was beautiful." Instant regret--Why did I say that?

"Yes. She is. And extremely intelligent. She's an expert on thoughtbases."

"Thoughtbase?"

"Well, the idea, which is still being developed to an operational level, as I understand it, is to construct a system for massive personalized storage of express thoughts. Basically, a complex database optimized for a range of different conscious and subconscious thoughts. I think memory is one of the categories she's most focused on."

"Why?"

"Well, it could be used for lots of things. Probably useful for improving the interactions each person has with the comp-sys and with others. But also, I think it would be useful for interacting with yourself, with your own thoughts and memories, your past selves, your unrealized dreams of future selves, and so on. Pretty interesting, but the details are beyond me really." He shook his head. "Anyway, I don't really want to talk about her. I'm much more interested in being with you." He looked into her eyes and smiled.

She smiled back. He was beautiful. Why hadn't she noticed before? His light blue eyes and soft tan face were framed in curly blond, and when he smiled, her eyes were drawn to him. She breathed deeply as her body began to react. Deep inside her, she felt a strong, building desire. She swallowed as her mouth came alive, wanting to touch him, to taste him. She shifted on the sofa so she could reach him with her lips. Their lips touched lightly at first and then she pressed them harder against his. He welcomed her, lips opening slightly, arms reaching around her to hold her close.

Part of her wanted to give in to the hunger rising within her, but another part hesitated and resisted the impulse, reminding her of who she was and her past, the loss of control. Their mouths opened, and their hands wandered. She felt herself slipping, being swept away in the flood. He pulled his head back for a moment and suddenly kissed her neck, nuzzling his head between her shoulder and ear. "Conlin," escaped her, "I love you."

The sex was wonderful, different from what she'd expected. Throughout their lovemaking, Kate somehow kept her hormones in check and avoided the chaotic intensity and extreme hallucinations that had troubled her in the past. It hadn't gone on for hours either. The relief was as good as the pleasure. Conlin seemed content. They laid together on the sofa, and he seemed sleepy, almost dazed. She looked at his eyes and for a moment, he was gone.

"Conlin, hey! Are you alright?"

"Huh? Yeah, I'm fine."

"What are you thinking about now?" Kate asked. She felt jealous and a little scared.

"Nothing. I'm just happy to be here with you."

"Are you being tempted by the Queen?"

"Queen Kate, yes, absolutely. Darn temptress, devilishly beautiful clone. Always flirting, pulling at me with those gorgeous green eyes. Mmmm, I can't help myself. I want more." Apparently, he did. So did Kate.

The second time was also wonderful, although less intense than the first. When they first had sex, they didn't think about what they were doing or how to please each other. It was a raw hunger that drove them. That same hunger still drove them, but Kate found herself thinking about what to do to please Conlin. It was more experimental. Each of them explored the other and, at the same time, themselves.

Afterwards, as they rested together, Kate wondered whether it had been good for Conlin. They had both climaxed, and she knew he enjoyed it. But somehow doubt crept in. That dazed look on his face haunted her. It was the only time he'd ever looked dead.

"What's wrong, Kate?"

"Nothing."

"Was it me? Did I do something wrong?"

"No, that's not it. The sex was delightful. I loved it. I love you." She smiled.

He didn't buy it. "You're not saying what's on your mind. I can see that you're thinking about something. Your eyebrows crease."

"They do not."

"Sure they do, Kate. Ever since I met you, I noticed. Now what's wrong?"

"Your eyes. They had that vacant look, after the first time we had sex."

"Well, OK, for a second, maybe, I had to completely disconnect. I hadn't before we started; it just happened so fast. But I did as soon as you asked about the Queen."

"But what was happening? What happens when you, when comp-mods have sex? Is it different?"

"Yes and no. The physical sex is obviously the same, although there is a range of brain functions that are enhanced. But I experienced that with you. I mean, it's part of how I function, I guess."

"You mean your senses were enhanced through a comp-modification?"

"Yes, exactly. It's all mediated by the brain. Sight, smell, touch, they're strong during sex. You were amazing." She could see he was getting excited just thinking of her.

She smiled. "But that doesn't explain the daze. I have to say, it scares me to see you dead."

"What? Dead? Stop saying that."

"Dazed, with vacant eyes. You know."

"Well, comp-mod sex progresses in stages. Coupling physically as we just discussed shifts to coupling in a two-person network, a binary system."

"Like you and Ayana would be your own comp-sys?"

"Uh, yes, I guess you could put it that way. That's one stage, and then it goes to higher stages, broader networks.

Anyway, we don't need to get into this. I disconnected, and I always will when we, you know, I've set the default. Don't worry, Kate. I won't leave you to join the comp-sys. I promise. I don't want to, ever. I want to be with you, and only you."

"OK, sure. I'm not saying you would or," she paused to think and then went on, "I'm just wondering what it's like, what you like."

"I like you, plain and simple."

Kate didn't want to continue the conversation. She loved Conlin and trusted him, but she couldn't displace the memory of his vacant eyes.

TWENTY-FIVE:

DATASWIM

San Francisco, California. August 2154.

To put it lightly, they humored her. The nurses were less condescending than the doctors, but all of them treated her like a child and a novelty, as if a human scientist was hard to fathom. It was hard to stomach their arrogance. Kate wanted to lecture them. Humans were sophisticated. They had very advanced technology that didn't depend on selling your soul. She could remind them of what they were before they merged with machines. But she held it in. Not worth it. Perhaps their arrogance was no different than hers, or at least, what hers had been before she went to St. Louis. Despite the aloofness, they treated her well. They let her observe. They answered her questions. If only they didn't treat her like an idiot.

A heavily wrinkled doctor, Doctor Hanssen, paid her a little more attention than the others. He seemed to be attracted to her. He never flirted overtly but his eyes wandered, scanning her body and getting caught in a short loop before having his attention pulled away. He smiled often. It made her uncomfortable, but she could play it to her advantage.

"Doctor Hanssen, I'm glad you've agreed to meet with me. I know you're very busy."

"It's my pleasure. Since you're on my schedule, I can give you my full attention." He smiled and suddenly seemed more fully present in the room, not on the comp-sys. His eyes focused intensely on the left side of her neck and drifted slowly down. "We're very intrigued with you. You've come all this way to learn from us." His eyes slowly crossed her breasts. She coughed, which he ignored. "A very intelligent decision. Surprising. I thought you all were in hiding, overwhelmed by conspiracy theories and afraid of technology." He returned his gaze to her green eyes. "But you've overcome that. We've much we can teach you." She felt his predatory advances but only smiled. A bio-mod would've known her internal disgust immediately. He was blissfully unaware.

"Yes, well, I think that's right," she said, her voice as calm as text. "I'm here to investigate infant mortality rates and learn about how the comp-mod community has driven the rate down so substantially."

"The advances we've made in medicine and technology are quite impressive, especially when compared with the standard of care in your hospitals." Again, his eyes wandered while he spoke. "I'm sure you do the best you can. Our prenatal data systems alone provide an incredible predictive map. We've been able to head off most complications that you probably encounter regularly."

"I see." She let her slight smile vanish. "Well, not really. I've not seen any of the data."

"You don't have the capability to interface directly. With the system or the data." He looked up and said, mostly to himself, "How might we deal with that?" His eyes fixed on her forehead as he contemplated the question.

Kate bit her lip because she almost referred to a database technology that bio-mods used.

He returned abruptly, "We'll figure it out. I've some ideas being examined." He looked back into her eyes. "You'd like to see the infant mortality data as well?" She nodded. He continued, "We've yet to compile a comprehensive dataset. We've some data on humans, but it's incomplete. I'd like to know what you think of it. We haven't obtained data from the bio-mons."

"The what?"

"Bio-mons, you know, bio-monsters. The animals. They kill off large numbers of their infants in experiments, running clinical trials in utero, on infants and even on children. I bet the rate is an order of magnitude higher than ours. All for the sake of what? Some twisted notion of perfection? To play God?" He was getting agitated, and so was Kate, but he didn't notice. Thank goodness he couldn't sense her biochemical feedback. He went on. "It disgusts me to think how they've perverted the human race."

"I agree." Kate clenched her hands together and forced herself to say. "Fricken animals. It disgusts me too. Of course, that's why I'm here. I don't think they've anything to teach that's worth learning." She suppressed the bile rising to the base of her throat and forced a smile, a seductive we're-on-the same-wavelength smile.

His attraction to her grew. He nodded and stepped closer to her. She stepped back. "Kate, I can help you. Go talk with Doctor Jon Rhavin. He is one of my old students, from a decade ago. He runs the hospital's data center. He should be able to get you what you need."

"Thank you very much, Doctor Hanssen. I will." She stepped forward as he turned toward the door. Her body relaxed.

"We'll get together next week to discuss your progress. I will free up some time in the evening. We'll have dinner. OK?"

"Sure. That sounds good," she lied.

He left, and she went to the bathroom. She felt like screaming at herself, like she'd committed a terrible crime. Something was wrong. She looked at herself in the mirror. Beads of sweat gathered, readying for a race. Her head felt light, and her stomach pushed everything in it toward her head, as if to fill the vacuum. The sensation was new. She vomited powerfully in the sink. She knew what was happening as it churned and rose, as her stomach muscles squeezed. But it was awful and scary. When it ended, she took water from the sink, swished, and spit. She washed her face with the cold water for a minute or two. When she finished, she felt much better.

Kate didn't feel good about what she'd said or how she'd manipulated Hanssen, but she was satisfied with the results. Best to head straight to the data center and find Doctor

Rhavin. In the hallway, two nurses walked by, and when Kate asked them for directions, they ignored her, as if they were mobiling, even though they seemed to see and hear her. She wandered for a minute until she came upon another nurse. To get his attention, she reached out and touched his arm. Startled, the annoyed nurse pointed her in the right direction, "At the end of the hall." The data center was not open to the public, but the door slid open when she arrived. A young woman met her. "Hello?" She stared at Kate with a blank expression.

"I'm here to see Doctor Rhavin. Is he available?"

"No. He's fully immersed." They stared at each other for ten seconds. Kate tilted her head, chin down, eyebrows up.

The woman said, "You're waiting for me to say more. Why?"

Kate asked, "Can you check his schedule or notify him that …"

"Give me a moment." She continued to stand in front of Kate, facing her, but her eyes glazed slightly. It wasn't a full vacant stare. Just distracted, a flash away and then back. "He has no time today. Come back Monday at 11:15."

***

Conlin made her dinner. She savored each bite while he sat across the table, tapping his fingers. He'd asked her about her first week at the hospital, but she shook her head and said, "After dinner. I'm famished."

"Well?," he asked.

"It's excellent. I haven't had anything like this. What exactly is it?" She put another piece in her mouth.

"Halibut with fennel and shaved orange peel. I'm glad you like it. I really missed seafood in St. Louis. And oranges too."

Kate nodded. "I can see why."

"Alright, so tell me about your day, your week really. You haven't said much."

"I wanted to let it sink in. The hospital is different. It's so quiet. I think everyone is on the system, communicating that way."

"Right. It's easier and quieter."

"Well, yeah, but it's more than that. It was like when I was out walking and everyone was mobiling."

"You mean when they moved through the hallways? People mobiled?"

"I don't know. I don't think so. But that's not what I meant. It's the way they communicated with me, how they interacted, or couldn't interact normally, I guess. People accepted me and seemed willing to help, some more than others. But even those who tried to help, they were still rude or, I don't know, incapable of relating."

Conlin open his mouth to say something, but refrained.

"You know, it reminds me off Joseph. When Fredric and I first met him, shook his hand, he just seemed off. No biochemical feedback, I think. I figured that later, but didn't pick it up at the time."

"How is that the same?"

"Well, I felt the same way when talking to most of the people at the hospital, but it was much stronger. I didn't get any biochemical feedback from them, but I felt like they were equally at a loss, missing feedback from me. Maybe because I'm not a comp-mod?"

"Ah, yes, that's right. We rely on simple relational programs to manage transactions ..."

"Transactions? Is that what you call conversations? Personal interactions?"

"Yes, I suppose. It depends on the context."

Kate rolled her eyes. People always pulled that bullshit move when they were caught but didn't want to admit it. It depends. It's contextual. Conversations aren't transactions, plain and simple.

"What's the big deal? Is it really any different than your biochemical feedback?"

"Yes, there's a big difference. Our conversations are never just transactions. Biochemical feedback enhances perception and deepens our social relationships."

"Same for us."

"I don't buy it. The comp-sys feedback seems to do more, to automate, or initiate scripts."

"Sometimes, sure. But ..."

"Conlin, so far, no one has been like you. No one."

"Well, of course not, I am exceptional, after all." He smiled and leaned toward her.

"No, I mean it."

He leaned back, sat up straight, and put his hands behind his head. "I do too." He took a very deep breath, held it for three seconds, and let it out slowly. "I am different. It's actually a rare skill that I have. I can relate effectively with other humans without mediation by comp-sys technology. It's why I'm able to work in the Midwest, live among the unmodifieds. Most other comp-mods couldn't pull it off. Not without a lot of practice. Even then, I'm not so sure."

Kate stared at him, a soft smile emerging.

"You know when I notice it most?"

She shook her head.

"When I first return to San Fran. It's hard to reintegrate without feeling the loss of ... I don't know what to call it."

"Reality?"

"No." His eyes met hers, and after ten seconds, he said, "Authenticity."

***

Kate gagged upon seeing Doctor Rhavin; her stomach rebelled. Fortunately, he was oblivious to her visceral reaction. Outside of vids, Kate had never seen such a hideously ugly human being. Of course, bio-mods were engineered aesthetically, and her sense of beauty was probably distorted, but something like this hadn't seemed possible. Among the unmodified humans, she'd noticed variations that many bio-mods would consider unattractive, even ugly. Noses that were too big or small; uneven, disproportional and asymmetric features. She'd found some variations refreshing, if not aesthetically appealing. But this was different.

Rhavin was grotesque. The middle aged man had a huge bulging forehead with strands of black hair pulled from the top and sides and pressed flat in greasy snake patterns. The top and sides were thick curly black, also coated in a film of grease. His dark bushy eyebrows hung over bulbous brown eyes, one of which seemed larger than the other. His pig nose was dominated by two cavernous nostrils out of which spilled more black hair that flowed into a thick mat of curls that covered the bottom half of his face and neck.

He smiled, a thin courtesy. That is when Kate noticed he had a mouth. "Ms. Genet. What can I do for you? I've only a minute." Kate shivered.

"Hello. I'm here from St. Louis."

"I know. I know your background, and why you're here, to learn about the maternity ward, observe our medical procedures. But what can I do for you?"

"I'd like to see all of your data on infant mortality." She tried to maintain eye contact but found her eyes drifting toward his mouth. Why doesn't he shave it off or at least trim it? What was he hiding underneath all of that fur?

"I'm sorry. You can't. You must know this. It's medical data. You're a doctor, right? It's not public." His voice grew louder and sharper, his irritation growing.

"Doctor Hanssen sent me to you. He said you'd help." Again, she returned her gaze to meet his.

"He did, you say." His eyes went stale, not blank, still focused, but there was no movement in the eyes or even on his face. Then he was back. He changed so rapidly that it was hard for her to mark. The switch was almost automatic, and Kate wondered, only half-seriously, whether he got an instruction from the Queen. He warmed considerably. He even smiled, this time for real.

But he still spoke robotically. "Go ahead. Tap in."

"I don't understand. How can I tap in?"

"My apologies. Of course, you cannot. You're incapable of seeing and manipulating the data directly in your mind." Frustration contorted his face as he spit out, "Do you need a printout? Some nice color graphics that you can carry off with you?"

She suppressed a laugh at his somewhat human outburst and interrupted. "Do you have a computer monitor or something with a screen that I can use?"

"We do." He stopped, processing. "But it's not really designed for you. We use it when someone is having problems with their implants or comp-sys connection because of a medical emergency."

"That sounds fine." She paused. "You know what, why don't you just assume I'm one of those patients? You know, a comp-mod injured and in need of some extra help."

To her surprise, his demeanor shifted again. "Sure, Ms. Genet. That's fine." The seemingly genuine smile was back. "You can get started today if you wish."

"Excellent. I'm ready whenever you are."

"My assistant will get you set up. I've got to get back to work." As he rushed off, she waited. Did he even realize how awkward he was? Their conversation had been so disjointed and obviously mediated. Although it ended well, it left a bad taste with her, a fakeness like the uncanny valley that made twenty-first century robots too creepy for mainstream. People couldn't handle a robot that mimicked humans so well. It was like the bots had come too close and thereby posed a challenge to authentic humans. Somehow Rhavin's momentary lapses into being normal made it much worse.

Within an hour, Kate was set up with an interface. It was a familiar technology, a virtual screen that she could manipulate physically and audibly in the air in front of her. She used her fingers to move it around, and she spoke commands, search terms, and notes to record. For an hour or so, she struggled to figure out how to initiate tasks and functions. There were no menus or program lists. Finally, she asked the assistant about a menu; the woman had no idea what Kate was talking about.

"How do I open up the database? How do I visualize the data? I'm not sure how to operate this."

"The system is designed for comp-mods. We don't rely on menus. Just think about what you want or query for available opportunities if you want to swim. Since this interface is designed for a patient with some disconnection, it responds to auditory stimuli rather than thoughts. OK?"

"I guess. Thanks."

Kate experimented for hours, but she didn't get very far. She spoke her thoughts, or rather she said what she wanted, "infant mortality data" -- but what she got back, what she saw in front her made no sense. Somehow the data was represented as light and dark, shades of grey, colors. She called out for labels but nothing happened. She thought, and spoke, in terms of the categories and menus and database design principles that she'd encountered throughout her life. But these meant nothing here. It brought vertigo, a lack of control that Kate hated. For a moment, she recalled room 542, the chaos. But it passed quickly as another idea pulled on her attention, a sense of opportunity, an appreciation of power and possibility.

The comp-mods lived in the data and experienced it differently. They must do research very differently. Curiosity and envy drove Kate to want something she'd never contemplated before. Could she get a comp modification, one that would allow her to experience the data as they did? A chill ran across the surface of her skin.

***

"Doctor Rhavin, thank you for meeting with me." Kate regulated her breathing to manage her excitement and anxiety.

Rhavin was busy. "Not a problem, but I do need to manage a few tasks. Rest assured that you have a sufficient amount of my attention."

"That's fine." She didn't mind because it allowed her to avoid eye contact as she sat on one side of his desk and he on the other with a half dozen screens in between them. "The interface technology you've allowed me to use is quite amazing, but I'm still having difficulties working with the data. It's difficult to understand, to see what it all means. I can't really analyze it as I would normally."

"It's not surprising. Comp-mods live in data from birth. The data center manages immense amounts of data along only very broad field lines, time and space and other macro-variables. We rely on distributed search and computation capabilities for various tasks. The entire system must be completely foreign to you."

"I'm curious." She pressed ahead with her plan. "What do you do to help injured comp-mod recover? I assume they don't use the interface technology forever."

"No, of course not. It's a terribly poor substitute. Why do you ask?"

"Suppose a patient needed to be able to swim in the data, more than anything else. In fact, suppose that was the only objective. What would you do?"

"That's a good question. Usually, integration with the comp-sys is a priority and the basic mods are reintroduced as a system." He stopped multitasking and turned toward her. His eyes brightened as he pondered the puzzle. "But if we weren't worried about that, we might use the ocular lens mod." His eyes went blank as he conferred with others. "Yes, that would do it. That should work. You'd be able to see, understand, yes, integration with the field data as well." He stopped verbalizing his thoughts. Kate waited for a moment, and then she coughed lightly. He didn't respond, so she coughed loudly. It caught his attention.

"This isn't my field. I run the data center, not the mod center. You should see Doctor Jung on the fifth floor. She works to get people reintegrated. I'll let her know you need an ocular modification only. This is best kept between us for now. She'll understand once she meets you."

"Will do. Thank you." This was the first step. Was she really going down this path? Why not? The prospect of getting an ocular lens to modify her vision seemed pretty straightforward, not so different from 21st century lens or even 20th century glasses.

***

"You're from St. Louis?" Doctor Jung was in her fifties, starting to grey. She seemed young at heart with bright blue eyes and oddly welcoming personality. Kate liked her immediately.

"Yes, I'm here to learn what I can about how comp-mod hospitals function. I spent most of my time in the maternity ward, but Doctor Hansenn and Doctor Rhavin have given me some help with other areas too."

"Excellent. I think it's a good idea. There is so much knowledge we could share. I imagine we've made many advances that your community hasn't even heard about given our lack of communication." She shrugged and then smiled. "You know, you're the first unmodified human I've met."

"Really?" Her voice suggested surprise, even though Kate wasn't surprised at all. Playing naïve seemed to work well with comp-mods.

"Yes. Do many of you come out here? I always thought you all feared mods and that was why you stay in the god-awful heat."

"Well, that's true of many humans, I suppose, but not all of us." Kate thought of Gina and Chief Jenks. "No, many of us aren't fearful of comp-mods. We've just adapted to the heat and live our lives where we grew up, where our families are, you understand."

"Yeah, that makes perfect sense." She looked at Kate like a best friend's approving older sibling, as if she'd passed some test and a bond had been set. "So what can I do for you?"

"I have been working with the interface system used for injured comp-mods, people who've lost their connection. I've been using it in the data center. It hasn't worked very well. I cannot understand or analyze the data. Doctor Rhavin told me to come see you and ask for an ocular modification. He thought it would solve my problem."

"I see." She froze, her eyes vacant for five seconds. It took getting used to, but Kate had anticipated it this time and so it didn't bother her at all. Kate just stared into her eyes and admired the soft sky blue.

Jung continued. "Yes, it would. It would help you. But we haven't modded an adult human in, well, I haven't ever, and it has to be decades since anyone else has. Running this through the admin channels will take a long time, I suspect."

"Can we avoid that?"

"I suppose if we only use the ocular lens mods on a temporary basis. They set over an extended period of time, normally a few days. If we allowed you to use them for a few hours while in the data center and then removed them, it wouldn't really be a full modification and so maybe we could ..." She stopped verbalizing her thoughts.

Kate waited a moment and then said, "That would be fine with me. I just need to be able to access the data for my research."

***

Kate realized that she'd been correct. The comp-mods did research very differently. They were so close to the data. The temporary lens she slid onto her eyeballs felt uncomfortable at first, but she got used to it quickly. The data center came alive. It was no longer lights, darks, shades, and colors. It was a raw, easy to manipulate, environment, almost a dream that she shaped with her own thoughts as she searched for relevant streams of data. She was immersed in it; she swam in the data pool throughout the room. She manipulated with her mind, but she also used her hands and even the rest of her body; she spoke, unsure whether the words had any effect or were simply reassuring.

Kate was struck by a strange sensation of intimacy. She understood the data environment as a part of her, as if she flowed into and was a part of it. She knew and perhaps even felt the many different overlapping categories that applied to various data. She immediately saw data that she desired to see and manipulated it with her own scientific instincts and curiosity. The infant mortality data formed into a constellation of events that she could explore in different ways, by diving and zooming into specific events or by shaping them along contours of similar features. She sought out connected threads within the constellation.

She issued commands to execute tasks, run statistical regressions, visualize the data in different formats and displays. Now, she could impose her categories and database designs, but doing so was incredibly artificial. So much actual data about reality would be lost if she forced her preconceived models onto the data, like forcing a square peg into a round hole. She gave up on that effort. It was better to feel, experience, and live within the data in all its complexity.

It was oddly liberating and enjoyable, intoxicating in a way only a scientist could fully appreciate. Kate imagined how she could use these tools in her own research. Imagine swimming in the genomic data, the possibilities!

Did the comp-mods live their entire lives swimming in data like this? Were they always manipulating their world by projecting their thoughts and constructing their perceived reality? Could they project their thoughts to construct each other's perceived reality? Imagine the potential conflict. There would have to be a meta-control, rules about what could be done with respect to others. But the idea of manipulation of constructed worlds brought Kate back to what always bothered her most about the comp-mods, the machine in the background or whoever controlled it, or simply, the Queen.

These thoughts frightened her, brought her back to the task at hand. She examined the data for hours. The infant mortality rate in this hospital was almost the same as at the bio-mod hospital. Deaths pre-birth or even at birth were incredibly rare, about the same rate as the bio-mods and less than the humans. This was incredibly impressive. The bio-mods should've been much farther ahead in the race to eliminate such deaths. Doctor Hanssen was justifiably proud of the prenatal data system he mentioned.

She put aside, essentially in one corner of the room, all of the data related to infant mortality. She'd need it again. But first she'd look at the data on allergic reactions. The comp-mods had allergies that were comparable with the humans, and they were able to identify and manage them effectively. Deaths from allergic reactions were incredibly rare. Kate looked for data concerning infant deaths caused by allergic reactions. She found none.

This was a relief. It was possible that there were no mixed couples who gave birth in comp-mod hospitals. It was also possible that the Biomen's drug cocktail was the cause of Adam's death, and since it was not used in comp-mod hospitals, no infants died. Kate could explain Adam's death. She could help other mixed couples avoid the cocktail. Mixed couples would be better off giving birth in comp-mod hospitals after all. Kate took a deep breath.

Her stomach felt empty, though she knew it wasn't, and her neck ached. She should have been satisfied, but there was a familiar itch, that nagging splinter that begged to be fully extricated from the flesh. She was pulled back toward the infant mortality data.

Kate siphoned the data on deaths within the first 48 hours. There were some, a lower number than in the bio-mod hospitals, but still significant to Kate. She tried to pull up the individual patient records, but she couldn't fully explore the events; there was some constraint. Apparently, patient privacy was protected. Still, from the data she pulled, she knew enough. There were sudden deaths that occurred within the first 48 hours, and it appeared that the deaths occurred within hours of modification procedures, initial comp-chip implants. The official medical explanation was heart failure, not an allergic reaction. It had to be the same phenomenon though. The numbers were too close.

The conclusion slammed her. There were mixed couples hiding in comp-mod territory, and their children also suffered cruel deaths within 48 hours of birth. Kate sunk down and sat on the floor in the middle of the room flooded with data. She held her breath and stared at the ceiling, searching for an answer. There were more mixed couples than anyone would suspect. The number of infant deaths alone proved this to her. But there must have been so many more. Most mixed couples would stay underground and avoid having children. What could be causing the babies to die? A genetic defect? An incompatibility that naturally emerged as the two groups evolved? She worried that both communities had no clue what was happening to the mixed couples and their children. The medical communities offered plausible explanations for the rare events, but they were based on incomplete information. The doctors had no idea that the couples were mixed, and so they couldn't do anything to save the babies. Kate exhaled. She would. She'd do whatever it took.

Twenty-Six:

Modification

Denver, Colorado. August 2154.

STAY PUT. THE SPOOK WILL TAKE CARE OF
HER.

I don't understand. If she'll be taken care of, why do we
need to stay.

SHE IS AN ASSET. ONE OF OUR MOST
PROMISING SCIENTISTS. HE'LL EXTRACT HER.
WHEN THE TIME IS RIGHT. YOU'LL BRING HER
BACK.

Understood.

San Francisco, California. August 2154.

Kate rushed home after spending hours in the data center.
Removing the ocular mods had been a simple procedure, but
it left her dizzy for ten minutes. Doctor Jung had been kind.
After removing the lenses, she asked Kate some questions
about the experience and then told her to get some rest.

Exhausted, Kate intended to walk home leisurely, but she
ended up jogging. The walkways were filled with mobiling

comp-mods, heading in both directions. She tried to go with the flow heading towards Conlin's house, but she still felt like a fish swimming upstream. Her rhythm was different, more variable and less stiff.

When she reached Conlin's house, she was a sweaty mess. He was waiting for her with a glass of water.

"Kate, what's wrong?"

"I'm so glad to be back here, to be with you." She took the glass and drained it. "Thanks. We've got to talk."

"Sure, let's head inside."

Kate told him everything she'd learned. She didn't say anything about using the ocular lens mods. She wasn't sure why she held this back, and doing so made her feel guilty, but her findings seemed more pressing.

He wasn't surprised. "Kate, this is what you expected, right?"

"I don't know. I guess. I suppose I thought it might be happening here too, although I don't know, part of me hoped it would just be the Biomen cocktail. You know, maybe it was the cause."

"Well, it is, right?"

"In bio-mod hospitals, sure. I think so. But not here. Here it's the comp-mod implants, I guess. I don't understand the mechanism exactly. It must be genetic. The infants have inherited genes from both parents, and that combination leads to problems. The doctors in Boston might have had it diagnosed correctly, as an allergic reaction. My best guess is that the genetic inheritance from mixed couples leads to a hypersensitivity to the modification technologies, and the infants are so fragile that they die from an extreme anaphylactic reaction. I don't fully understand it though. Figuring it out will require more research. But I don't think that actually matters."

"What do you mean?"

"What matters is that it's entirely avoidable, if only the doctors knew, if only the couples didn't hide. You understand? We could have saved Adam and the others. I mean, if Nicola and Joseph hadn't pretended to both be bio-mods, Adam would have lived. The doctors wouldn't have given him the cocktail. Same is true for the others, I suspect. It's a serious problem only for the children of mixed couples, but if no one knows about the risk, they can't avoid it."

"Yes, I suppose." His face contorted with worry. "Kate, there are other considerations. What if the hospitals wouldn't admit them, or if the doctors wouldn't deliver in the first place?"

"What? That's ridiculous."

"No, not at all. Look, there are many reasons why the mixed couples hide. Look at us."

Kate nodded.

"I'm not disagreeing with you in principle. I'm only suggesting that this is complicated. We need to be careful, to think about how best to proceed."

"I don't see what else we can do."

"Besides what exactly? What is your plan, Kate?"

"We have to publicize what we know."

"To whom? How? Think about it. Are you ready to come out and admit you're a bio-mod? Here in San Fran? I don't think that would be a good idea. You're not authorized to be here. You don't have papers. Besides, people would treat you very differently, as we've discussed. Not everyone, but enough."

"I know."

"And it's not just about you. All the others hiding, they might not be ready, and you know, depending on how you publicize what you've found out, there could be repercussions, a lot of pressure. It could lead to more scrutiny. I don't know. I haven't thought it through fully either."

"I understand, and I agree that we should be careful. Maybe we should talk to someone at the hospital?"

"Let me think about it. I might know someone who can help us. But in the meantime, we should keep it quiet. You should continue to learn what you can at the hospital."

"Agreed."

***

Kate continued to go to the hospital and spend a few hours in the maternity ward. She tried to maintain the same pattern of observation she'd practiced over the past few months in the various wards she'd visited. She stuck to the plan and then, during her free time, she'd visit the data center to take another swim in the data. Doctor Jung seemed excited to help with the ocular mods, and even Doctor Rhavin observed her and seemed intrigued. Kate's genetic expertise led her to look for patterns that the comp-mods hadn't deemed important. Doctor Rhavin increased the scope of Kate's data access privileges.

Kate tried to figure out how the bio-mod half of a mixed couple could hide in comp-mod territory. Joseph had a much easier time in Boston, she suspected. Humans and comp-mods could pass themselves off as bio-mods relatively easily. There wasn't a comp-sys monitor assessing your membership credentials. It was different here. She hadn't met anyone else claiming to be human, and everyone treated her like such a novelty. Of course, it could be simple statistics, just a very small population spread out and probably hiding in less populated areas. But Kate thought of another possibility. Maybe the bio-mods joined the comp-mod community. Maybe they got comp-modifications. Why not? She'd been using one effectively.

Most comp-mods thought bio-mods were incapable of comp-modification. Conlin had explained this to her. Most comp-mods, even those who didn't think of bio-mods as degenerate animals, thought bio-mods were incapable of comp-modification because, as Conlin put it, "they'd altered their brains and basic biochemistry" or as Kate translated, "bio-mods have inferior brains and they've poisoned their bodies." Although she didn't belabor the point with Conlin, Kate spent a lot of time thinking about it while at the hospital. The whole line of reasoning made no sense. The demeaning myth might have been convenient because it allowed comp-mods to elevate themselves over bio-mods, but it was mere propaganda, probably generated by the Queen, and it was simply untrue. Bio-mod brains had evolved along superior paths for generations, increasing memory, cognitive function, even emotional intelligence—there was simply no basis for a claim of inferiority. If comp-modifications harness, tap into, or augment human brains, then it should work for bio-modified brains and get even more advanced. This was Kate's experience, after all. And bio-mod bodies were not poisoned; all medical data on bio-mod health suggested otherwise.

The more she thought about it, the more she convinced herself that bio-mods could get comp-modifications, and they probably did. At least, the bio-mod half of mixed couples living in comp-mod territory must have done so. It was the best way to blend in, to fit in.

She investigated but found nothing in the data. No evidence of comp-modification of humans or bio-mods. Nonetheless, she was sure that it was happening. It made perfect sense. If a bio-mod could get the comp-modifications, she'd be able to participate in the comp-sys. For a moment, she thought of Nicola with comp-mods, and her mind wandered into dream. She saw Nicola with Joseph and Adam, alive. All three were smiling and outdoors somewhere, which distracted Kate because of bright sunlight that was so different from the hospital room.

Then the image in her mind shifted, and she saw herself instead. What if she got a full set of comp-mods? She'd be trusted by others and be able to trust Conlin unequivocally. No more doubts about that vacant stare she saw only once but couldn't forget. She could have sex with Conlin the way that he really wanted. She lingered on that last thought.

***

"You've done excellent work. The specs are being analyzed, but I'm confident we'll be able to crack their security system and inject our presence without ever being detected."

The agent nodded.

Mr. Shephard continued, "Their reliance on old systems, I mean, almost 50 years out of date by their own standards and ancient by our own, that's their Achilles' heel. It does present a challenge to crack and infiltrate, and we'll have to build a local communications sys that allows peering across units and that aggregates and communicates with our net. But those are surmountable obstacles because of your excellent work."

"Thank you, sir. It has been an interesting assignment, and frankly, my cover work, which you know is a real passion of mine, was also quite successful. I'd like to go back and continue, especially if I can be of use during the next stage."

"That will be fine. Your supervisor will coordinate the details, and then I'll sign off. You've earned it." He smiled and waited a moment. "Is there anything else to report?"

"No, sir. Well, not officially. But I do have something I'd like to bring to your attention."

"Unofficially? Cover work, then. Something about the humans? Adaptation technology?" Mr. Shephard sat on the edge of his seat, curious about the unexpected intel.

"No, it's about us and the bio-mods."

***

"Doctor Jung, I want to be a comp-mod." Her unwavering voice startled Doctor Jung, who looked surprised, scared, and dumbfounded.

"What?," she stammered.

"I want to be a comp-mod. I appreciate what you've done to help me access the data, and I've made a lot of progress with my research. But I've also seen how amazing the comp-mod technology is, how it can open up new horizons, and to be honest, I've fallen in love with someone, someone here in San Francisco."

"My goodness, I wouldn't have guessed that you'd ask for this. I'd like to help you, but I'm not sure. Let me think. It would be very interesting, but I've never modded an adult human."

"You do it for infants, and you do it for adults who've lost their connection. Can't you treat me just like an injured patient who has lost her connection?"

"I'm not sure what the hospital administrators would say. You're right. I do it for children. But I haven't heard of anyone working with adult humans in a very long time, decades probably."

"But it should work fine, as it did back then, right?"

"Sure. I think we'd have to do it offline, and it would have to be incremental. To work offline is surprisingly difficult, because every physical space has hundreds of embedded sensors that would pick up the experiment."

"I assume it has to be done here."

"Yes, absolutely. We can use the Box."

"The Box?"

"It's a room in the basement that is sensor free and off the comp-sys. Some friends of mine found it, and we use it to escape the collective and form our own little experimental network. We play some of the old school fantasy games." She smiled sheepishly and looked like a teenager. "Maybe you can join us sometime."

Kate smiled back. "Sure, why not? But let's figure this out first. When can we start?"

"Tomorrow night. I need to set up the room and obtain the mods. Should be easy enough. This is not a complicated procedure actually. Much easier than childbirth. In any event, let's meet at 7:30 in the basement, the room number is 011."

"Thank you, Doctor Jung."

"It's my pleasure. This is very exciting. Please do keep this quiet. Once we've successfully completed the procedure, no one will care much. But it will only create headaches and probably make it impossible to do if the word gets out beforehand."

"I understand."

***

That evening, Conlin and Kate were both quiet. Each apologized for being tired and expressed concern for the other. Neither said what was on their mind. They settled into bed, caressing each other and intending to make love, but sleep beckoned. Kate made one last effort before sleep took over, and Conlin happily joined. It had the makings of a quick adventure, but it grew steadily and lasted much longer. Conlin seemed surprised, as Kate grew more passionate, and that awakened him. Kate imagined something more than what they were currently doing; she imagined what it would be like to see, smell, and feel Conlin even more than she could at that moment -- and somehow, she did or at least she thought she did; she imagined what it would soon be like to establish a direct emotional and mental connection with him as they took their lovemaking to the next level -- and somehow, she did or at least that is how it felt at that moment. Conlin and Kate strove for more together, and together, they reached a different plateau that evening. Afterwards, they just looked into each other's eyes, smiling, and in love.

***

As she took the steps to the basement, Kate began to have second thoughts. She'd been quite confident about three things that motivated her decision. Now, she started to doubt them. First, she thought that the bio-mod halves of mixed couples in comp-mod territory must have hidden by becoming comp-mods, but maybe not. Perhaps there was another explanation. Maybe the parents concealed the mod history some other way, by pretending to be an injured comp-mod and thus offline. By pretending to be human. By some other technology. Who knows? Kate had no clue, and she became less confident about her initial hypothesis. Second, she thought that if she could pass as a comp-mod, then she could publicize what she'd found out. She wouldn't have to worry about reprisals. But that view now seemed naive. Somehow they'd know what she was. Third, she assumed that sex with Conlin would be much better if she became a comp-mod. It would be more of what he really wanted and had experienced throughout his life. Their wonderful sex last night oddly cut both ways, in part strengthening her belief that comp-modification would enhance everything yet in part making her wonder if she was being a little crazy. Last night had been perfect.

She recognized that her doubts were perfectly rational. This was a big step. It was the right step for her and Conlin. She could fit in here and live with him. She could handle it, no, she would love it, so long as she could retain the capacity to choose, basically, her free will, and not become a drone. She'd retain control. That was critical. She trusted Conlin. He said he always had a choice, and he'd shown her day after day, by choosing to be with her.

Her mood lightened, and she felt playful as she descended, almost dancing down the steps. "I'm returning to Santa's Workshop," she muttered, and she laughed. With each step down the stairs, Kate said "I'm a bio-mod" then "No, I'm a human" then "Now, I'm a comp-mod" then "No, really, a bio-mod" then "but basically, human" then "plus, a comp-mod." She didn't know whether to laugh or cry, but she felt like doing something to let out her emotions. She stopped and leaned against the wall to her right. She took a deep breath and resumed her descent in silence.

***

"Kate, I'm glad you're here. This is very exciting. We have this room to ourselves for at least an hour. The procedure should only take thirty minutes. You're still up for it?"

"Yes. I'm a little nervous, that's all."

"Nothing to be nervous about. All we're going to do is install four devices, two above your ears and two on your eyes." Kate blanched. "Please don't worry. The ocular chips are quite unobtrusive, as you know. We place a thin film in each eye, and the film will set within a week. That is, it will bind all on its own. During the binding process, your vision may become a little blurry or distorted for a day or so. It's hard to say. We normally implant these on infants. We have a few of them for adults as replacements in case of damage, but the adults have had the implants since day one and so they've adjusted; they're used to it. Just don't rub your eyes or try to remove them. They could come out, and then we'd have to start over. OK?"

"Sure."

"The other two chips do a lot of things, but three primary modifications are sensory enhancement, comp-sys interconnection, and a wide range of brain function management. You'll see."

"You mean, like mobiling?"

"Exactly. That's right. It will take a decent amount of training, however. You've not grown up with it. I can work with you in the evenings for about an hour, maybe three times a week."

"That would be wonderful."

"There are some other mods that I've decided to hold off on. As I said before, we'll approach this incrementally and monitor everything. I've set up a sensor network in the room so we can gather all of the data and monitor everything. This is really the only scientific experiment of its kind that I'm aware of. It's very exciting."

"Sure. Should we get started?"

***

The procedure was simple. The ocular implants were slipped on within a minute. They felt a little uncomfortable but familiar. After applying a local anesthesia, Doctor Jung did something just above her ears. It took about fifteen minutes. Kate couldn't see or feel much, except Doctor Jung's breath. She applied some type of thick ointment, like glue. "All set. It should bind and heal very quickly, within a day. And as soon as I activate your chip set, you should begin to be integrated. But first, how do you feel?"

"I feel fine." Anxious for a sudden change, she ignored the minor irritations. "When will you activate them?"

"I can do so right now, actually. The bio-brain interface technology is quite incredible. You know, I take it for granted because I'm so used to it."

Kate could care less. She wanted to interrupt and get her to move things along, but she took a slow breath to calm herself.

Doctor Jung went on. "It's remarkable. It used to take days, then it was hours, but now, it's almost instantaneous."

"How will you activate them?"

"The set itself is interconnected and has a unique frequency tag. I just need to send an activation signal. Once we do, you're on, if you know what I mean. I just want you to be ready and to tell me exactly how you feel. When you're settled, we'll establish a two-person network, and then we can communicate directly, and I can help you navigate. Are you ready?"

"No," she almost said. Her mouth was open just a little. Her tongue touched the top of her mouth, beginning the word, but then her lips closed, and she nodded assent.

***

A slow jitter buzzed in her ears, her eyes blurred like she was looking through water. Kate heard Doctor Jung breathing and speaking to her, no, her lips didn't move, she was inviting her to join, sending her thoughts. Kate didn't reply, not yet; she didn't do anything. She just allowed herself to feel, to observe, like a child sitting at the bottom of a pool, in wonder at the distorted rays of light.

Everything accelerated. Kate was thrilled by the depths and acceleration of feeling and being. Swimming in the data center had been incredible, but this was on an entirely different scale. Her senses exploded with sensitivity she couldn't comprehend. Her body thrummed with energy and, as her brain accelerated and expanded her subjective experience and understanding beyond anything she'd imagined possible, her heart accelerated and expanded, and then it stopped.

***

Kate looked up at her father. He was holding her tightly, looking down at her face. He was the happiest she's even seen him. He seemed on the verge of tears, indescribable joy pouring out of his face, his broad smile. He was elegant in his happiness. She tried to tell him how much she loved him. Nothing came out, but somehow he knew. He said, "I love you, Katie, my baby girl. You are my perfect baby girl."

Her father held her tightly. Her mother peered from the side, just beyond his arm. Love and happiness flowed from her eyes as well.

Kate knew with a sudden immediacy that was completely unfamiliar to her that this was some sort of programmed experience, a script for the dying, an opportunity to bear witness to her life; it drew on long-hidden memories that the comp-sys somehow retrieved from the deep recesses of her brain. And with this realization came another— she was going to die in less than a second. A horrible sudden death spasm was a millisecond away. She shouted in pure mental anguish that she loved them. She knew with the same immediacy and certainty that they didn't hear her.

***

Kate woke. There was a commotion she couldn't fully understand, except through an intense smell. She smelled Doctor Jung and others. The smells overwhelmed and attacked, knocking her out. Blackness.

***

Kate woke. Again, commotion beyond comprehension. Again, the smells of Jung and others. But she fought to not smell, to not focus on the smells. She tried to see. There were many people standing around her; she must have been lying down.

"She's here. She's awake. Kate, can you hear me? We removed the ocular mods and tried to remove the others, but it's not working. The reactions slowed."

"Doctor Jung, that's enough!" A firm male voice Kate didn't recognize. "Doctor Genet, we've stabilized you. That's all we can say right now."

The room cleared out, except for one. It was Conlin.

"Kate, I don't understand. I don't know why you did this. I know it's not the right time to talk about it. But, I love you. So much. Please, fight. Stay alive."

Blackness.

**

A shadowy figure hovered over her. There was a buzzing noise coming from a device he held. He whispered beneath the noise. "Doctor Genet, are you awake? Yes, I see that you are. Don't say anything, not a word. Just listen. I will be back, if I can. I'll get you out of this prison. I promise you that. But until then, hold on and fight. Stay alive. I'll get you home." Kate struggled to see him better, but when her eyes adjusted to the dark after a series of rapid blinks, there was no one there. Was she in prison? She couldn't move her arms or legs. They felt heavy, as if wrapped in heavy linens. She couldn't lift her head to see.

***

"Kate, it's Conlin. You're stable, but not recovering. Somehow most of your body's systems went into shock. The doctors told me not to say anything to you. I'm supposed to stay positive and reassuring. But you need to know, because, because you need to fight. Stay alive, Kate."

***

Nightmares fought for her. She could hear them bickering. The powerful sex dream rose above the others; he wanted another opportunity to own her, especially with death on its way. This was his chance to live forever, to be the death dream.

A dream of Adam emerged victorious, and Kate returned to room 542 for what seemed like an eternity, an endless series of retellings.

Though she cherished moments where she saw Adam and once more felt his love, the bitter end hurt tremendously. Worse, she realized, was her inability to act, to do anything, the lack of control and feeling of helplessness. Kate fought to wake up, to live. As the dream died and she woke, she sensed and felt relief.

***

"Nurse, nurse! She's awake." It was Conlin. He stood beside her. "Kate, you look much better this morning."

The nurse entered. "She's here. Doctor Millio's on his way. Vitals look good. Doctor Genet, how do you feel today?"

"Alive. I'm," her voice creaked, "I'm feeling fine. What's happened to me?"

"I can't say much, Doctor Genet. You had a heart attack and that seems to have triggered a series of system failures. Frankly you're lucky to be alive. You're a fighter, that's for sure." The angelic nurse's smile lit up the room. "Everything is fine now."

Kate could barely move. Her body weighed a ton, like she'd been recast in steel, and her head ached with a slow, constant thrum. She had a difficult time focusing her attention. It was like her eyes moved with the rhythm of her PTV's windshield wipers during a light rain. Each time they opened, it took a moment to focus. "My eyes, they seem off beat." It was maddening.

"Off beat? Look, they'll adjust, Doctor Genet. Try not to get agitated. We removed the ocular lenses." She continued to inspect Kate, to look at her with probing eyes and manipulate the data generated by sensors throughout the room and attached to Kate.

Kate began to notice what she'd lost. The depths she'd seen and felt. The rich and variable smells. The world seemed so dull. She'd always thought the bio-mods had evolved the most advanced sensory organs, especially those with the intensely focused sensory modifications. Everyone had benefited from the basic genetic modifications. Yet the moments when she was a comp-mod were so much more intense. She wondered if it was the comp-mods alone or the combination of bio- and comp-mods. Perhaps she was the only person to have ever seen and felt such depth of experience. Kate smiled at that thought.

"Kate, I'm so glad you're awake and feeling decent. I was so worried."

"Conlin, I'm sorry."

"Nurse, can we have a minute or two?"

"Sure." She left.

"I know that now's not the time, Kate, but I need to tell you. I love you, but I'm so incredibly angry with you. I don't understand how or why you could do this without me. The idea that you'd try to become a comp-mod, it doesn't make sense, not after what you said about us."

"I know. It happened fast, I guess. I thought about the mixed couples and how bio-mods would have to hide by becoming comp-mods."

"No, that's not possible. I could have told you that. I did actually. We discussed this, right? I had no idea what you were planning. But we did talk about your theory."

"Yes, and you thought bio-mod brains couldn't handle it, that our bodies were incapable. But none of that makes sense, Conlin. On all objective physiological measures, bio-mods are substantially more advanced than humans and I suspect comp-mods. Keep in mind what we've done for a few generations with gen tech."

"But, Kate, how do you explain what's happened to you? Obviously your brain and body couldn't handle it. Maybe it's not a question of whose brain is more advanced according to some objective measure. Maybe we've both advanced, just down different diverging paths. Maybe they're incompatible."

"I suppose. But I used the ocular mods. There wasn't an incompatibility. I swam in the data, and it was wonderful."

"Yeah, but you weren't fully integrated, and they didn't bind, right?"

"Right."

"Look, what matters is that you're alive. They've got you in a special unit because they don't want it getting out. No one can know what happened."

"Like Adam's death. The truth about mixed couples."

"No, I didn't say that. I don't think it would be a good idea to say anything about that right now. But now, more than ever, we need to keep quiet. I'm not sure what they'll do about you being bio-mod in the first place. You don't have papers. It's a real mess. We need to figure out a plan, and I did speak with someone who said he could help."

"Who?"

"I can't say." He looked around the room.

"When can I leave?"

"Soon, I hope. A few days maybe. I'm not sure. We need to see what the doctors say."

"I want to go home."

"You mean, home my house or home Rochester?"

"I don't know. Both. Neither. Gina's." She smiled and laughed lightly.

"I'm supposed to go back there to complete my work. But now, I'm not sure it would be safe."

"I know. I miss her though. I miss being there with you."

"Me too."

"Would you come to Rochester with me?"

"Not my first choice, but if you needed to go there, then sure."

***

"Doctor Genet. Good afternoon. I'm glad Conlin contacted me again, and brought me up to speed. You're going to be fine. Don't worry."

"Thank you. Doctor?"

He smiled and barely shook his head. "No, I'm not a doctor. Mr. Shephard will do."

"Where's Conlin?"

"He'll be back, in just a few minutes. I asked him and everyone else to give us some time to get acquainted." The room was empty.

Kate looked around the room and whispered, "Are you here to take me home?"

He seemed puzzled. "Why do you say that?"

"You were here to, oh, never mind. It's very jumbled."

"Yes. You've been on quite a journey, I imagine. Conlin filled me in on your experience with the Trinellis."

Kate was shocked. Why would Conlin tell him about that?

"Don't worry. I know all of it. Your secrets are safe with me. And I might be able to help you."

"How? With what exactly?" Fear crept into her gut and began to poke with its long nails.

"Well, first and foremost, with living. Kate, I can help you live. That's most important, you know. You're stable for now. But, and they don't know this yet," he smirked and then frowned, "you're dying. Slowly."

Kate sank back into the pillows that propped her up in a seated position.

He continued, "The doctors saved you from the rapid attacks on your systems, but you've still got them in you, the mods." He pointed above his own ears. "I'm not sure they're necessary though. I think the ocular mods you used before the procedure were probably enough to trigger the switch. Maybe, maybe not. Hard to say. We've lost track. But either way. The switch has been triggered."

"The switch? What switch?"

'The Kill Switch."

He paced around the room and then suddenly, he stopped. "I've something I want to show you before you die. Heck, maybe it will save your life."

TWENTY-SEVEN:

A SIMPLE CHOICE

San Francisco, California. September 2154.

Mr. Shephard broke his rules, the rules his father, and his grandfather, and great-grandfathers had set and passed on. He showed this woman the memories, more than just the selected scenes he'd occasionally needed to persuade or motivate others. This time, he showed enough to see how history was made, how the present was constructed, the origins of the kill switches. Once he decided to do so, he felt an odd sense of relief. It would be good for someone besides him and Donduardo IV to know. He had no children yet, and so he hadn't started the grooming process.

Rooftop of the Willis Tower, Chicago, Illinois. September 2036.

"It was only you two." Flynn said in his soft voice. "In the Greenbrier. There were no other clients. Only you."

"No, that can't be," Jonathan said. "I saw others, other like us, in the sofas, being escorted by the beautiful women."

"Just a show. You two were all that mattered. I knew that then, and look where we are today, just a decade later." Flynn smiled, a mesmerizing flash of teeth.

Jonathan and Donduardo nodded. It had been an incredible ride with so many huge accomplishments. Their technological advances were staggering. Jonathan had pioneered the sensory extensions beyond anyone's wildest dreams, and at the same time, Donduardo had pushed the boundaries of bioengineering, bridging the gap between pharmaceuticals and genetics, making bio-modification possible. Yet the regulatory game had been a most difficult labyrinth. Flynn had guided them through it, helping them to avoid pitfalls and endless circuits.

"You listened, you committed fully. Now, you own all the right people at the federal and state levels. You've got a bunch of independent think tanks, Public Liberty and the Let me be FREE Foundation are my favorites, preaching just what you want them to, just what the public needs to hear. You fought regulation by the F-fill-in-the-blank-C tooth and nail, and it paid off, because when you finally conceded the error of your ways and supported the regulation, it looked just the way you wanted. We fuckin' wrote the regs for them, by God." He laughed and laughed. "You've got your markets locked up tighter than a constipated nun." He laughed and laughed. "No one is ah enterin', that's for darn sure." His laughing settled. He waited until both Jonathan and Donduardo were looking at him, and then he said, "And now you got one more obstacle. It's in the room. It's you. Each other."

Jonathan and Donduardo were confused. Donduardo said, "What are you talkin' 'bout? I don't see how. We're tight too, you know."

"Oh, I know. I know. But my job is to see what's coming, and help you navigate the obstacles, so you can create the future. In a few years, it'll be the two of you, at the top, dominating your markets, setting the agenda. But you'll end up competing, don't you see? You'll be looking to shotgun each other with the government puppets you been buying, and your customers, your people, are going to have to choose. Am I right?"

Jonathan saw it: a brief vision. Sensory modification was an obvious market where they were close to competing right now, and they'd converge in the future. People would gravitate toward one or the other technology path and the opportunities it afforded. Jonathan could see it. They'd end up competing. It seemed a long way off, but possible, and increasingly probable the more Jonathan dwelled on it.

Donduardo must have been thinking the same thing because he said, "You might be right. We could end up competing, at least in some contexts. But why don't we just join forces now. We could merge, right?"

Jonathan nodded, "Yes, that's a good idea. Flynn?"

Flynn shook his head. "No, that'd undo much of what we've done already, open the door to increased regulatory scrutiny, invite antitrust officials to peek under your hoods, and my hood even. No, there's a better option, a safer option.

Divide and conquer, divide and rule in peace." He laughed. "Can you render your technologies incompatible?"

Jonathan and Donduardo didn't answer. They shrugged, trying to figure out what Flynn was thinking.

"If merging to one would be acceptable to each of you, then why not establish mutually exclusive domains within which you're each Kings!"

All three smiled. They shook hands and agreed.

***

Jonathan and Donduardo sat in a dimly lit room with a team of their brightest scientists and engineers. Rob Flynn stood in the back, mostly hidden by shadows. Only his bright smile gave him away.

"Simple code. A kill switch, basically. It can be done within the core. As soon as the system detects any of the indicators of bio-manipulation, it can shut down any number of bio-systems. We have some flexibility with how we engineer that."

"Yes, and the same can be done on our end. It will have to be a little different in execution, of course. But a biological kill switch also can be done at the core with a simple bit of code. And similarly, the reaction can be engineered."

San Francisco, California. March 2095.

Mr. Shephard's grandfather, Jerome Shephard, spoke, communicating aloud and not just through his thoughts. "Son, it's critical that you understand. I am responsible for our people. You will be responsible. You must understand. The kill switches began as simple engineering tricks--intentionally designed incompatibilities, but we couldn't control the reactions, and the code is buried. Nothing to be done about it." He stopped as if thinking about what to say next.

"Of course, the original idea was to divide the markets. That led to the territorial division we now live with, although that was not by design. Warming drove it. It was probably inevitable though. Maybe Flynn knew. There's always been an Us and Them, you see, since the dawn of time, since humans conquered the earth. Driven by competition for scarce resources, religion, race, politics, and all sorts of fears and human biases, we've always struggled against ourselves, and caused such incredible suffering." He paused again and then in a deeper tone, he slowly explained: "But this time, son, it led to peace and prosperity. We are better off, and they are better off. The kill switches keep us apart, and so does all of the idiocy about monsters and robots. It's contrived but that's fine. You've got to learn that. We don't want to remix. The kill switches would get triggered. People would die. Worse, everything could unravel, everything we've built. People might abandon the tech. It must remain a secret."

San Francisco, California. September 2154.

"Kate, I've shared these memories with you for a reason. You're the only one I've ever shown them too. You must keep them to yourself. As I have had to do all of my life. Do you understand?"

She nodded, "Yes, I understand." Kate was still processing everything she'd just experienced. She'd lived this Jonathan Shephard's memories. It had been incredible, so real, another deep swim. The technological path of the comp-mods began with this Virtual Porn Guy. It was mind-blowing. The meetings with this Flynn character. The integration of kill-switch codes in computer code and genetic code. She struggled to piece it all together, to understand what it all meant. She wasn't given time.

"Now, maybe you can understand why, why I have to ask you to remain silent about the kill switches, about the deaths. There is no way to explain them without opening Pandora's box. None of the doctors know. Not here or on the Atlantic side. No one knows, besides you, me, and Donduardo the Fourth. You don't know him, but he's the chief executive of Biomen. It's an awful price to pay, I admit. But we must pay it. For the hundreds of millions who live wonderful lives in peace."

"Why can't the mixed couples know? Even if they just know that they can't have mods."

"It's not that simple, Kate." He sighed and slowly shook his head. "There's no way for them to know without others knowing. There's no way to keep the lid on the box once it's pried open."

"I don't know. I have to think. I need to talk with Conlin."

"You don't have that luxury. You're dying, Kate, and so is your child."

"What? What did you say?"

"You're pregnant, Kate. We've known that since you activated the mods. Our prenatal systems picked it up immediately. The embryo is stable, but it will die, just as you will die, unless you let me help you."

"I'm pregnant?" she whispered. She tried to think about it, to process what it meant. She thought of her parents and how happy they'd be for her, and then she thought of Conlin and she felt stronger. She looked at Mr. Shephard and asked, "What do you want?"

"Kate, listen, I want you to work for me. You can continue to do your genetics research, in the Midwest or on the East Coast, but you'll work for me. And you'll keep our secret. In exchange, I'll keep you and your child alive. You'll both need my help. I can block the kill switch codes. It takes a particular device, an expensive device, and I'll set it for monthly reactivation, which only I can do. You stick to our deal, you and yours stay alive."

"I don't know. I have to think. I need to talk with Conlin." Kate's mind raced. She was pregnant. For her child, to save her child, she'd have to sacrifice her freedom, her control, become what she feared most.

She thought of Adam, Joseph and Nicola and her heart broke for them. Adam died because of a technological switch they intentionally engineered into the basic computer and genetic code? It didn't make sense. It didn't seem fair. She couldn't imagine staying quiet while others like them suffered the same fate. Yet she also thought about Jerome Shephard and his message to his son. He seemed like a good man. He didn't talk of power or wealth or being a King. He spoke of responsibility, of peace and prosperity. Who was she to unravel it all?

"You have a simple choice, Kate. You can choose life, for you and your child, a life with Conlin. Doing so also means life for so many more. Peace and happiness for all really, as close to world peace as we've ever seen on this planet. You are dying, and so is your unborn child. But I can save you both. I will save you both, if you choose wisely."

Kate whispered. "I choose life."

***

Denver, Colorado. September 2154.

RETURN HOME. MISSION ABORTED.

Is the asset lost?

NO. SHE'S ALIVE BUT THE SPOOK REPORTED SHE'S BEYOND OUR REACH FOR NOW.

Understood.

***

Mr. Shephard was relieved. "Kate's fine. You did the right thing coming to me, Agent Rice. She's agreed to my terms. The three of you are free to go. Your cover might get more complicated, or maybe not. I leave that for you and your supervisor to figure out."

"Will my supervisor also handle Kate?"

"Yes, in time."

***

Kate couldn't move, even if she tried, but she didn't bother. She felt cold and weighted down. Her body was pressed by a thin white sheet, not taught but snugly tucked in along three sides of her bed. Her toes were distant mountain peaks, her breasts twin hills. No one else was in the hospital room; she noticed the complete absence of biochemical feedback, nothing to trigger her senses or even just tickle them; she craved a soft brush. Only her face felt the crisp yet stale air, which had a faint, metallic odor. Was it the air or sheet that trapped her, she wondered. Neither. It was her submission. She wanted to scream but suppressed the urge. She should be happy, to be alive, to be with Conlin, for the baby within her. And she was, intensely so, but only as long as she maintained focus on them. But that was a struggle, like recalling a dream or a childhood memory, or lately, Adam. When she succeeded, happiness set an anchor and drove her to plan for their future, but then the trap sprung again. She could make no plans of her own.

Kate lay still, terrified of what she'd become—Shephard's drone.

Thanks for reading Shephard's Drone. If you enjoyed it, please consider leaving a review on your favorite website or social media platform, and tell a friend.

If you'd like to find out more about my work, follow me on Twitter.

 @BrettFrischmann

If you're interested in how technology is currently affecting humanity, check out my nonfiction book Re-Engineering Humanity.

Available on Amazon.
http://author.to/ShephardsDrone